SHOP! OR A STORE IS BORN

SHOP!
OR
A STORE IS
BORN

Jasper Carrott

ARROW BOOKS

Arrow Books Limited
62–65 Chandos Place, London WC2N 4NW

An imprint of Century Hutchinson Limited

London Melbourne Sydney Auckland
Johannesburg and agencies throughout
the world

First published by Arrow Books 1988
Reprinted 1988

Typeset by JH Graphics Limited, Reading, Berkshire

Printed and bound in Great Britain by
Anchor Brendon Limited, Tiptree, Essex

ISBN 0 09961700 5

Jasper Carrott gratefully acknowledges the
assistance received in the writing of this book
from NEIL SHAND and STEPHEN PUNT

1

It was 8.45 am on a dull bleak Monday morning
in Kensington High Street, near Knightsbridge,
London. The last remnants of the sales staff who
worked for the Beehive department store scurried
quickly across the goods yard situated at the back
of the store. There was always this rush at
8.45 am because at 8.46 am the clocking-in
machine changed its black numerals to tell-tale
red on their clocking-in cards. Lateness at the
Beehive was a heinous crime, along with spitting on the pavement and failure to purchase
the weekly edition of *War Cry*.

The Beehive was part of the Knowles empire,
a little-known and little-cared-for organization
that had as much effect upon world commerce
as the SDLP had on British politics. It was an
empire which stretched along Kensington High
Street from a line adjacent to the fire hydrant
marked HF212 to a similar line two feet left
of the concrete bus stop two hundred feet further
west along the pavement. Within these confines
rose five storeys of stunning Victorian medioc-
rity. Constructed in the late 1880s, the building
had no redeeming feature whatsoever. It could

not be classed as a tourist attraction; the high-rise council flats of Stoke Newington were a great deal higher up the list of London's beautiful buildings than the Beehive's monotonous austerity. There was no way the Beehive would ever be recognized as a listed building, although it had been said that given a few more years, the list to the vertical would be pronounced enough to achieve that notoriety.

The one word that best summed up the Beehive was consistency. Practically everything was consistently faceless and uninspiring, from the staff with an average age of sixty-two to the owner, Mr Alfred Knowles.

In present-day commercial trading terms the Beehive was indeed an oddity. When you entered through the set of creaking revolving doors you were immediately struck by the virtual non-existence of commerce. Customers on the trading floors were as numerous as car boot sales on the island of Sark. One could be forgiven for thinking the store was closed down, were it not for the sales assistants, hovering like emus, ready to waddle towards the rare species of clientele that patronized the store.

The staff themselves matched the building perfectly, their drab and dowdy appearances complementing the decor with unerring accuracy. What they knew about turnover/profit ratios, shelf brand leaders and subliminal customer awareness would vie with the amount of information on the average race jockey's tax return. The majority of the staff were near or past

8

retiring age. What young people were employed came mainly from desperation, having been considered unsuitable even for government youth training schemes.

It was fair to say that each employee had their own personal story that if related to an insomniac would remove the necessity to swallow any amount of Mogadon. Each had a future that would put fortune-tellers out of business.

The conduct expected from the staff was one of high morality. The Beehive, from conception, embraced a Christian code founded upon the work ethic, that is, a hard day's work for a miserable day's pay. They were expected to observe strict sexual abstinence outside marriage and the Ten Commandments at all times. In the store's heyday, any transgression of these codes would warrant immediate dismissal, but these days, with the difficulty of finding staff, standards were not as they used to be. If the truth be known, the Beehive harboured a cross-section of perverts whose dubious practices were rarely equalled outside the House of Commons.

Entrance through the revolving doors was always obstructed by Jim the commissionaire. Once one of Oswald Mosley's staunchest supporters, he had mellowed with the years and was now content to be secretary to the Intercity Firm of Football Followers. Jim's main directive was to keep undesirables out of the store. Undesirables to Jim meant Jews, spiks, wops, dagoes and anyone whose colour of skin did not resemble that of a supernova. He wore a small gold cross around his neck which, he felt, absolved him of all sin.

Once through the revolving doors, customers would be met with scented waves from the perfumery department – a strange mixture of rosewater, sandalwood, musk and embalming fluid. The counter was manned by Mrs Loving, an eighty-year-old spinster with an enormous double bun of hair tied on the top of her head. This was dyed light brown, severely lacquered and resembled to all intents and purposes a burnt cottage loaf. Over sixty years of serving scents and cosmetics had had a deleterious effect upon her skin. The constant application of thousands of trial samples of different perfumiers' products had broken down her body's immune system to counteract outside bacteria.

The resulting dermatitis resisted any attempts of modern medicine. She was tried for a part in *The Singing Detective*, but was rejected on the grounds that no one would believe the skin lesions were real. The effect upon sales of her condition was to render them virtually nil, but it did have the positive effect that when people entered the store and saw Mrs Loving, they rapidly dispersed to the other departments for fear of infection.

Each department at the Beehive would be almost deserted for most of the day, except for lunchtime when a small flurry of people would descend upon the Buttery located on the first floor. This at least had achieved reasonable sales figures of late due to the increased interest in natural and unprocessed foods. The staff of the Buttery still baked bread and cakes on the premises. The contents always consisted of wholemeal stoneground flour, wild unprocessed honey and only the freshest of ingredients. With hardly an E number or artificial ingredient in sight, the food and beverages were virtually the same quality and standard as those served one hundred years ago. For those people concerned with health, the Beehive Buttery had been an oasis in the desert for many years.

The Beehive was a traditional store in every sense of the word due to the original concept instigated by the brothers Knowles. Timothy Knowles and his brother Jacob had been very successful businessmen trading in London in the mid 1800s. Their fortune was based upon loans to the working class which were recouped with considerable interest, way above that of accepted trading practice. Their insistence upon prompt repayment was accompanied by extremely brutal retribution for those who failed to meet the payments on time. This ensured they were feared throughout the area of London known as the Docklands. Just how rich the brothers might have become through this extortion no one could say, because they underwent, as a result of an encounter with a Christian Scientist, a remarkable conversion.

A fresh disciple to the new religion had owed the brothers a considerable amount of money. On his failure to repay, they decided to visit the poor man's hovel and extract their due.

11

When they burst into his home, the miscreant fell to his knees and began fervently praying to the heavens for money. Not being devout Christians themselves, they ignored this supplication and prepared to 'dust him over'.

As they were tying him upside down by his ankles, a miraculous event happened. An extremely well-to-do man in bowler hat and frock coat, carrying a black Gladstone bag, entered the room and proceeded to ask of Timothy Knowles how much was owed to him by the praying man. Informed that it was well over forty pounds, the visitor opened his bag and gave Timothy a manila envelope. He then left immediately, without a word. On opening the envelope the brothers found it contained forty brand new one-pound notes.

Releasing the unfortunate convert from his upside-down position, they began to question him about the sequence of events that had just taken place. The convert explained that it was God's will, that God was omnipotent and that if one followed the good book to its literal word, then this type of miracle would become commonplace to them.

Intrigued, the heathen brothers decided to discover more about this strange form of Christianity. Over the next few weeks a remarkable conversion took place that at once relieved a great deal of fear and misery in the Docklands area and became a talking point for many years at pubs and clubs throughout the whole of London. It seemed that they had seen the error of their ways. No one was too sure exactly how it happened but it was not long before people who owed them money received letters from the brothers telling them not to repay the debt to them, but, if it was within their means to do so, to donate the money to charity. The brothers within a short time became renowned for their generosity and charity work. Their Christian Scientist conversion eventually led them to a deeper acceptance of other Christian faiths.

The Beehive was Timothy's own idea. The money they had made from their extortions would not last for ever, and brother Jacob agreed it would be sensible to set up a business that would benefit the community as a whole. Thereby, a store was born.

From day one the idea was to make the store a success, pay the staff and distribute the profit to those in need. The goods were to be of the highest quality, thereby enticing the moneyed gentry to patronize the store and, by passing on their money to the deserving poor, a reasonable distribution of wealth was accomplished

The brothers married, and Alfred Knowles was born to Timothy Knowles on 1 August 1891, three years after the Knowles' official opening.

It was nicknamed the Beehive because it epitomized the principles of communities working diligently with each other for the benefit of all concerned.

Timothy and Jacob wanted the store to remain

within the Knowles family in perpetuity, and so laid down rules and conditions preserving the original ideal to be specifically followed by the descendants in order to keep the ownership of the store.

Alfred Knowles, the current manager of the Knowles dynasty, had followed the conditions with a diligence that could not have been foreseen. Any attempt to update and modernize the store was severely frowned upon; he would have no truck with present-day forms of commercialism, and many such trading practices were anathema to him.

The extent of his observing the spirit of the law could be seen wherever one went within the bounds of the Beehive. The hardware and ironmongery department was a classic case. Here could be found many products long since obsolete or deemed unnecessary in the late twentieth century. Replacement washers and valve cylinders for handpumps, tin galvanized baths, dolly washers, blue bags, solid cast-iron smoothing irons, various styles of washboards, large mechanical traps to catch everything from mice to ferrets, the stock was endless. It was piled high to the ceilings rusting with age and dilapidation. Concessions were occasionally made to recent technical developments. An electric mangle sat proudly in the middle of the floor, along with electric kettles and bed warmers. In between the stacks of merchandise were dozens of units consisting of tiny drawers that held countless thousands of nuts, bolts, screws, tacks, pins, hooks, hinges and brackets for every conceivable indoor and outdoor handyman's job that ever existed. It was a stocktaking nightmare that every year took eighteen months to complete and so no one ever really knew how much of whatever it is there was.

If one climbed the stairs to the next floor, the music department was almost as bad. Here large oak-encased phonographs with huge sound horns attached to the sides stood side by side with early radiograms and wireless sets reminiscent of a 1933 Ovaltinies advertisement. Fragile 78-rpm records were stacked row upon row featuring such artists as Al Bowley, Rudi Vallee and Gertrude Lawrence.

In charge of the music department was a Mr Caffey, a medium-sized man with medium-sized features and medium-sized shoes. It's fair to say that medium just about summed up his general appearance. He would be able to go unnoticed anywhere, attract not one jot of attention, be almost invisible – if it were not for the way he walked. The length of his stride could be measured in inches. A giant step for Mr Caffey would propel him the width of a ruler. An abnormality of the pelvic girdle restricted the movement of the top joints of the femur, and further abnormalities of the hip and knee joints combined to afflict him with a gait that could best be described as a mincing stumble.

The balance required to stay upright with this structural formation was formidable. When moving forward, Mr Caffey would dip violently from the waist at an angle well beyond ninety degrees. Just as you would expect him to slam his face into the floor, he would seemingly defy the laws of physics and loop upwards whilst tottering four or five steps before his back arched into a letter C, bringing him to an immediate halt. The process would then be repeated until his destination was reached.

There were variations to this display depending on whether or not he was in a hurry, or if perhaps he had to turn a corner. To manoeuvre a right- or left-hand turn was difficult because of the pivotal action required. He had developed a technique whereby to turn right or left he would first of all head in the opposite direction. By throwing his weight to the right, say, his left leg was relieved of enough pressure to turn in the opposite direction. Then dipping quickly down and left, the resulting torque on his hips spun him round to face the direction in which he wanted to continue his journey. Sometimes the initial weight transference was too strong and he had to go in the opposite direction anyway. But still, in the main it worked and it had the advantage that no one asked him to carry anything.

His love for classical music was unquestionable and much to his satisfaction, the store's attitude to the present-day popular music matched his own. The infernal jungle rhythms and caterwauling of modern singers and groups made Mr Caffey spit and wish he could stamp his feet in rage, except that would make him fall over.

Not that he hadn't given 'pop' music a chance. He had tried stocking the very latest 'hit' single records only recently, but as he suspected, his customers found them as distasteful as he did and so the fifty copies of Anne Shelton's *Bring Back Your Arms* lay unsold in the stockroom.

Much more to Mr Caffey's taste was the melody of Strauss, the stirring emotions of Gustav Holst, or his favourite Sibelius. 'Ah, Sibelius,' Mr Caffey never tired of saying, 'not only a genius but a man who could walk well.'

It would be a rare day indeed if in the vicinity of the music department the customers would not hear the strains of a Sibelius symphony winging its way to their ears. They would also hear a considerable amount of cracks and crackles as the worn-out 78-rpm records met the blunt end of the steel phonographic needle. If the customers' curiosity led them to the source of the disturbed music there was a good chance they would see a familiar Beehive spectacle.

This would be Mr Caffey standing in front of a pair of giant phonographic speaker horns conducting the symphony with a large pointed baton. It was as near as any orchestra would want to be to Mr Caffey considering his unique style of conducting. With each sweep of the arms and vigorous stabbing of the baton Mr Caffey would curl and dive, spin and mince with a timing that had no relationship whatsoever to the music's intricate metres.

Mr Caffey was always very keen to tell people of the time he conducted the Lewisham Amateur

Symphony Orchestra in a performance of Mozart's *Eine Kleine Nacht Musik*. What he omitted to tell his listeners was that the orchestra members were so confused by the gyrating, bobbing conductor that they all got up and went to the pub.

As one moved from the music section, each and every floor and department had a dull and dowdy appearance seemingly matched by its attendant sales staff. Yet when each representative was studied it would appear as if every one of them was a unique creation. How the store continued to survive would puzzle even the most casual of observers. The gifts of surplus profits to charity had dried up many years previously and only by a combination of pitiful wages to the staff, an insistence upon a purchase being in cash, and interest from a trust fund set up by the original brothers, could the store pay its way. However, the site that the building occupied was worth untold millions, a fact that was not wasted upon those with more selfish concerns than would be entertained by the Beehive's founders.

Eric Dunnet was dreaming. He was dreaming that he was in a villa in Spain with an old woman he couldn't recognize who wanted to go out to the beach, but he was telling her no because he had to wait in for a telephone call from Sonny Liston about the grapefruit. That's when he woke up. On his back, eyes wide open immediately, staring at the ceiling and wondering what had possessed him to paper it with posters from the London Planetarium. He went back to his dream. Why Sonny Liston? Why grapefruit? And what was Sonny Liston going to tell him about the grapefruit?

He felt a body stir next to him and he turned his head to the left, idly wondering as he did so whether all right-handed men shared their beds in the same way. His eyes opened even wider. Crawling along the pillow towards him was the most frightening insect he had ever seen. Some sort of centipede. A killer centipede! His central nervous system went into overdrive. A casual passer-by at that moment – an unlikely event as Eric Dunnet lived on the fourth floor of a West Hampstead terraced house – would have seen Dunnet's body rise, like a jump jet in human form, for fully six inches from the mattress before folding upwards and inwards upon itself and then pitching over the side of the bed with a terrible scream.

His companion had also been dreaming. She had been dreaming that she was an old lady with Sonny Liston and that he wouldn't go the distance with her because he had to phone somebody about the grapefruit. It made her so mad she wanted to scream – and that's when she woke up. Somebody was screaming and it wasn't her.

Thora opened her eyes, looked up at the ceiling and thought: My God, I've spent the night sleeping in the London Planetarium. She became aware of a heap of clothing at the foot of the bed. It was shivering and making strange noises. It reminded her of the beggars in Calcutta. The heap of clothing was saying something. 'What's what?' she heard herself reply.

'That thing. That killer centipede on the pillow.'

Thora opened her eyes again. 'That's not a killer centipede,' she said. 'It's an eyelash.'

'What?'

'It's a false eyelash.'

Dunnet was silent for about seven and a half seconds. 'Why are you wearing false eyelashes at your age?' he suddenly shouted. Like all of Dunnet's women, Thora was of advancing years. Some men look for a mother figure; Dunnet was looking for a grandmother figure.

The impact of this brief outburst was undermined by his inability to unravel himself from the sheet and the duvet. His companion looked at him and thought he most closely resembled a ginger ferret who'd been trapped in an unbaked Vienna roll. But not as sexy.

Thora said, 'Is there any coffee?'

'In the kitchen.'

'Are you making any?'

'Well, I wasn't.'

Oh! she thought, I knew I should have left when he was in the bathroom looking for his royal jelly and Michelin tickler with the 'added rubber studs and banding for maximum pleasure and heightened enjoyment'. She'd forgotten just how charming the post-coital male could be.

'I would,' said Dunnet, 'but I'm late.'

'What do you do?' she said, scratching herself noisily.

'I'm managing director at the Beehive.'

'Beehive? In Ken High Street?'

'That's right.'

'That's a terrible dump.'

Dunnet didn't answer. He never did when people talked about the Beehive. He gazed instead at the pin-up picture of Mother Teresa on the wall above his bed. She was his ideal woman, and featured regularly in his late-night erotic fantasies. He strode off into the bathroom. Until that moment his mood had been its usual early-morning mix of nausea and regret topped up with a liberal splash of alcoholic remorse.

To the mix he now added depression.

She was right of course. The Beehive was a dump. He knew that. Practically everybody in the world knew it. The only person who didn't seem to know it − or, if he knew, didn't care about it − was Alfred Knowles.

Dunnet looked into the mirror above the vanity unit − he couldn't bring himself to call it a sink. The mirror had added complexion-enhancer which made anyone who stood in front of it look like George Hamilton. All Dunnet could see was a lightly tanned, slightly fudged impressionist painting. Alcohol does that to you the morning after. With a glint of hatred in his eyes he said aloud: 'Why doesn't the old fart die so I can make a fortune . . .'

21

2

In Harold Street, Mayfair, there was a small door between the gentlemen's outfitters and the Taylor and Tranchmont Art Gallery. Over the door was a hanging sign made up of red and silver foil discs that shimmered with every waft of wind that blew frequently down the street. On a breezy day it was difficult to make out the words, but today was reasonably calm and the name on the sign could clearly be deciphered: 'Hamilton Club', and in painted words underneath, 'A Gentleman's Club – 24 hour non-stop strip'.

The Hamilton Club was not noted for satisfying the needs of the studious intellectual. Its membership consisted in the main of seedy businessmen and petty humanity who enjoyed nothing more than a good dribble down their macks.

Entrance to the club could be gained by ringing the front doorbell and waiting patiently for the door to be opened by one of the several club employees specifically trained for the job. The training lasted approximately two days. Each employee had first to pass the qualifying standards, that is, (1) an inability to pronounce any word of the English language with more than two syllables and (2) the skill to employ any form of physical combat necessary to persuade the customer to change his mind or pay the bill in the quickest time possible. Each employee would be carefully instructed as to the mechanical necessity of turning the handle on the door before opening it. This was easier said than done, for the door had two handles that had to be turned simultaneously. One was the standard knob handle and the other was a Yale lock. Such was the dexterity required in placing the left hand on the Yale and the right hand on the knob and turning the top one anti-clockwise and the bottom one clockwise, and at the same time moving the feet backwards to allow the door to open, that many would-be door attendants had failed to learn the complicated manoeuvre in the two days set aside for this intensive course.

The member requiring entrance on this cold, grey, January afternoon was a strange sight indeed. Hunched over the bell, covered in an enormous black cape, face hidden behind the high collar, the Bishop of Lambeth anxiously awaited the arrival of the doorman. At last he heard him coming. The man started mumbling, 'Left hand clockwise . . . Right hand anti-clockwise . . .' The door finally opened and the Bishop hurried inside. The door then closed quickly behind him, a sure sign the doorman had passed the second half of the training course.

He was taken into the dimly lit interior of the club by the scantily clad receptionist in only shoes, fishnet tights, skimpy briefs and a bandana. The chill from the door brought out goose pimples all over his bare flesh.

Late afternoon meant that the club was fairly quiet and the only members present were two males watching a soft porn video in the corner of the bar. The Bishop relaxed slightly as he recognized them both, one a respected polo organizer and the other a TV presenter. Moving quickly through the club the receptionist led him into a back room where he came face to face with Mr Big, the club's owner.

Mr Big was one of London's gangland leaders. He was big in all respects except size. In his stockinged feet he was several inches below four feet, but with the help of stacked high-heeled shoes, he could just topple over the magical forty-eight inches.

Mr Big was greatly aware of his lack of stature and any jocular remark or sniggering aside regarding his dwarf-like appearance would be met with a physical rebuff from one of his henchmen. This task usually befell Mangle, his constant bodyguard and companion. What Mr Big lacked in size, Mangle more than compensated for. He was built like the proverbial brick outhouse, the only difference being the outhouse looked more intelligent. If his forehead had been any lower, it would have met his chin. His huge seven-foot frame hovered behind Mr Big awaiting any word of command his boss cared to give him.

The third person present was Rupert, Mr Big's 'brains'. Mr Big never made a legal move without him.

Somehow London's gangland never had the romantic appeal of its American counterpart. For a gangland boss to boast 'I control the numbers racket on East Side' has a classier ring than trying to boost one's importance by claiming 'I control every bingo hall in Walthamstow.' Nevertheless Mr Big was a powerful man. Indeed he controlled every bingo hall in Walthamstow, and moreover had just seized control of the lucrative Trivia Quiz machine racket in south-east London, apart from Lewisham where the notorious Gravel sisters Bobby and Jackie still reigned supreme. It was a brave man indeed who would take on Bobby and Jackie. Those who had tried had ended up being mutilated after a particularly vicious perm and rinse in the sisters' high street salon.

The Bishop eyed the trio with apprehension, and for good reason. It was not the first time he had visited the club: in fact, if anyone observed the comings and goings of the members, the Bishop would have been noticed attending more than most. His predilections for the sins of the flesh were sated on those premises at a rate usually associated with American presidential candidates. The threat of eternal hellfire did nothing to quell the range and tastes of the Bishop's carnal desires. Upon his very own instructions the Bishop had devised and constructed a 'confessional box' wherein the

penance handed out had nothing to do with Hail
Marys or rosary beads. The young and not so
young ladies providing sensual gratification
never ceased to be surprised at the Bishop's lusty
appetite. No matter how trivial the sin they
confessed in the box, their terms of atonement
involved the most vigorous flagellations and
purges – administered by the Bishop.

The Bishop's less than pious desires had to be
paid for. Over several years of attendance at the
club the Bishop had run up a debt with Mr Big
that ran into many thousands of pounds.

Mr Big's generosity had nothing to do with
insurance for himself in the after life. There
wasn't a Commandment he had not broken more
times than Herod had boils. On the contrary,
Mr Big was quite happy for the Bishop to get
into debt. Not only was it good for business
having a Bishop on the premises, but it also
meant a good deal less interest from the police
authorities who were reluctant to cause embarrassment to the higher ecclesiastical orders or
other related Freemasons. Besides, Mr Big knew
from past experience that such debtors in
influential places would always come in extra
useful at the most unexpected times.

Mr Big felt that this maybe was one of those
times. He called the gathering to order. 'Good
afternoon, Bishop,' he welcomed in a voice sur-
prisingly loud for such a short man. A faint
Geordie accent could be detected from his early
upbringing in Redcar and his borstal days in
Galashiels.

'Good afternoon Mr Big, Rupert, Mangle,' responded the Bishop.

Mangle grunted and Rupert nodded.

'I've called you in, Bishop,' said Mr Big, 'to definitely decide on what . . .'

'Sorry to interrupt, Mr Big,' butted in Rupert, 'but you've split your infinitive. It should be definitely to decide or to decide definitely.'

'Thank you, Rupert, how daft of me.'

Rupert was gangland's best grammarian, and extremely irritated with misuse of the English language.

Mr Big continued, 'I have asked you to see me, Bishop, about the rather large amount of money you owe me.'

The Bishop shuffled uncomfortably.

'What I want to know,' enquired Mr Big, 'is when do you propose to pay off the monies owed, and in what manner?'

All three villains awaited the reply.

The Bishop, whose finances were over-stretched not only with Mr Big but many other creditors, had no real answer. Instead he would apply to Mr Big for furtherance of his generosity. In a tone that he used frequently to exhort his congregation for funds for the church restoration the Bishop said, 'Demands upon my funds from deserving and worthy causes are, you will appreciate, considerable in this day and age of materialism. Wages of the clergy, as you know, are not excessive. My overheads alone take up the majority of the remuneration, personal donations from business and commercial interests in my diocese have not been what they were, and I have to say a great deal of difficulty would be entailed in me finding the necessary resources to repay you.'

Mr Big listened to the Bishop's whining and with just a hint of menace said, 'You are aware of course that people who in the past have reneged upon their responsibilities have met with some very unpleasant experiences.' As he finished the sentence Mr Big turned and gave Mangle a brief glance.

Mangle, understanding basically the gist of the conversation, if not all the words, gave the Bishop a baleful glare.

The Bishop, understanding full well Mr Big's inference, could only gulp and enquire if there was anything he could do to further Mr Big's interests.

It was time for Rupert to interject. 'Tell me, Bishop, I believe you are familiar with the Beehive department store.'

The Bishop, startled, moved uncomfortably in his seat.

'Well, er . . . yes, I have shopped there at infrequent times in the past. Why do you ask?'

'Are you familiar with Mr Eric Dunnet, the managing director?'

'I have met him,' said the Bishop, a sinking feeling now wending its way into the lower regions of his stomach.

'From my information,' said Rupert, 'not only have you met him but met him frequently. Now we'd like some information.'

'I will tell you all that I can,' murmured the Bishop, 'but really, er . . . I don't think there is much I can tell you that you probably don't already know.'

'Perhaps you would let us be the judge of that,' said Mr Big.

'Right. Well,' said Rupert, 'what do you know of Alfred Knowles?'

'I know he is the owner of the Beehive, a God-fearing man who has helped the Church many times in the past. He tends to keep himself to himself and has little to do with the outside world.'

'Why doesn't he want to sell the store?' said Mr Big.

The Bishop paused for a moment, wondering how much they knew and how much he should say. He decided that ignorance would suffice for now and replied, 'I am not too sure. They do say it is because he is senile and doesn't fully appreciate the virtues of the store's commercial viability.'

'Oh, come now,' said Rupert, 'I think you know a little more than you're letting on.'

Mangle, sensing that his talents might be needed, stood up and moved menacingly round behind the Bishop.

The Bishop thought that ignorance was perhaps not the ploy to use on this occasion and offered a little more knowledge to see if he could pacify the interests of his interrogators.

'Well, I do believe there are some unusual conditions relating to the ownership and control of the store. It is said that only the sons of the founders of the store and their sons can inherit the business. Alfred Knowles, as far as I know, has no heir and therefore has no one to pass it on to.'

'Then why doesn't he sell it?' said Mr Big. He motioned to Mangle to move in closer. Mangle moved up to stand behind the Bishop and placed his large hand on the Bishop's shoulder.

The Bishop was nervous now, and realized they could know more than he first thought.

'He. . . . can't sell the store,' stammered the Bishop.

'And why would that be?' enquired Rupert.

'Because of the original conditions set out by the founding brothers.'

Rupert looked at Mr Big and said, 'My information seems to be correct.'

'Carry on, Bishop,' said the diminutive boss.

'Well, as far as I know the conditions state that the store must be handed down until such time as there is no male heir. The business and property cannot be sold because doing so would be in contravention of the original conditions and the inheriting sons would be disinherited. That is why, I believe, Mr Knowles cannot sell the store.'

'Now then,' said Rupert, 'what happens if, as seems likely, the heirs run out? Alfred Knowles has not married, and there being no other inheritors, who gets the business?'

With this question, Rupert, Mangle and Mr

Big all moved very much closer to intimidate their victim. After several seconds, Mangle's other hand clamped itself vice-like to the Bishop's other shoulder and gave his body a gentle shake. The Bishop now knew what it felt like to be in a Magimix. Upon cessation of the violent rattling, the Bishop said, 'The business goes to the Church of England.'

'What, everything, the whole lot?' said Mr Big.

'I am informed that is the case,' said the Bishop.

Mr Big nodded to Mangle and Mangle released the Bishop, who sank gratefully back into his chair hoping that the shaking had not dislodged some vital organ.

'Who else knows of these matters?' asked Rupert.

'Not many people,' said the Bishop. 'Alfred Knowles of course, Eric Dunnet would know and, I believe, the company solicitors. It is possible other people know, otherwise how did you get your original information?'

Mr Big ignored the question and came straight to the point.

'What sort of scam have you got going with Dunnet?'

Rupert tut-tutted at Mr Big's use of American slang.

The Bishop, reckoning that cleanliness was next to godliness, came clean.

'Mr Dunnet has suggested that when Mr Knowles dies and the business reverts to the Church, we come to a business arrangement.

As the Beehive lies within my diocese, I will be the Church's representative in accepting the deeds and titles. The store is of course worth a great deal of money.'

'And the original conditions allow the Church to sell the property?' said Rupert.

'As I comprehend,' said the Bishop, 'when the business is passed over to the Church we have full jurisdiction as to its future.'

'What about your superiors?' said Mr Big.

'I am in the position,' said the Bishop haughtily, 'to convince them of the large amount of money that would accrue from the sale and with such large amounts involved, I do not foresee them causing any problems. So you could say, Mr Big, that when Alfred Knowles dies I shall be in a position to repay your debts, with interest.'

Mr Big got down from his chair and walked around the room pondering this new information. After several minutes of silence, he turned and said, 'You've been most helpful, Bishop. I wonder if you would do something for me.'

The Bishop, in no position to refuse, acquiesced readily.

'I would like you to arrange a meeting between Mr Dunnet and I.'

'No, Mr Dunnet and me,' said Rupert.

'I'll deal with this!' snapped Mr Big, looking at Rupert in surprise at this attempted control of operations.

'No, I meant it's Eric Dunnet and *me*, not Eric Dunnet and I,' said Rupert. 'A common grammatical error that people often make.'

'Ah,' said Mr Big, 'of course, Mr Dunnet and me. Will you oblige, Bishop?'

The Bishop agreed and said he would be in touch.

'Well, Bishop, a most interesting meeting,' said Mr Big. 'Now there is a young lady upstairs awaiting your arrival. She has some terrible misdemeanour to confess which I am sure you will be only too happy to absolve.'

The Bishop's eyes glinted with immediate lust and for the moment his mind was taken off what would be a very awkward time to come.

3

'Phone down to the hardware department and get them to send a ladder up, will you, Mr Middleton. Jacko's stuck between the third and fourth floor.'

Mrs Clarkson of children's wear was staring up at Jacko's lift, stuck between her floor and the next. Jacko was the lift attendant at Knowles. He'd had the job for over twenty years.

The policy of using disabled persons to operate the lifts was an admirable practice, and the store was perhaps one of the first organizations in London to appreciate their need, like everyone else, to be accepted into the humdrum of everyday life.

This benign attitude did have its drawbacks on occasions. Today was a bad day for Jacko. As with all things at the Beehive, the lifts, too, dated from the late 1880s. The lift shaft was situated in the middle of the store to allow maximum customer convenience for access to all departments, except that the customers rarely used the lifts. The Beehive's clientele consisted mainly of ladies and gentlemen approaching the latter days of their existence who had been shopping there for many years and knew better than to risk a ride in the lifts, preferring instead to walk up the staircase that encircled them.

It wasn't that the lift was unsafe. The shaft itself was made of fine grade steel and formed a metal cage which ran open-meshed from the basement to the top of the fifth floor. Inside the cage was the lift, fronted by a metal gate that concertinaed to allow access to a teak-panelled interior which could accommodate up to seven persons including the operator. This early predecessor of the high-speed elevator was operated manually by means of a brass lever, situated on the right, that controlled three separate operations − up, down and stop.

The co-ordination required to stop the lift manually so that its base would be level with a department floor was not something that would normally trouble Jacko or the other lift attendants. However, Jacko's co-ordination could fluctuate between reasonably competent and abysmal. Today it was abysmal.

A quartet of elderly spinsters, visiting the store for the first time, assumed that the quickest way from ground floor to the carpet department on the fourth was via Jacko's lift. They could not understand the commissionaire's almost forceful persuasion that they should consider hoofing their way up four flights of stairs if time was of any importance, particularly as one of the spinsters required the stabilizing capabilities of a Zimmer frame.

They entered the lift fully expectant that their

35

journey to the fourth floor would be brief and presumably incident-free. Their expectations were threatened immediately by Jacko's insistence upon the Zimmer frame being ejected from the lift due to its cumbersome size, which would impede further customers who might require entrance to the lift on subsequent floors.

It was pointed out to Jacko that if the Zimmer frame were to be prised from the knuckles and trembling fingers of the incapacitated lady in question, there was every chance she would plummet to the ground in a painful heap. Jacko was in no mood for compromise. Had he not spent his entire forty-five years coping with an ungainly lack of balance? The hump over his right shoulder forced his right arm, which was somewhat shorter than his left, into a position that made grasping the handles of the lift gates extremely time-consuming. And it was a cold day. At least this woman had had many years of normal limb function. It was not his fault she now needed mechanical aids for mobility, and anyway he would return to the ground floor, put the whole lift at her disposal and transport her separately to the fourth floor to rejoin her friends.

The idea of leaving their friend abandoned on the ground floor clutching a Zimmer frame did not appeal to the other three spinsters and they remonstrated with Jacko as to his inflexibility, insisting that their friend be included in the ascent. They were not to know that when Jacko was confronted in this manner his physical co-ordination deteriorated alarmingly. A wave of agitation was starting to roll round the children's wear department, where the lift was situated. The assistants, all familiar with Jacko's unpredictable moods, could sense that a situation was building up. Someone instructed the hardware department to stand by with the ladder.

Finally Jacko reluctantly agreed to include the Zimmer frame in the party of four and prepared to shut the outer gate in the hope that some progress could be made.

Straddled across the small gap between the lift floor and the ground floor, Jacko started to hop up and down in the hope of attaching his right hand on to the gate handle. Normally, he had a little stool that he would step on to reach the handle, but today he had a point to prove that whether it be stools or Zimmer frames they were to be deemed unnecessary for the capable.

His hopping up and down had an alarming effect upon the lift itself. Suspended by four metal cables, it had a propensity to sway from side to side or judder up and down. It was now juddering to the rhythm of Jacko's hopping, and all four spinsters were tightly gripping the Zimmer frame. The children's wear assistants now fully realized that Jacko was having not just a bad day (the sort where he would sulk on the fifth floor and refuse to answer the lift bell), but a full-blown pearler of a day, where if previous events were anything to go by, the lift would be out of commission for the rest of the week.

They knew better than to go to Jacko's aid and lift him up so that he could grasp the handle. Mr Peke had tried that once, and Jacko had hit him with the stool and accused Mr Peke of indecently assaulting him. Indecently assaulting a disabled person is an accusation one finds hard to live down, particularly in the children's wear department.

And so Jacko was left to hop up and down until with a scream of delight his right hand, like a salmon taking the bait, had eventually clutched the gate handle. In triumph he hurtled backwards, dragging the gate with him and with a deftness belying his disabilities hopped into the lift and clanged it shut with remarkable force.

For a few brief moments, the shuddering lift came to a complete standstill, much to the relief of the encaged spinsters, who momentarily relaxed their grip on the Zimmer in a little hasty relapse of concentration. But no sooner had the lift achieved a motionless state, than Jacko proceeded to repeat the performance in an attempt to hook the handle of the inner gate.

Where the outer floor had previously helped support Jacko's vaulting and bouncing, the lift alone was now taking the full force. It was free to swing and judder at will, and it did just that.

Jacko was not so fortunate this time and although brushing the handle his hand failed to clasp it with sufficient strength, due to it being a cold day. Jacko's cavorting became more demonic and the lift was in such a state of tremor that it elicited the first cry of many from the now severely concerned inmates holding on to the Zimmer for dear life.

By now a small group of customers had joined the children's wear assistants to observe the spectacle being enacted before them. They saw Jacko, panting like a whippet, admit defeat and resort to the stool. His frustration at being unable to close the gate without it only made him more determined than ever to deliver his cargo intact and alive to the carpet department.

He struggled on to the stool to grip the handle. Getting down was, however, always a problem. Usually Jacko would ask a customer to pull him gently away from the stool while he closed the gate, all in one sweeping simultaneous movement. The spinsters were in no state to understand what was required of them, and the one nearest Jacko took it that to speed the proceedings along he wanted her to kick the stool from under him. She duly obliged.

Unprepared for this sudden demand of strength upon his right arm, Jacko fell to the floor screaming with pain. He was now blind to any objective in life other than showing he was as capable as anyone else of operating this lift. Grasping what was now an overcrowded Zimmer frame, he yanked himself to his feet and with a mighty hop, grabbed the handle with his left hand and hauled the gate shut.

In triumph he took hold of the brass lever

to set the lift in motion. The ascent to the carpet department started with a downward flight to the basement. Realizing this, Jacko immediately reversed direction by ignoring the stop section and ramming the lever into the 'up' position.

The lift juddered in violent protest at this savage misuse of its functions, and swayed so hard that one side clanged against the shaft. Then it started its upward momentum. Jacko, convinced matters were now under control, gave a victory smile as he passed up through the onlookers in the children's wear department. His convictions were short-lived – he missed the carpet department floor by a good eight feet. Annoyed, he slammed the lever back in to 'down' and the lift plummeted to the basement and then up to the fourth floor with several abrupt stops in between. None of them were anywhere near a level that would allow the spinsters to exit.

During the violent manoeuvring, the Zimmer frame had given up any hope of keeping four frail spinsters upright and had toppled over, sending them all sprawling. Two of them were clinging to Jacko's legs for support, while the other two rolled about the floor in unison with the swaying lift. Their cries for help were heard all over the store by now, and customers and staff gathered round the lift entrance and stairs to watch. The spinsters, in a state akin to jet lag and on the verge of being violently ill, were gesticulating to the watching crowds to do something, turn off the electricity, shoot Jacko, anything.

At one point the lift stopped with only a three-foot difference between its floor and that of the carpet department, but Jacko, ever the perfectionist, wanted it inch-perfect. His pride was at stake. There followed hundreds of little jerky ups and downs while he tried to get the levels absolutely level. To no avail. The lift, not built for such mistreatment, gave up the ghost by snapping one of its cables, and in a shower of sparks of welding-type proportions came to an abrupt halt between the carpet and garden furniture departments.

The near-unconscious spinsters clutched the bars of the gate and pleaded to be rescued.

The ladder was dutifully brought up from hardware to start the tricky business of getting four very ill spinsters out of the lift and down to the second floor where the store medical unit was situated.

Jacko refused to submit to such an ignominious exit, and was determined to stay with his lift until it was returned to the ground floor . . .

4

A large Daimler limousine pulled up outside
the entrance to the Beehive. People in the street
stopped and stared at the distinctive decoration that covered the entire car. Once belong-
ing to a famous member of a sixties beat group,
the car was painted in every conceivable colour
to convey an impression of a psychedelic journey
once taken by the artist during a particularly
bad trip. The onlookers, intrigued by this
antique of the flower-power era, then observed
the equally intriguing set of passengers alight-
ing from the vehicle.

Jim the commissionaire, at first, was most
suspicious of this exotic vehicle. Feeling sure
it contained people of foreign descent, he
prepared a diatribe of racist insults. He walked
over to the car to deliver his verbal attack and
was stopped in his tracks by the emergence of
Mangle the seven-foot troglodyte. Putting a large
hand on Jim's chest, he propelled the commissionaire backwards at a high rate of knots
whence he had come, through the revolving
doors. Mangle opened the passenger door and
helped Mr Big negotiate the large kerbstone.

Completing the trio came Rupert engrossed in a *Roget's Thesaurus*, looking up the variations on 'apportionment'.

At the wheel was the well known 'wheel', Spinsky, responsible for all Mr Big's transport requirements. Seeing his passengers safely into the store via the revolving door, Spinsky sped off down the High Street making sure to leave enough tyre smoke to impress the awe-struck sightseers.

Inside the store, Mr Big led Rupert and Mangle on a guided tour. Walking past the perfumery counter, Mrs Loving arose from her chair in the hope of making a sale. In doing so she released a great dermis cloud of smog-like proportions into the atmosphere. Mr Big hurried on to the safer area of the curtain department.

'Rupert,' he said, addressing the wordsmith, 'see what I mean? This could make the most fantastic amusement arcade in the whole of Europe. Look at the area of this ground floor. You could probably get three or four hundred slot machines in here. Each department would house all the different types of machines you can get. Space Invaders one end, What The Butler Saw the other, one-armed bandits at the entrance. London will have seen nothing like it.'

Rupert, not entirely convinced, took in the miserable surroundings and tried to envisage Atlantic City coming to High Street Ken.

Mr Big directed them up to the first floor. 'Look, look.' He was getting excited. 'Here we could have snooker tables, pool tables, football machines.'

Hurrying to the third floor, Mr Big was now beside himself with excitement. 'Here there could be massage parlours, a Bacchanalian room, the possiblities are endless. We could have our offices on the top floor and you have not seen the basement yet, but it's ideal for jacuzzis, saunas and just so many things!' exclaimed Mr Big, jumping up and down and clapping his hands with glee.

Mangle who just, sort of, got the gist of something he was not quite sure of, wondered if there was an area where he could practise maiming.

Rupert wasn't too sure about all of this. 'I can see the possiblities, Mr Big. Without doubt it's the perfect position considering all the tourists that visit this area, and space there is a-plenty, but you may have one small problem.'

Mr Big paused briefly in his joy. 'What might that be, Rupert?'

'A small question of planning permission.'

Mr Big continued his skipping. 'Rupert, you underestimate me. Mangle, tell Rupert, who is the planning officer?'

It was the word 'officer' that made Mangle stumble. 'Office' he understood, but the third syllable 'cer' did not relate to the first word.

'Duu . . . hhh . . . one of them 'igh up knobs who owns an office?'

Mr Big, used to his henchman's unexercised

brain, gave a sigh. He never gave up with Mangle. His ambition was to get him through the door-opening course with distinction. 'Never mind,' he sympathized. 'Let me explain to Rupert. The planning officer, Rupert, is the man at the Hamilton Club who wears the Zorro cape, mask and the Noddy slippers.'

Rupert was silent for a moment and then a smile crossed his face.

'Mr Big, there are times when your gangland expertise fills me with awe.'

'You're most kind, Rupert. Now let's keep our appointment with Mr Dunnet.'

Dunnet's office was Executive MFI, low-budget Hollywood. The combination of nylon carpet and plastic wood furniture generated enough static electricity to run a small generator. His taste in modern tat was at variance with the rest of the store's Victorian tat.

Dunnet was bemoaning the harshness of life. The bills on his desk resulting from his personal social excesses all bore a vivid shade of red. There was one for £327.00 from the Flower Emporium demanding payment for orchids, red roses and flower arrangements that he had sent to his many elderly lady friends. There were other bills from car sales rooms and credit card companies, all adding up to many thousands of pounds. What frustrated Eric was that he was sitting at this very moment on a site and premises that, if he could only get his hands on a fraction of what it was worth, could fulfil all his wanton desires and ambitions until he keeled over with the sheer ecstasy of indulging them all.

His obstacle, of course, was Alfred Knowles. How much longer would that old fogey spend on this earth! He had toyed many a time with the idea of doing away with the ancient git, but whilst most criminal acts he would consider without conscience, murder was not one of them. His thoughts were interrupted by the voice of his secretary Melissa accompanying her knocking on the door.

'Mr Dunnet, the three gentlemen are here for your 2.30 pm appointment.'

'Right, send them in please, Melissa,' shouted Dunnet, and tidying his desk he prepared to meet the three strangers. He was curious as to who they might be. The Bishop of Lambeth had phoned several days previously with a request to meet them. He felt that it could be to their mutual advantage. The Bishop's tone of voice had certainly contained an urgency that indicated as such.

After a few moments' wait there was another knock. Melissa opened the door and led in the three visitors.

Dunnet was quite taken aback as to their appearance and quickly realized he did not have a chair big enough for Mangle to sit in, or indeed a chair small enough for Mr Big to climb on to. The problem was solved by Mangle sitting on the edge of Dunnet's desk and propping Mr Big on his knee. Rupert, ever conventional, sat on an appropriate chair next to his boss.

After the formal introductions, Mr Big opened the conversation. 'Very nice store you have here, Mr Dunnet.'

Dunnet, trying to get over the odd presence of these three men, mentally questioned the sanity of anyone who thought this place had anything whatsoever to recommend it.

'Thank you, umm . . . Mr Big?'

'Correct,' said the dwarf.

'Whether or not it's a nice place is a matter of controversy.'

'Excuse me,' said Rupert, 'I think you will find it's pronounced contro*versy*, the stress being on the versy not the trov.'

Dunnet, perplexed, wondered why he was having an English grammar lesson from a total stranger.

'Forgive Rupert,' said Mr Big, 'he's such a perfectionist where grammar is concerned,' and then commanded Mangle to stop bouncing him up and down on his knee.

'Let me get straight to the point of why we are here, Mr Dunnet.' Eric sat down behind his desk to listen to this strange little figure.

'Let me first say that we are aware of your understanding with the Bishop of Lambeth regarding the Beehive if and when it subsequently passes to the Church.'

The effect on Eric of this statement was as if he'd been jabbed in the rear with a cattle prod. '*What* understanding?' he spurted.

'Let me state this. The Bishop has been most

47

forthcoming in his confidences to us. He has explained the arrangement you have for these premises when the owner, Mr Alfred Knowles, goes to meet the big retailer in the sky.'

'I don't know what you're talking about!'

'Let us not insult each other with trivial banter. I will just say this. After the demise of Mr Knowles, I have plans for these premises that will be worth a great deal of money to me and other people concerned that I am dealing with. We would be prepared to make it worth your while to consider coming to an agreement with our goodselves.'

Eric, preparing to lie through his molars, wondered if he'd heard right. 'What sort of agreement?'

'How does a hundred thousand pounds sound?' said Mr Big.

It sounded very good to Eric. So good that it forced him bolt upright in his chair, banging his knees on the desk. His mouth moved without emitting any sound save for a dry croak that prompted a coughing fit of magnitudous proportions.

'One hundred K!' spluttered Eric.

Mr Big, realizing that he might have aroused Eric's interest, confirmed the figure.

'My partners and I are very serious about this property Mr, er . . . Dunnet. If you would check with the Bishop you will find that we are most honourable in our dealings and would appreciate your assistance in an attempt to achieve our ambitions.'

Eric could not believe his ears. Here was someone, whom he had never met, offering him a
great deal of money. There must be more to
this than met the eye.

'What would you have me do,' said Eric, 'for
this extremely generous amount of money?'

'We both know,' said Mr Big, 'that when Alfred
passes away, the Church gets the property and
the Bishop will have full jurisdiction on the
Church's behalf to determine the future of the
store. The Bishop is extremely anxious that my
consortium reimburses the Church, how shall
we say, adequately. Your silence as to the
beneficial terms on which we will acquire the
buildings would more than make up for the gift
we would like to make to you and I would hasten
to add that, depending upon how beneficial the
terms are, there could be another cheque on
its way to your bank account that would make
this one seem like a DHSS payment.'

'And that's it?' said Dunnet, hardly being able
to believe his luck if all of this was true.

'Certainly,' said Mr Big affably, 'there are a
few points which I am sure Rupert here would
like to go through with you over the coming
weeks, but nothing too much untoward, just a
few guarantees here and there. What do you
say?'

Eric composed himself with a great deal of
unaccustomed aplomb and said that he would
think about it.

'Splendid,' said Mr Big, 'we need not take up
any more of your time. Rupert here will be in

touch and I look forward to a favourable reply.'

With that Mangle popped Mr Big back on to the floor and the trio left the office, satisfied that the arrangements would suffice to provide the required assistance.

As Melissa closed the door on their exit, Dunnet danced a jig around the room, kissing the statement he had had that morning from American Express. Sitting down he immediately phoned the Bishop of Lambeth and confirmed with the Lord Bishop the details of the meeting he had just had. When he had all he wanted to know, he replaced the phone and hand-wrote a letter to a Mr Big, c/o The Hamilton Club, the gist of which agreed to his proposition and ended with the fact that Eric would look forward to a certain amount of remuneration as soon as possible.

Within the week, Eric had paid all his bills and was the proud owner of a Jaguar XJS HE in Sebring Green.

5

As the last notes of *Happy Birthday* concluded,
so the gathered employees of Alfred Knowles
burst into *For He's a Jolly Good Fellow* with
an apathy largely reserved for those celebrities
who open new post offices.

Not that Alfred Knowles, now ninety-seven,
was disliked. Nobody really saw him to have
an informed opinion. No, it was just that
everything about Knowles department store had
apathy running like holiday-rock lettering
throughout every department, office and soul.

Alfred Knowles sat in his wheelchair summon-
ing up enough breath to attempt to extinguish
the eight dozen or more candles set out before
him on a cake that was an exact replica of the
store he owned. They were perched on the
sloping roofs and turrets of the building and
lined the marzipan pavements that represented
the part of Kensington High Street that fronted
the store. The candles ablaze, Alfred blew with
concentrated gusts of halitosis to douse the
flames so that the confectionery could be divided
and consumed by the staff present.

The staff themselves weren't too keen on

devouring the delicacy. Along with the gasps of wind emanating from Alfred's mouth, little flecks of spittle emerged that cascaded and glinted in the candle beams, alighted upon the glaze and blended quite nicely with the tiny silver balls with which one is obliged to decorate any celebratory cake. As the slurry poured from the vortex of Alfred's crimson face, the candle flames resisted any further attempt at ignition and quickly spluttered into saturated submission.

Grasping the silver-handled knife, Mr Knowles plunged it into the cake with gusto, neatly splitting the bedding department from soft furnishings and forming a neat triangular wedge that contained perfumery on the ground floor, music on the first, bedding on the second and complaints tucked away in the skylight on the roof.

Coming forward to grasp the first slice was Eric Dunnet. Alfred not only despised his managing director, but regretted the day his brother Ronald had sired the revolting brat. He regretted even more the fact that he'd been saddled with the bastard child.

Ronald Knowles had escaped action in the war by convincing an army medical officer he was allergic to cordite, potatoes and corned beef. He was promptly called up and put in charge of catering at the Aldershot gun ranges. Whilst achieving his aim of avoiding action it also gave him the opportunity to indulge in his favourite pastime, dallying with the many available females at the barracks and, not far away, the Kensington store.

At the end of the war, Ronald spent most of his time gambling and avoiding innumerable irate husbands returning from the front, looking to use their new-found killing techniques on Ronald. One bombardier in particular was extremely displeased on his return to find that his wife was bearing Ronald's child. The woman herself was a slim unattractive brunette in charge of haberdashery at the Beehive, and had let herself be seduced by Ronald in exchange for extra tins of corned beef and a promised rise in salary.

Their afternoon of illicit passion had been conducted on Wednesday half-day closing in the bedding department. The luxurious Viscount spring mattress on which they writhed was so smooth and all-enveloping that, transported to such states of sensual excitement, contraception was overlooked completely.

The bombardier made regular visits to the Beehive in the hope of catching Ronald on the premises. Each time he carried the new-born infant in his arms, determined to confront Ronald and make him take full responsibility. The bombardier didn't want the brat anywhere near him or his house, and anyway, the baby was ugly. Its sole interesting feature was a birthmark on the bum.

Ronald had warned all the doormen and store security staff to let him know when the bombardier was anywhere in the vicinity, so he could scamper away into some secret corner of the building and hide until he could no longer hear his name, with added expletives concerning his own parentage, bellowed round the premises. Eventually, such was the bombardier's frustration with Ronald's refusal to be confronted that he left the bawling baby, basket, bottle and all, in the hands of the new lady assistant in haberdashery, informing all and sundry that it was their responsibility now and they were welcome to the monkey. He further informed them that he still wanted Ronald's blood and went into graphic description of what he would do to Ronald's bodily orifices, plus something to do with Ronald's teeth and an act of circumcision. Ronald heard all this quite clearly as he quaked in the boiler room behind a pile of coke.

The bombardier refused all inducements to accept the child back, leaving Ronald's uncle Alfred in somewhat of a dilemma. What could he do with a three-month-old child on the premises, squawking most of the day, his haberdashery assistant complaining bitterly that it was not part of her duties to be a surrogate mother? Ronald was refusing to accept any responsibility for the child; it would certainly put a damper on the numerous amorous affairs in which he was still indulging.

Alfred, never one to deflect an opportunity, came to an agreement with his brother. He, Alfred Knowles, would take over the parental role concerning the child, providing Ronald would refrain from entering the store altogether and leave sole responsibility of the Beehive to him. Ronald would be paid handsomely for this provision and would still have a fifty per cent share of the company, provided he bequeathed all voting rights to Alfred, leaving him in complete control. Further, if Ronald would see his way to putting a great deal of distance between himself and the Beehive, Alfred would see to it that he received regular wages to be sent anywhere in the western hemisphere.

This would achieve two aims. One: Ronald would be out of his hair. The husbands and suitors now pestering the store wanting to rearrange his brother's genitalia was reaching epidemic proportions, and the fact that he could now tell them that Ronald was legitimately 'away' would be a considerable relief. Two: Alfred would be able to run the Beehive just as he wanted to. He would strive to keep the store for gentlemen and ladies who would insist on only the finest of traditional merchandise, those customers who appreciated the finest accoutrements of civilization and who would spurn the mass-produced garbage that seemed to mesmerize those with lesser breeding.

So it was that Ronald packed his belongings and with ten thousand pounds bulging from his money pouch, he boarded the *Queen Elizabeth* to sail to New York, where he would start afresh amongst a community he felt was more attuned to his way of living and morals. Eric, his son, was swiftly taken care of. Alfred hired a buxom mother of three healthy children to foster Eric, paid for a good school education and generally looked after him at a distance not enough to trouble his Christian conscience.

Eventually he persuaded the foster mother to officially adopt Eric, and promised to pay adequate amounts to support the child. He made it a condition that she would never tell Eric of his background, and so he grew up without knowing that the boss he despised was his uncle.

As a child, Eric was blessed with his mother's scrawny looks and pale complexion. From his father he inherited selfishness and a propensity for failure. His school career was remarkable, not for academic achievements, which were below average, but for his hucksterism. One of his first exploits was to sell school milk to the local milkman. Eric realized that by becoming milk monitor, he had control over delivery of the milk to the thirty or so children in his class. By paying twopence a week to each pupil to forgo their milk, he could then sell the whole crate each day to another milkman and make himself two shillings and sixpence per week: an admirable scheme that would have run more than its two-year course, had it not been for the suspicions of the local school medical officer, Dr Robson. He was more than puzzled as to why the pupils of form 3A Derryfields Senior should have such an abnormal incidence of rickets. It took only a cursory interrogation of the class to determine the reason for this lack of calcium and Eric was, as an example to others, pummelled in front of the whole school by a sadistic headmaster with a Dunlop size-ten plimsoll.

Eric's entrepreneurial designs achieved local celebrity status. He actually made the front page of the local paper when they did an exposé on the 'Fagin of Derryfields Senior School'.

Eric had organized a little posse of first and second formers to go on shoplifting forays into the local town centre. He would take orders from his classmates for diaries, chocolate, pens, records and suchlike, then instruct his urchins to steal them to order. Eric discovered early on in his life that for some reason he instilled quite naturally into people a strange mixture of trust and fear. This characteristic he put to good use, and the urchins readily succumbed to the lure of his will. What alerted the press to this Dickens-like ring of hooligans was a case of over-enthusiasm by a young first former called Umbers.

Umbers was instructed by Eric to obtain a garden spade for a fifth former who wanted a present for his father's birthday. What Umbers lacked in nous he made up for in enthusiasm. The filching of a garden spade was not so easy as it seemed. The local hardware store had a keen-eyed lady assistant who trusted nobody, and in particular, not the shifty little first formers from Derryfield.

Umbers, distraught at the thought of failure and Eric's subsequent displeasure, did his best to find another source. On scouting round the High Street shops in the lunch hour, he found himself at the back where a large building project was underway. With the construction workers ensconced in a pub for their lunch, the site was clear for Umbers to peruse.

It would appear all the implements for digging and shovelling were locked away to prevent people like Umbers acquiring them. At a loss and in near panic at the thought of Eric's retribution, Umbers had a brainwave.

And so it was at quarter to two in the afternoon, Umbers arrived at the school gates driving a mechanical digger.

His face was a beam of delight, anticipating the shower of gratitude and appreciation that Eric would bestow upon him. The beam quickly faded as the digger failed to respond to any attempt to halt its progress. It ambled down the school drive, heading inexorably towards the new science lab extension.

The science teacher, Mr Winnersthorpe, was conducting a private lunchtime lesson for four sixth formers on the explosive properties of hydrogen and its use in electronics, when a mechanical digger, entering by the brick wall, brought the instruction to an abrupt and near fatal conclusion.

In the subsequent interrogation, Umbers confessed all and Eric, who thus sold his story to the local press, would have been expelled but for an anonymous and generous donation towards a new science lab, fully equipped. His uncle, threatened with exposure by the little sod's adoptive mother, had had no other option.

Therefore it came as no surprise to Alfred that, his greed and manipulative qualities to the fore, Eric was leading the queue for the first slice of cake.

As the rest of the staff queued up dutifully for their share, Alfred viewed them with a despairing eye. There was Miss Marchmont, the store detective, attired in her customary deerstalker hat and tweed cape, inspecting her section of birthday cake with a large magnifying glass and intense suspicion. Miss Marchmont was suspicious of everything and everybody. Over the years she had cultivated an air of superiority and mystery so she could better emulate her childhood hero Sherlock Holmes. Ever since she had read the novels of Arthur Conan Doyle, she had wanted to believe every word written. They were not novels to her, but true accounts of a genius, a man born to rid the earth of crime and evil, a guru who went unrecognized, a master who was misplaced in the realms of fiction. She, Judith Marchmont, would see to it that Sherlock would be resurrected to his true place of enlightenment. She inspected the cake more closely.

The droplets of saliva appeared as large globulets through the lens of the magnifying glass. Her disgust hidden so as not to offend Mr Knowles, she looked round for her constant companion, a fat, waddling bulldog.

'Watson! Here boy!'

Watson heaved himself up from the corner

and flabbed his way across the room, accelerating as he suspected the prospect of food.

She bent down to pat him and then, checking to make sure no one was looking, slipped the whole segment of cake including candles to Watson. The dog wolfed it down complete in a flash. Anyone noting this remarkable feat would have been immediately reminded of an iguana licking up a large crusty beetle. The cake and candles disappeared down Watson's throat totally without the aid of his fearsome set of molars, so that his stomach acids would have to deal with the original state of construction.

Watson sat down waiting hopefully for a repeat performance, but having done her duty Miss Marchmont was in no haste to obtain another slice. She bent over to pat Watson and usher him back to his corner. As she did so, several of the males present gave admiring glances to her rather pert form. It was widely suspected of Miss Marchmont that underneath her tweeds and trews was a fine figure of a woman that sadly never saw the light of day.

In an effort to emulate her hero she had taken great pains to appear masculine, even to the extent of clamping a pipe between her teeth. Tobacco made her sick, so she had to settle for pulling draughts of pure air through the bowl and stem. The pipe would appear at moments of great concentration when, pondering with deep perception, she would try to unravel the plunderings of the kleptomaniacs she was convinced infested the Beehive.

Alfred looked around for Hacket, the Company Accountant. There he was, skulking in the corner that had just been vacated by Watson. Hacket was a timid wretch of a man, totally controlled by Dunnet. He had a stutter that was little short of appalling. Any stressful situation or difficult occasion and Hacket would become almost silent, his speech deserting him except for the odd syllable expunged between interminable passages of silence.

No amount of therapy had been able to cure this unfortunate disability, although there had been a breakthrough several years previously when it was discovered that his diction could return to something near normality if he sang everything. His oratory problem did have its advantages, in particular when he was discussing the company's books and affairs with the tax authorities. The government representatives on taxation matters would sit mesmerized for hours on end as Hacket would attempt to read even the most rudimentary parts of the annual tax returns. The balance sheet alone would take the best part of a fortnight, and even the most dedicated civil servant would refrain from asking for any clarification rather than risk Hacket replying, mouth agape in a fruitless attempt to communicate.

It was therefore to the company's benefit that many a shenanigan in the accounts was spared the inquisitive gaze of the tax collector. A benefit of which Eric Dunnet was well aware.

Hacket's singing technique could be very successful, too, at times. When Eric set fire to some old stock to claim the insurance on it, he got Hacket to phone the fire brigade and send the warning.

The receptionist handling the calls became confused by this strange man who, each time the lines connected, could utter only single syllables. Halfway through the fifth attempt at conversation he burst into song, and to the tune of *Colonel Bogie* relayed the information that there was a fire at the Beehive in Kensington High Street and to send a fire engine immediately.

She was obviously dealing with a drunk and slammed the phone down. Hacket tried again, only this time he used the opening refrain from *Guys and Dolls*. After a rendering of most of the current popular hits, the receptionist finally thought there might be some grain of truth in the peculiar proceedings and so sent a fire engine round to the Beehive. It was of course hopelessly late. Eric had the insurance agent assessing the claim well before the first hose was attached to the fire hydrant in the High Street.

And so, along with Dunnet and Hacket, Miss Marchmont and Watson, Alfred glanced around at the rest of the drab lot that made up the backbone of the Beehive's apology for a commercial establishment. None of the prim and properness he was brought up to respect, no stiff white collars and Brylcreemed hair.

Alfred Knowles had not grown old gracefully. As each birthday arrived and he woke up to find himself condemned to embarking on another year on earth, he wondered what was the terrible sin he had committed to warrant such a punishment from God. Others thought he was such a miserable old bugger that God was just putting off the moment when he'd have to welcome him at the Pearly Gates. If he got any more miserable he could establish a world record — even outstripping all those sour Russian peasants who seemed to live forever on a diet of vodka and black bread.

Alfred would certainly go to heaven. He had led a blameless life — well, if you forgot the incident at the Henley Regatta when he substituted sennapods for the olives. If he was guilty of any sin it was the sin of snobbishness. Alfred was a terrible snob.

He had devoted his working life at the Beehive to making it the sort of store that duchesses would be proud to be seen in. For years it was his pompous boast that he had grovelled to more than half the members of the British aristocracy. He didn't call it grovelling, but others certainly did.

Not that he'd ever actually licked a duke's boots — well, not while the duke was still wearing them — but he had in his time been playfully horsewhipped by a belted earl who'd found a cockroach in a pair of pyjamas, and many a dowager's brolly had caught him in the mezzanine. He didn't mind if they all spoke to him with three or four plums in their mouths, so long as the plums came from the Beehive.

He liked nothing better than to descend from his rooftop apartment to the ground floor of the store and count the horn-voiced dowagers whose booming tones caused chandeliers to shake and had the assistants in glassware scrambling to get the stock off the counters before it was shattered into a thousand pieces.

He would point out proudly to visitors: 'We've got three-quarters of Debrett here today and quite a lot of Burkes as well.'

He grovelled, he fawned, he was so oily and oozy that had he wrung his hands he would have dripped on the carpet.

He still remembered his first encounter with the Duke of Southwark. 'Oh, so you're the shopkeeper person, are you?' 'Yes, your grace.' 'Do you know anything about cars?' 'As a matter of fact I do, your grace.' 'Good, fetch mine.'

They walked all over him but he didn't seem to mind. Providing they were wearing handmade shoes. Those were the days. None of that rubbish about a dustman being as good as a duke — unlike today when a dustman could end up a duke. He longed for those far-off times when the English gentleman spent his days huntin', shootin', fishin' and droppin' his Gs.

It depressed him that those days were no more. He looked round today and hated everything he saw. He hated hamburgers, people who ate in the street, drank in the street, kissed in the street. Men who wore earrings, policemen without moustaches, women in culottes, buses that only had a driver, instant tea, French apples, plastic cups, litter, little triangular containers of milk that squirted all over you, and anything wrapped in plastic. This feeling of disenchantment had been with him for years. In fact on his ninetieth birthday, as a present to himself he took out a life subscription to Exit. They welcomed him, saying how much they hoped he would breathe new life into the organization.

Then he was made president of Exit, and during his year in office the society went from strength to strength, with membership down by more than two hundred per cent. This was largely due to Alfred's inspired campaign to introduce smoking as a part of intensive care for elderly heart patients. Now he was coming to the end of that year in office and he was still alive – a situation he was going to have to do something about, because part of the unwritten constitution of Exit was that one way or another, when the president left office, he did so in a box.

Alfred dejectedly made his way to the sanctity of his office next door to put the finishing flourish to his bizarre if dramatic plan to be rid of all this nonsense and Eric Dunnet too. With a sigh he wheeled his chair over to where he had plugged the electrodes into the mains. The plan was simple, as most good plans are. He would ask Dunnet into the room and get him to help attach the electrodes to his body. He would say it was a new machine to help his heart cope with the demands of his old age. Dunnet would be too engrossed in his own affairs to realize it was a voltage pump, a lethal device designed to facilitate a near-painless instant death. He would be sure to pick an argument with Eric, a violent one that would be heard next door, and when a suitable moment arrived and the volt accumulator had built up enough charge, he would throw a bucket of water over himself, throw the switch and prepare to meet the great retailer in the sky. At last he would be rid of this wretched world, but best of all he would have incriminated Eric Dunnet.

Alfred was aware that Dunnet had other plans for the store. He had lost count of the times property speculators had been dismissed from his office with their ears throbbing from the effects of his tirade against the get-rich-quick brigade, their lack of morals and anyway, weren't they the ones responsible for the downgrading of his beloved high-class clientele by their money-grabbing socialist policies, their envy of the better bred. He would have nothing to do with them. But Eric, he suspected, had every intention of benefiting from the store passing to the Church. And there was always the dread that he'd find out about his heritage.

He busied himself about the office, preparing his planned death, waiting for the party next door to draw to its close . . .

The party was coming nicely to an end. The

slices of cake, eaten only from the bottom up, lay bedraggled on plates.

Watson hauled himself around polishing off what bits he could find on the floor. His mistress was listening with intent and a tiny bit of apprehension as the managing director was emphasizing the need to introduce Islamic law to deal with shoplifters.

'Don't stop at the bloody wrists, tear the whole arm off, that's what I say. A few empty coat sleeves dangling round the store and that'll put a stop to it.'

'I quite agree, Mr Dunnet,' said Miss Marchmont, 'but who will do the arm tearing? It would be a most unpleasant task, one that few people other than sadistic psychopaths would attempt!'

'I'm not a sadistic bloke,' insisted Dunnet, 'but believe me when word gets round that you don't use anaesthetics, that it's just torn off, you watch the crime figures drop.'

'Sta. . .sta. . .sta. . .tistics show tha. . . tha. . .that in I. . .' A feeling of dejection descended as people realized Hacket was about to communicate.

Dunnet figured out Hacket was about to attempt the word Islam or Islamic, and knowing he'd got some twenty or thirty seconds more to develop his theme, he continued. 'Those Ayatollahs have got it just about right, anyone gives you trouble snuff 'em.'

'Is. . . Is. . . Is. . . lamic countries the c. . . c . . . c. . . c. . . crime rates are w. . . w. . . w. . . w. . . w. . . way d. . . d. . . d. . . down com. . . p. . . p. . . p. . .' Hacket always had trouble with Ps.

Thankfully the phone rang to relieve the dejection.

'It's for you, Mr Dunnet, Mr Knowles would like to see you in his office.'

'I wonder what the old man wants now,' mumbled Eric, and leaving Hacket choking on his Ps, he walked through the door into Alfred Knowles' office. 'You wanted to see me?' He splayed himself out in the office armchair.

Alfred wheeled his chair around from behind his antique desk and came to a halt as near the door as was possible without appearing too strange.

'Yes, Eric,' said Alfred, and in a deliberately provocative voice he continued, 'I'm going to sack you from the company.'

Eric jerked violently upright in his chair.

'Furthermore, I'm well aware of your collusion with those so-called property buyers, the deals you've set up. I know what you're up to Eric, and I'm putting a stop to it once and for all.'

As Alfred expected, Dunnet rose from his chair and in a mixture of sneering disbelief and white-faced panic, yelled, 'What are you talking about, you stupid old bastard?'

'Exactly what I've just said.' He replied in a voice slightly louder, matching Eric's for the benefit of the people at the party next door.

'You're finished! Finished. I'm fed up with the way you conduct yourself, your business, your social life and your despicable lusting after women of mature years.'

Alfred's voice had risen now to a decibel level. The party came to a full stop as people craned their ears to listen to what was happening. Apart from Watson snaffling the last of the birthday cake, the one sound that could be heard in the room was Hacket still trying to pronounce 'compared'.

Eric, taken aback by the verbal onslaught, started to scream with rage. 'You can't sack me, I won't let you, I've got lawyers, accountants, I'll challenge you in court, why you geriatric, senile, stupid lump of plasma, don't think you can—'

Alfred cut him off in mid flow.

'Too late, Eric, tomorrow the papers will be despatched to you, do what you will but whatever it is, it will be too late; your scheming, selfish, evil doings will be no more and there will be many a person here glad of that! Tomorrow, Eric, tomorrow will be the most pleasant day of my life.'

The staff had by now all edged closer to the door, from where they could hear the argument a little more clearly.

Eric went into a furious tantrum of vile adjectives describing old people in wheelchairs. Alfred merely wheeled his chair over to the electrical apparatus and calmly applied the electrodes to his temples and heart area. Clutching two extra large cylindrical metal tubes, one in each hand, he smiled and asked in a calm voice, 'Would you like me dead, Eric?'

'You don't know how much I want you dead.

The hours I've spent wishing you dead would surprise even you, Alfred. The sooner you die the happier I'll be!'

Alfred had suspected as much and indeed had hoped for such a statement, but what venom! Even better.

'Come over here, Eric.' Alfred motioned Dunnet to step around the desk. 'Here, hold these.'

'What's going on?' cried Eric, for the first time taking real notice of the contraption by Alfred's feet and the wires and electrodes emanating from it.

'Just hold the tubes for a moment.' Somewhat perplexed, he grabbed the tubes from Alfred's hands.

'What on earth are you trying to do, electrocute yourself? I mean, don't let me stop you!'

Eric's fingerprints were on the tubes. He now had to get them on the electrodes.

'It's a birthday present to myself,' said Alfred. 'It monitors your heart beat, blood pressure and biorhythms. It helps me to relax when I am under pressure. You should try it some time. Here, just adjust the electrodes for me, will you?'

Eric thought that if the machine could measure his own rate and blood pressure right now, they would blow the bloody thing from here to Marble Arch. He adjusted the electrodes on Alfred's head.

'Pass me that bucket of water in the corner, would you please, Eric?'

Even more puzzled, he crossed the room to fetch a large pail of water that was placed under the old 'Fire Emergency' sign. As he did so, unbeknown to Alfred his foot caught the wire that led from the voltage pump to the three-pin plug in the socket on the wall. Stumbling slightly, Eric took the bucket across to Alfred. 'Thank you, Eric.' In one sudden movement he had poured its entire contents over himself.

Eric looked on in astonishment, now very confused, and even more so when Alfred started yelling. 'Stop it, Eric, don't, you'll kill me! What are you trying to do?' The geriatric then let out a gurgled scream as he pulled the switch that would send two thousand volts juddering through his body.

When nothing happened Alfred pulled the switch again and then again and then furiously backwards and forwards — he couldn't believe he was still breathing.

Eric, not fully understanding these events but realizing that something was drastically wrong here, dashed over to the door. There was a military tattoo being hammered on the oak-panelled door by concerned staff wondering what the hell was going on. He opened the door a little and popped his head through. 'Yes?' he enquired.

'What's happening, Mr Dunnet, we heard terrible noises, is Mr Knowles all right?' Miss Marchmont was at the forefront of the crowd, her magnifying glass at the ready, asking the questions.

'Right as rain, Miss Marchmont, he's just a little excited at the birthday present I've bought him.' Eric popped his head back and closed the door.

'What are you up to, you devious old clown?' he hissed, rushing over to the old man dripping wet in his wheelchair. A three-pin plug was dangling down from the end of the lead that Alfred now held in his hand.

'You pulled the plug on me,' cried Alfred. 'You knew all along what I was going to do!'

'Knew what?' said Eric, and then his astonishment returned as he saw Alfred pull a rope, attached to his desk, with a noose on the end. 'You won't outdo me, Eric Dunnet!' Whereupon Alfred and his wheelchair belted over to the window. Pulling the noose over his head he opened the window and shouted, 'Don't, Eric, don't, I don't want to die. Eric *stop*!' With that he hauled himself out of his chair and attempted to exit from the window.

Eric started to get some inkling of what was going on.

'Oh no you don't, you devious little bastard!' He dashed over and started to haul Alfred back in.

The drumming on the door started up again.

'Are you all right in there, what's happening?' Miss Marchmont again.

Having got Alfred back in his chair once more, Eric rushed back and popped his head through the door again. Through the spy glass one eye surveyed him, a big brown one, three times the normal size. 'He gets livelier as he gets older, doesn't he?' said Eric with a forced laugh.

72

Miss Marchmont craned her neck round the door. As she did she saw the boss of the Beehive, dripping wet, halfway through the window, his legs fast disappearing.

'*What's* Mr Knowles doing hanging out of the window?' queried Miss Marchmont, glass to the other eye now.

Eric turned around. 'Oh, my God!' He slammed the door on the woman and her magnifying glass. 'He's feeding the birds again!' he laughingly trilled as he caught the turn-ups of Alfred's trousers. He yanked furiously and with a mighty heave, hauled the old man back into the room.

'Curse you!' shrieked Alfred, panting loudly as he lay on the floor.

'My God, are you *mental*,' hissed Eric. 'Why the hell are you trying to kill yourself?'

'If I thought you had the intelligence of a gnat I'd try to explain. I hate you, don't you understand, I have a loathing for you that surpasses all loathing!'

Crawling on all fours, Alfred reached a large cupboard that covered one side of the wall. From inside the bottom compartment he pulled out a large shotgun.

Eric gave out a yell of anguish. 'Don't pull the trigger!'

'Keep back or I'll blast you off the face of the earth,' warned Alfred, whereupon he turned the barrels round and put them in his mouth. 'Goodbye, Eric,' he mumbled flabbily.

As he turned his thumbs to pull both triggers, so Eric bent down and pulled the carpet on which Alfred was half-lying. The gun popped out of Alfred's mouth and both barrels unleashed their deadly load of lead shot into the glass partition of the old cupboard with an almighty double boom followed by the shattering of one-hundred-year-old brittle Victorian glass. There was only one noise louder – that of the battering on the door by the entire cast of partygoers.

Eric shouted through the ever-so-slightly-ajar door, 'Boy, I hope you're having as much fun out here as we are in there!'

Miss Marchmont had had to forgo her place in the front of the battering ram and be replaced by Hacket, now so excited by the whole proceedings he had forgotten all about Islamic crime statistics and was demanding to know what was happening to the tune of *The Dambusters*. 'What was that big banging noise – that we all heard clearly in here – and is there something going on – that you are trying to hide?'

There followed a heated discussion between Dunnet and the rest of the party as to the whys and wherefores of entering the room or not entering the room, all accompanied by Hacket's new snatches of a well-known military refrain.

Whilst the din continued, Alfred took the opportunity of clambering back into his wheelchair. He was becoming a mite exhausted as he spun the chair round and headed for the medicine cabinet in the opposite corner of the room.

As retiring president of the Exit organization,

the stock of arsenic was more than sufficient for his purposes. He always kept arsenic on hand for desperate members who wanted to leave the earth post-haste. Half a dozen tablets and eternal rest was anybody's.

Should he chew them or swallow them with water? He had no chance to discover which was the quickest way. In a high state of agitation, and certainly under no illusions by now that the old sod was trying to implicate him as his murderer, Eric had jammed a chair against the door and rushed over to knock the pills flying from his hated boss's hand. As he did so the wheelchair spun round and the rope, still around Alfred's neck and attached to his desk, began to curl itself around his arms and body.

Eric saw his chance of a respite. He frantically spun the chair round and round until all the rope was bound around the figure in the chair, thereby immobilizing him temporarily. Stuffing a handkerchief into Alfred's mouth, he grabbed the wires from the voltage pump and tied the chair to the desk.

'There, that'll keep you out of mischief for a while! I'll deal with you later.' Eric composed himself and entered the party room, ready to do some fast talking. But as he closed the linking door he turned back and shouted through for all to hear, 'Thank you, uncle, lovely party, but why anyone should want to buy you a starting pistol I'll never know!'

'A starting pistol?' sang Hacket.

'Yes,' said Eric and with as much plausibility

as he could get away with, brightly announced, 'When you get to his age it's damned difficult to try to buy something he hasn't got.'

'But why would anybody want to buy him a starting pistol?' enquired Miss Marchmont.

Eric, stuck for an answer, ignored the question and began to clear the room of the party-makers. 'Right. The party's over, and there's a whole lot of people out there desperate to spend their well-earned money on our wonderful merchandise.' He ushered the people out of the door, including a very suspicious Miss Marchmont and Hacket, who had stopped singing by now and had recommenced trying to convince everyone of the low crime rates in Islamic dominated countries.

Eric returned to deal with Alfred Knowles. As he walked through the door Alfred was staring at him intently, water still dripping from his hair, the rope bound loosely but still immobilizing any actions he cared to make.

'Now would you kindly tell me what that nonsense was all about?'

Still Alfred stared intently, not moving.

'I said, would you care to tell me why you are trying to implicate me in your murder?'

Further enquiries upon Eric's part were not only falling on deaf ears, they were falling on dead ones. As Eric moved forward terror and panic rose to activate every single nerve in his body. He desperately unravelled the rope from around the torso and listened anxiously for any sound of life. He shook the old man violently by the shoulders, and screamed, 'Wake up, wake up, you cretinous bastard!' He laid his boss on the floor and remembering what he could from some obscure St John Ambulance instruction book, he tried to give Alfred the kiss of life.

To no avail. The old man had achieved his aim, albeit not in the manner he had intended. The tension, excitement and sheer physical exhaustion had all been too much for Alfred's heart, and it just stopped. Simple as that!

Eric got back up and started pacing the floor. What was he to do? The best thing was what he would normally do; fake something, cheat, lie, deceive, blame someone else perhaps, that would come later. First thing was to tidy Alfred up. He dashed round, found a towel and started to dry his hair. Sitting Alfred in the wheelchair, he straightened his collar and tie, combed his hair and gently moved him over to the private lift installed in the office. Opening the doors carefully, he put Alfred in and closed the doors.

He then set about cleaning up the office, making a mental note to have the cupboard glass repaired as soon as possible. Walking back down to his own office, he sat down and contemplated his next moves . . .

The Beehive had a sale once a year. Any merchandise that was unpopular or had outlived its usefulness was marked down in price and offered for sale to the public.

Normally at sales prices do come down. However, some of the items of merchandise at the

Beehive had been there so long that no matter how much they were marked down, they still cost more than the original purchase price. For instance, whalebone bodices in the ladies' underwear department had originally sold for 3/6d. As inflation put the price up every year, the retail price was now somewhere in the region of £85. However, they were on offer in the sale for £19 19s 6d, marked up in old money for the benefit of the majority of the customers, and £19.97½ for the new-fangled decimal coinage. The price tags on the bodices had been changed so often that the holes left by the pins could actually pass for decoration. Alfred Knowles' insistence that nothing in the present day could match what was made fifty to one hundred years ago reigned supreme.

As with all stores, the Beehive had succumbed to loss leaders, those heavily reduced goods usually brought in especially for the sales. Normally the Beehive sale would last for two hours, everyone buying the loss leaders and leaving the rest of the stock where it was.

The crowd outside the main doors numbered six hundred or so. Avarice predominated in the faces squidged up against the glass. At nine o'clock the doors would be opened and the rampaging mob would scatter around the store, pouncing like hawks on sale bargains, scuffling and arguing with the other hawks as to who got there first.

Sale day was like no other day in the year at the Beehive; it was the day when all their regular customers refused to cross the threshold. The Beehive staff, not used to such hectic activity as selling goods, in the main got totally confused. All mayhem would be let loose.

The computer age had yet to be introduced within the confines of the Beehive, and the system of recording sales and dispensing receipts and change did not differ from the very early days. A maze of pneumatic air tubes intertwined with a mesh of wires ran overhead. Both systems were necessary for conveying money and bills from all departments to a central cash point situated on the first floor. The transactional materials enclosed in brass cylindrical containers would then either be popped down one of the air tubes, or attached to wires and by mechanical means transported to the collection points. When the tubes were opened to receive the containers, a great roaring noise could be heard caused by the powerful suction constantly running through the tubes. Normally heard perhaps half a dozen times a day, this was no problem, but in the two hours of chaos on sale morning the noise would be similar to that of Niagara Falls. Combined with the increased voice levels required to make oneself heard above the din, it meant that most of the sales staff turned off their hearing aids.

At one minute to nine the countdown began. All staff were at their stations when the tannoy informed them to be ready, and as the seconds ticked away the tension rose over all departments.

At exactly nine o'clock Jim the commissionaire turned the keys in the locks and opened the floodgates to the manic herd. From past experience he knew full well to get out of the way as quickly as possible, or risk being stampeded to unconsciousness.

The scavenging mob sallied forth to all departments, the menswear section bearing the full brunt of one charge because of its very heavily reduced stock of pre-war merchandise that had recently come back into fashion — Oxford bags, floppy trews, deerstalker hats all at a cost that would barely account for the price to present-day manufacturers of the fly buttons.

The menswear department was situated in the basement, and accessible from the lifts or the stairs around the lifts. The only other access was from Alfred Knowles' private lift.

Normally Alfred Knowles would not be seen dead at the Beehive on sales day. This was to be his one exception.

As the bargain hunters thronged around the smart tab-collared shirts, laced cravats and wide-shouldered suits, their sole attention was to the product and the price. Children of the sale-hungry mothers were left to their own devices and ran around at will, meddling with anything that they fancied. One five-year-old girl, mesmerized by the buttons controlling Alfred's private lift, was merrily tapping them with the butt of a shooting stick.

Upon the third floor the now rigid form of Alfred Knowles began its descent to the basement.

The crowd in the menswear department was getting more frenzied as the bargains started to disappear and it would appear that anything and everything for sale was being snapped up. The harassed sales persons were shoving containers into pipes and pulling on wires to send their transactions flying across the roof of the basement. The girl was now staring intently at the strange figure sat in the wheelchair slowly descending before her eyes.

As the lift came to a stop, several people, their purchases clasped to their breasts, saw an opportunity of making a quick exit and so opened the lift gates. Helping Alfred out of the lift they shoved him forth into the flurry of customers seething and pulsating in their frantic attempts to secure a 'once in a lifetime' offer.

Alfred, in his wheelchair, circumnavigated the department as the crowd heaved and pushed. Such was the pitch of the mob's dementia that Alfred, quite understandably, was mistaken for a mannequin. People helped themselves to his garments convinced they were part of the sale stock and, in their present state of mind, also convinced they must be a bargain.

'Everything must go' – and so it did. Alfred, minus everything except his underpants, ended up next door in the china department. Even his wheelchair had been stripped by the hordes, the wheels gone and the chassis now supported by two piles of bricks.

By 11.30 am the store was once again its normal deserted self. The customers had fled, stripping all before them and leaving as usual the antiquated stock that had become almost welded to the counters and displays.

Mr Merryweather, the head of the china department, discovered Alfred Knowles' corpse and raised the alarm.

6

The police constable from the coroner's office sat on a hard, wooden, high-backed chair in Miss Marchmont's office. There is, he thought, with the sort of deductive reasoning that was one day to take him to the job of driver's mate for Securicor, something not right about this chair. And being a simple, straightforward sort of fellow he said as much. 'There is something wrong with this chair.'

'Ah, you've noticed, constable. You're in the wrong branch. Methinks you should be in plain clothes.'

PC Willey considered his grey suit, grey shirt, grey tie, grey socks and black shoes and thought you can't get plainer than that. He stood up and looked at the chair. The seat was too small for the averagely upholstered male to park anything but the rear portion of his buttocks, leaving the front edge to pierce a serrated line across the fleshy part of the upper thigh. The back was angled inwards by some fifteen degrees from the vertical which put even more pressure on the thighs.

'That's my interrogation chair,' said Miss

Marchmont. 'It's an identical copy of one I saw in the Museum of Medieval Torture in Barcelona – as used by Don Garcia Cojones, chief torturer and bingo caller to Philip of Spain.'

'Who do you interrogate?'

'Why, tea leaves of course. Wrongdoers, miscreants, felons, delinquents, malefactors and misdeameanists who would plunder and loot the Beehive were it not for my eternal vigilance.' Watson growled. 'And of course Watson's eternal vigilance,' she said quickly.

PC Willey, when not grappling with the ergonomic problems posed by the furniture, had been keeping a watchful eye upon the recumbent Watson, returning as it were the watchful eye Watson had been keeping on him. He had a love-hate relationship with animals. He loved them, they hated him. He knew it was only a matter of time before Watson tried to sink his teeth into one of his legs. He was just grateful he'd read his stars that morning – 'Somebody could be putting the bite on you today' – and wrapped his legs in plumbers' lagging.

'Will you forgive me if I don't sit down, Miss Marchmont?'

'Yes, of course, do whatever makes you feel comfortable, and please, call me Judith,' she said. 'Do you have a Christian name, constable?'

It was a question he dreaded. In a moment of unthinking cruelty PC Willey's parents had christened him William Walter. 'Yes, I do, Miss, but as I am on duty would you mind sticking to constable. Perhaps if I was to see you off-duty then I would be happy to tell you.' Miss Marchmont blushed; she hoped, prettily.

'Now as you will be aware, Miss Marchmont,' said PC Willey, 'it is the custom of this country to hold an inquest when a person snuffs it, I mean passes on, in what could be described as unusual circs. And I think you will agree that the circs in which the body of Mr Alfred Knowles was found were highly unusual. It's not every day a ninety-seven-year-old man, naked save for his underpants, is found sitting tied to a wheelchair, from which the wheels have been removed, mounted up on a pile of bricks. The coroner's inquest will be on Thursday at two of the o'clock when you will be required to attend, along with any other witnesses the coroner feels he may want to question.'

The coroner's court was temporarily housed in a Portakabin on the top of the council multi-storey car park. This was because the council was in the process of knocking down the coroner's real court to build an omni-sexual leisure complex and street credibility centre. There were advantages and disadvantages to the new arrangement. An advantage was that there was no problem finding a place to park. The disadvantage was the stretched plastic roofing which, taken with the stilts upon which the Portakabin stood, created a drum effect which deafened all the occupants when it rained. The thunderous roar did nothing for the dignity of one of England's oldest legal offices. The inquest upon the death of Alfred Knowles was conducted to the accompaniment of a light drizzle, a sound not unlike the patter of a thousand starlings on speed.

Miss Marchmont listened attentively to all that was said because she knew that Watson would want a full report. Mr Dunnet was telling the coroner how he thought that Mr Knowles had been acting strangely on the night of the party but had put this down to watching too many soap operas on the box. She didn't trust Dunnet. Hadn't done so since a succession of elderly ladies had complained about a man who looked like a floor walker, and whose breath reeked of aftershave, approaching them in the corsetry department and asking: 'Could I interest you in a double-gusset corset made with the older swinger in mind?' One woman had hit him with her shopping-trolley and threatened to call the police.

Miss Marchmont critically appraised him as he returned to his seat in a suit she knew he had borrowed that morning from men's haberdashery, along with the tie, the shirt and the shoes. She only hoped he'd remembered to use his own underwear. Honestly, she thought, would you let your mother marry this man?

When all the witnesses had had their say the coroner stood and announced that he was retiring to consider his verdict.

Retiring to consider a glass of whisky you mean, thought Miss Marchmont, who couldn't remember seeing a varicose nose before. She went out to the car where Watson was listening to Radio Four and told him all that had been said. He didn't seem very interested. He just wanted a biscuit.

Miss Marchmont had just got back to her seat when the usher asked the court to rise. The coroner entered, his nose pinkly leading, and sat behind his desk. 'I have considered the evidence in this case, which I have to say is one of the most bizarre I have encountered in all my years as coroner. Now it is my duty on behalf of Her Majesty the Queen, Her Majesty the Prime Minister, the Home Secretary, the Lord Lieutenant of the county, and the High Sheriff to return a verdict through those powers vested in me on how the deceased, Alfred James Knowles, died. After listening to Mr Dunnet I was tempted to believe that the deceased had contrived his own end. However I ruled that out. I considered another person's involvement because somebody must have placed him and his wheelless wheelchair on those bricks.

'Personally I would like to bring in a verdict of murder. I think verdicts of murder are good for society. A few murder verdicts a week soon bump up the crime statistics which is a useful tool for getting more money for the police, and of course murders sell newspapers and which of us doesn't like to sit down for a few minutes in the morning with a good murder on our knees? It's my belief that murders cheer people up and suicides depress people. So that's another reason for not returning a verdict of suicide – however much as I'd like to I can't bring in a verdict of murder either. So considering all the possibilities, half the probabilities and a few of the plausibilities I return a verdict that Alfred James Knowles died from unnatural causes.'

Unnatural causes, my eye, thought Miss Marchmont. It's murder. Wait till I tell Watson about this. She hurried from the court.

Lawson, Chaddesley & Peck were a longstanding London firm of lawyers, solicitors and notaries. Its organization and staff, it could be said, was a parallel to that of the Beehive; its musty shambling Victorian offices were situated in that part of London renowned for its sobriety and arcane rituals so beloved of all the legal fraternity.

The head of the firm, Albert Peck, grandson of one of the founders, George Peck, sat in front of a large woodwormed kneehole desk observing with some distaste the group of people assembled in his office. Staring back apprehensively and in a state of expectation was Eric Dunnet. Sitting next to him was Hacket, in the early stages of saying 'Good morning'. Behind them sat Miss Marchmont, on her lap Watson idly looking around for scraps of food. The rest of the dozen or so people attending were hopeful distant relatives of the Knowles family.

Mr Peck started to address the meeting in a high-pitched nasal tone reminiscent of a squealing tram. As he did so his enlarged epiglottis travelled in many various directions which immediately captivated the attention of anyone to whom he was talking. It was only with a large measure of concentration and strong willpower that the listeners' attention could be focused on the actual content of his speech.

'Good morning, ladies and gentlemen, we are gathered here this morning for the solemn and formal occasion of reading the last will and testament of the late Alfred Knowles.' As Peck whined out the family name the epiglottis tremored violently up and down.

'For those of you unfamiliar with the Knowles family tradition,' continued Peck, 'let me explain the binding oaths and traditions instigated by the founders of the Company . . .'

Eyes glazed, he joyously launched into a detailed explanation of the legal terms governing the store. Peck whined on for a further twenty minutes, rambling into the topic of morals and ethics. The attention of the audience rapidly reverted to his epiglottis, except for Hacket still striving to mouth the first consonant of morning.

Dunnet, bored with what he had heard one hundred and one times before in various forms from his boss, took his attention away from Peck's throbbing neck and glanced around the room. Much to his delight his eye fell upon a pert and trim young lady in her middle sixties. She had one of those hats that had to be screwed on to her head, from which protruded brown and silver hair. Eric hoped to catch her attention, the lust within him, for a moment at least, distracting his thoughts from the expectations of the will.

Mr Peck's meanderings finally ground to a halt. He announced that without further ado, he would now read the will. He reached into the drawer on his right-hand side and pulled out a large brown envelope, withdrew its contents and placed them before him. He started to read.

'I, Alfred James Knowles, being of sound mind and body, have set here my name and seal in the presence of the Archangel Gabriel, Moses, John the Baptist and the Virgin Mary.'

The incredulity of the listening relatives was plain to see.

'As you may realize, ladies and gentlemen,' screeched Peck, 'Alfred James Knowles was, as we say in legal jargon, "pretty much cuckoo".'

'You mean he was insane,' said Miss Marchmont.

'Exactly,' replied Peck, 'unless there are four people existing with these exact biblical names, all having some sort of personal relationship with Mr Knowles. An unlikely case, I think you will agree.'

The confusion in the room could only be settled by Peck's patient if high-pitched explanations of the proceedings to follow.

'You must realize, ladies and gentlemen, that we only received this will from Alfred Knowles several days before his untimely death. The ramifications are such that it will be some time before matters can proceed, and the rightful recipients can be determined. In the meantime, Mr Dunnet takes control of the affairs of the Beehive, but of course, no major decisions may be taken until this unfortunate set of circumstances has been resolved.'

'What is to stop me doing what I like with the store right now?' shrieked Dunnet.

'Well, Mr Dunnet,' replied Peck, 'we are under strict instructions from the inaugural set of conditions that if the will is disputed in any way, my firm is to act as trustees to see that the original conditions are maintained with the spirit of the initial concepts.'

'Is there any chance of explaining that so that we can understand?' shouted a now confused and extremely agitated Dunnet.

'It means, Mr Dunnet,' said Peck, 'that until this whole business is sorted out, we run the store together.'

Eric slumped down in his chair, perplexed and dumbfounded. What had promised to be a straightforward operation, the Beehive delivered to the Church and thus the generous Mr Big, was now unbelievably complicated by the screwball mind of his jackass employer.

Miss Marchmont tapped him on the shoulder. 'I think, Mr Dunnet, this whole affair smells, if you get my drift.'

Eric remained silent. Miss Marchmont took out her magnifying glass, and peering at Peck with a left eye, she focused upon the epiglottis. 'Never trust a man with a violent epiglottis!' exclaimed Miss Marchmont. 'We shall have to keep a careful eye on Mr Peck, won't we, Watson?'

7

Six thousand miles away, in a room in downtown Los Angeles, Kelsey Ringwood sat upright in his TV chair facing a bank of nine TV monitors. Upon each of the monitors a picture flickered. A different picture. Kelsey Ringwood was in a state of terminal ecstacy as he gazed at the screens. A faint sheen of perspiration lay across his features, here and there reflecting the flickering light from the screens. He was in some pre-nirvana trance which he occasionally interrupted with a sharply spoken command into the mouthpiece of the telephone that he held in his right hand.

Had the windows not been draped in heavy-duty velvet that excluded every last chink of natural light from the room, the pilot of the LAPD traffic helicopter who frequently hovered alongside the building monitoring the traffic on the nearby freeways might have taken him for a freelance television director or a mission controller for NASA. Kelsey Ringwood was neither of these things. He was a TV shopping junkie. In fact, he was a junk junkie. He'd spend hours in his TV chair, telephone and credit cards at the ready, buying up whatever rubbish the video age's answer to the snake oil salesmen and hucksters of yore were pushing. Sometimes he'd buy items by the gross, but mostly he just bought stuff that was gross.

The nine TV monitors – Sony seventeen-inch Trinitron FSTs that he'd bought from a Japanese family in the San Fernando Valley whom he'd called on with the intention of selling a set of household brushes – and the TV chair were the only items of furniture in the room.

The TV chair was rather special. It had been designed by a drunk who lived in Santa Monica. Not while he was drunk, but during a rare sober moment when he realized that the one thing he liked to do when he was getting juiced and stoked up for a trip to Blackout City was watch television. Presumably because it was the one thing that actually made more sense the drunker you got. And like an ugly woman – or an ugly man – it also looked better the drunker you got. With that knowledge in his mind he set out to create The Chair. In shape it was not unlike the old electric chair that once stood in the Governor's office at Sing Sing prison. It was covered in naugahyde, the skin of the nauga, the king of the plastic jungle, with foam cushioning on the arms, the seat and the back.

It was the arms that testified to the designer's capacity for forward planning. Built into one arm were a series of holes, four in all. Three of them were just the size to hold a quart bottle of Jack Daniels, Gordons or Stolichnaya. The fourth held a glass. In the same arm there was also a small button which when pressed released a metal tray, projecting out from the arm like an ashtray. This was the icemaker. It could deliver four cubes of ice made from Canadian Branchwater every eight and a half minutes.

The other arm was a state-of-the-art electronic control panel. It had built into it a telephone, a telephone answering machine, a micro tape deck, and a televison remote control that was capable of calling up fifty-six separate TV channels, controlled sixteen video recorders, and brought in satellite transmissions from around the world, including – when the wind blew from a certain direction – CIA transmission of *Road Runner* cartoons from its station in Bangkok to the South-East Asia desk in the Pentagon. Built into the arm at the front was a small microwave oven which generated nine hundred watts of power and was capable of ruining most food in less than twelve seconds. Once a man was in that chair he need never move out of it – at least, not until either nature called or the booze ran out.

How Kelsey came by the chair was typical of the way Kelsey came by most things. Somebody saw him coming. On this occasion he was out in Orange County trying to sell car wax and polish to the good people who lived on Richard Nixon Drive, one of those streets that lies by the beach. It had not been a good morning. Two women had set the dogs on him when he'd said, 'I wonder if I could interest you

95

in my wax.' Three others had tried to drag him inside for the free demonstration – and they made it quite clear what it was they wanted demonstrating. One of them, with skin the colour of a cowboy's saddle and a look that said she'd been ridden twice as hard, pressed him up against the garage door directly under the basket ball net and called out in a voice that came all the way from Marlboro' Country: 'Give it to me baby and no hurtie hurtie.' He grabbed his car wax and ran.

He was still trying to get his breath back when he saw somebody changing the name outside a house that stood back a little from the road, presumably to allow passers-by to savour in full the intriguing mix of architectural styles – English stockbroker Tudor, Spanish early colonial and late California schlock. Kelsey watched as the man stepped back to admire the new sign. *Dunpukin.*

Kelsey thought it was probably some old Indian name. They did say the Shoshonas once passed this way. Aloud he enquired, 'Indian name?'

The sign shifter said: 'Wa?'

Kelsey said: 'Your house name, is it Indian, I was wondering what it meant?'

The sign shifter said: 'It means what it says – Dunpukin' – I've dun pukin, I've finished throwing up in the mornings. I've signed the pledge, seen the light, rolled up the carpet, flushed the tube, cuddled my liver, hopped on the wagon, kicked the monkey, blown out the dragon, I've kicked it man, I'm clean.'

At the word clean Kelsey swung into action. 'Yeah, but if you want to be really clean then you need some polish, and do I have polish.'

'Well, do you?'

'Does the Pope shit in the woods?' Kelsey had read in some selling manual that the successful salesman could always establish a rapport with his customer by using the odd colloquialism.

'Well, why don't you come inside and show me your polish – I've got a chair you're going to love sitting in.'

Forty-five minutes later Kelsey was heading back up the San Diego freeway to Los Angeles, his cases on the seat beside him. Normally they would be in the boot but this afternoon the boot was full of a chair he had loved sitting in. He was a hopeless salesman but a wonderful salesmanee.

On one of the nine seventeen-inch Sony Trinitron FST monitors a woman with teased hair and a jelly mould face was offering five sets of Carmen underarm hair rollers for the bargain price of just two dollars ninety-five. 'A life time of underarm coiffeur! See those heads turn on the beach when you wave a friend good-bye. Ringlets, afro or plain old-fashioned waves can be yours with your own personal underarm crimper.'

Kelsey fingered the credit card that lay on the arm of his chair. It was just one of the eighty-six credit cards that Kelsey had available for moments like this. Kelsey loved his plastic, and it had to be said, the plastic liked Kelsey. Just when it looked as though he had exhausted every last cent of available credit, when his personal debt was beginning to resemble the arms budget of a third-world country, why then another credit card company would arrive with the morning mail offering him a Founders Membership – 'Free writing set/calculator and wristwatch/travel bag/condom holder – tick for your free Founders gift' – and he would have another X thousand dollars of rolling credit with built-in ceiling flexibility and negotiable credit levels.

Kelsey never ceased to wonder at the ease with which he was given credit. He could only assume that the various credit managers of all the companies he dealt with had at one time been bankers in charge of lending money to Mexico and any other country you cared to name in South America. They presumably checked out his rating on the Big Computer at the Credit Rating And Payment Potential Organization, and when they discovered that eighty-six other companies allowed Kelsey to owe them quite a lot of money, they reckoned they could grab a piece too.

His latest card, the one he was fingering as a particularly hirsute Philippino demonstrated underarm hair styling on screen, was the new Greed card. Kelsey made up his mind. He spoke into the phone.

'Telesale 2? This is Greed Card No. 2401 367 8211. The expiry date is 21 June, 2093, and my name is Ringwood. I'd like three sets of Carmen underarm rollers . . .'

'You already have mountains of underarm hair rollers,' came a voice behind his right ear. 'You also have nostril lasers – "Defoliate your nose now!" Musical pooper scoopers, bullet-proof vests with bullet-proof underpants attached in case your attacker is a feminist. You have . . . you have entire warehouses filled with this crap for Chrissake. You don't need any more!'

It was as though God had spoken. It *wasn't* God of course, he knew that. It was Jake. Jake shared the apartment with Kelsey Ringwood. His friends thought he looked a little like a gorilla with a receding hairline. He was one of those men – thank the Lord it rarely happened with women – who had a lot of thick black hair all over his body. When he went swimming and floated too close to the beach, coastguards used to try to shoot him.

Jake was 'in computers'. Whenever he told people that, he invariably thought 'What a half-assed thing to say. People aren't in computers. People, unless they're extremely bow-legged or enormously fat, aren't even round computers. People are *at* computers.'

In, at or around, Jake was brilliant with computers. He was to the floppy disc what Neil Simon is to the Broadway play. He was the king of the hackers, the uncrowned emperor of the unauthorized entry. He never had to knock to get in and he always let himself out without disturbing a soul. It was Jake who had programmed a computer with every copy of *Playboy*, *Penthouse* and *Hustler* magazines. For a week afterwards the computer had responded to every enquiry: 'Not now, I'm reading.' He it was who had programmed a computer to play the Brandenburg concertos on a mouth organ. It sounded vile, and the computer became known as the model whose Bach was worse than its byte. It was Jake who succeeded in hacking into Jackie Collins' home Amstrad and linking it to the operations computer of a Strategic Air Command. The world was given forty-six long-range missiles that could bonk Russia to oblivion.

Jake and Kelsey met when Kelsey had applied for a job as a canvasser with Hi-Tec Public Opinion Polls, or Hi Pop as they were known, a dubious polling outfit funded by a group of extreme right-wing Texas businessmen who wanted to spread the message that Fascism could be fun and give every blond and blue-eyed boy of fourteen a uniform. Jake was there in his capacity as freelance systems analyst. Hi Pop thought he was fixing a fuse. In fact, he was re-programming their computer to think Left instead of Right and to completely reverse whatever public opinions the pollsters produced.

Jake decided Kelsey was 'his sort of person' when he overheard his job interview with Hi Pop's senior pollster, a sagging creature of some fifty-eight summers and ninety-three winters who looked as though she'd been left out in the rain too long.

'Now let's say,' said senior pollster, chewing

on her pipe, 'that you're carrying out an opinion poll on behalf of the Friends of Ronnie Reagan.'

Kelsey said, 'Why should three people want to commission an opinion poll?'

Senior pollster said, 'Levity is not encouraged, Mr Ringworm.'

'Wood,' said Kelsey.

'Mr Woodworm,' said senior pollster, a woman with a fine head of hair (unfortunately she'd left it at home that day). 'Now Mr Wormwood, how would you attract a passer-by's attention in a shopping precinct?'

'Shout, "There's something on your shoe!"?'

'That's not the answer I was looking for.'

'Whistle?'

'Neither is that. Our canvassers never shout nor whistle, well not in company time,' she said with a smile that would have iced coffee. 'We explain that we are conducting an opinion poll.'

'What about if the guy comes from Krakow, do you say do you have an opinion, Pole?'

Senior pollster lowered her clipboard, not amused. 'Mr Wormwood, a recent survey revealed that ninety-seven per cent of all potential opinion pollsters have made that joke. Do not regard yourself as one of the world's original thinkers and wits. I don't think you have the stuff of which great opinion pollsters are made. I suggest a position more suited to your talents – perhaps soaping wheels in a car wash?' And with an imperious toss of what hair she had – it lay in rolls on the top of her head, more breadlocks than dreadlocks –

and a fetching trip on the doorstop, she was gone.

Jake emerged from behind the three tall metal cabinets that housed the Hi Pop's 4000K megabyte computer memory, a floppy disc dangling from his mouth like an unrolled cigarette. 'Hey 'an 'at 'as 'errific.' He took the disc from his mouth. 'Sorry man. Hey, that was great, you really stuck it to the all American prune. Wanna come and have a beer?'

Their friendship had begun that day and was quickly cemented when Kelsey offered the homeless Jake a room in his apartment. Jake was homeless because his air stewardess girlfriend, or ex-girlfriend as she now was, had kicked him out of her bed, her apartment and her life after he had electronically connected her telephone answering machine to the public address system at Los Angeles International Airport. The entire concourse halted when they heard 'American Airlines announce the departure of "Hi this is Big Boy and I'll be banging on your door tonight and guess what I'm gonna be banging with".'

Kelsey lived in an apartment that belonged to his mother in the old Fairbanks building, in what was now downtown Los Angeles. His mother was currently away. She had been currently away for three years. She was house hunting: the problem was, the house she was looking for had to come with a husband. The last Kelsey had heard from her was a postcard from Atlantic City in which she said she had a magnificent specimen in her sights and she couldn't wait to pull the trigger. His mother was a mistress of the passing euphemism and the single entendre.

Jake said, 'Do you mind if we switch these things off?' With one last lingering look at the Carmen underarm hair rollers, Kelsey pressed the standby button on the remote control set into the arm of the TV chair and all selling ceased.

Jake said, 'We are going to have to do something about your somewhat less than magnificent obsession. It is now way beyond a joke.'

The intercom on the street door buzzed. Jake switched on the DoorvuScan. The Fairbanks Building might be an ancient monument by Californian standards, but its security system was pure Fort Knox. Whenever anybody pressed a button to gain entry to any of the forty-nine apartments in the building, three forty-K spotlights came on and bathed the intruder in the sort of light only found these days for the Sarah Brightman song in an Andrew Lloyd-Webber musical. Standing there now in the full brilliance of the carbon glare was an LA mailman in the standard issue uniform of bullet-proof vest, visored crash helmet, chain mail trousers and metal-toed boots. Jake spoke into the microphone. 'Yeah, what is it?'

The mailman was barely audible through his visor. 'Mailman, special delivery.'

'Oh God,' said Jake, 'more parking tickets.'

'Or,' said Kelsey, 'another credit card for me. I'll go down.'

'No you won't. I'll go.'

Kelsey called after him, 'I wouldn't bother taking the lift.'

'Broken again?'

'No,' said Kelsey, 'I think the landlord has let it to a family of boat people.'

As Jake set off to negotiate fourteen flights of stairs and the assorted bodies that lay upon them in alternating states of oblivion, ecstacy and despair, Kelsey switched the screens back on.

The girl on screen four with matching hair and teeth — she had the sort of smile that could fade crimplene at twelve paces — was selling a complete home dentistry kit, including an extra set of old magazines for the waiting room. Hey, thought Kelsey, that would be really neat. A dentistry party, and if guests didn't pull a partner they could always pull some teeth. He reached for the phone to order half a dozen and looked up guiltily at the DoorvuScan. He saw Jake was locked in some sort of struggle with the mailman to get him to hand over the special delivery letter. Kelsey had given up fighting mailmen. He just gave them ten dollars. Nobody did anything for nothing any more. He put the phone back. Maybe Jake was right. Maybe he should be doing something about his habit of buying things.

Habit, hell. It was as Jake had said, an overwhelming compulsion, an obsession. Perhaps he should see a shrink. He'd already been to two. The first one had been a complete disaster. The shrink was a neo-Freudian Jungish Adlerian behaviouralist and Kelsey had said to him: 'Doctor, everywhere I go, people try to sell me things,' and the shrink had said, 'Rubbish, how much will you give me for the couch?' The second one wasn't much better. He had said that Kelsey was looking for his mother. Kelsey said, 'What do you mean, looking for my mother, how am I going to find my mother in four thousand jars of Navahoe Nectar — guaranteed to get rid of pimples, spots, warts and stubborn rust?' He'd bought the jars from a passing pedlar whilst sitting in the shrink's waiting room.

The shrink explained, 'Can you remember the first time you thought, now, that I must have?'

'Yes,' said Kelsey, 'I was in senior high school.'

'Good, and what was it you wanted — a Harley Davidson motorbike, a new car, your first filofax?'

'No,' said Kelsey, 'it was the tassel tosser who worked stag nights at the Dean Martin Wino Bar on Wiltshire Boulevard.'

'I see. And how long was your mother a tassel tosser?'

'Now wait a minute,' said Kelsey, 'my mother never tossed a tassel in her life.'

'Perhaps she tossed her tassels when you were in her womb and you've been trying to get back there ever since. Now when did your mother leave home?'

'About four years ago.'

'And when did you last hear from her?'

'Two years ago, I got a card from Atlantic City.'

'That explains everything,' said the shrink.

'What do you mean, that explains everything?'

'What do people buy in Atlantic City?'

'Well, it used to be saltwater taffy, but these days it's gambling chips.'

'Apart from the chips.'

'Well, I suppose they buy junk.'

'Right, and what do you buy?'

'Junk.'

'Precisely. Don't you see, your subconscious is telling you that if you keep buying junk, one day you will purchase a piece of junk that will lead you back to Atlantic City and your mother. That will be four hundred dollars, cash, and I don't give Green Shield Stamps.'

That was the last time Kelsey had seen a shrink. If anything his buying sprees had gone from bad to worse. Now he seemed to be buying all the time. In the beginning he had been a bout buyer – he'd buy something about eight am in the morning and about twenty minutes later he'd have to buy something else, and in some perverse way he compounded what was already a desperate situation by taking that job as a brush saleman, working door-to-door in the townships and wealthy enclaves of Southern California. Sometimes he actually managed to sell something. He noticed this was usually if he was following a bunch of Mormans. If he knocked on the door after one of the haircuts had pitched his spiel, the lady of the house would be so relieved to see that it wasn't the Mormans back again that she'd buy the entire stock, especially if he noticed a Mezuzah by the door. He'd slap on a skullcap and it was a breeze. Sometimes of course, they just turned the hose on him. But what he hadn't yet learned to do was to walk away when a fellow salesman opened the door. You could always tell if it was a salesman, they were the only people who invited you in. Some of them even offered to carry his bag of samples, so they could put it to one side while they got on with the business of selling their junk to Kelsey.

This complete lack of sales resistance was why Jake no longer allowed him to remain in the apartment alone. Jake swore that if he did word would get out and every salesman in the West Coast would be pressing their bell.

Jake came back into the room with his 'My Hoover Sucks' T-shirt hanging out of his trousers.

'Goddam mailmen, you know they want fifteen dollars now before they hand over a letter! I said to that guy, "What would happen if I reported this?" He said, "Don't even think about it, you'd never get another letter as long as you live." Anyway they're both for you.'

Kelsey took the envelopes. One was over-printed with the legend 'O'Goldberg's Hollywood Warehouses – The Gateway To The Stores'. He opened this one first and read aloud:

Dear Mr Ringwood,
We is writing to infirm you that de rent on de warehouse full of dat garbage you keep

buyin' is now seriously overdo. Dis constoots a breaking of your contract which could be followed by a breakin of your legs. If you unnerstan our meanin. Get de money by de end of de week. Or else.

Yours in friendship and prompt payment
Penny Arrabiata (Ms)

Kelsey dropped the letter on the chair. 'Do you suppose they take credit cards, I mean this is heavy stuff, I mean we could end up as a part of the Santa Monica Freeway Extension!'

Jake said, 'What's with the "we", Keemosabe. Face it, Kelsey, you don't have any credit, you've used it all up.'

'I thought you were going to do a bit of hacking with the big Wang and get me out of this jam. I mean you said you could break the Pentagon purchasing codes so I could charge all my stuff to the government. I remember you said it would make a change for a tax payer to buy a load of junk on behalf of the government.'

'I'm still trying,' said Jake, 'but these things take time. Anyway, who's the other letter from?'

Kelsey examined the pale cream envelope he was still holding in his left hand. It was very good quality heavy woven paper and in the top left hand corner discreetly printed was the name Schwartz and Schwartz, Attorneys at Law, 130 West 57th Street, New York, New York 10036.

Jake said, 'You see? Now they're suing you.'

Kelsey opened the letter and started reading. 'Not exactly — listen to this.'

Dear Mr Ringwood,
Would you please contact me as a matter of some urgency at the above address where you may well discover, if you'll forgive the cliche, something to your advantage.
Yours faithfully,
Gloria Beresford
Attorney at Law.

'Now what do you suppose that means?'

'Only one way to find out,' said Jake, picking up the phone. 'What's the area code for New York. . . ?'

8

In a small neat two-bedroomed flat high above
a tobacconist in Baker Street, Miss Marchmont
was having a one-way conversation with Watson.
The small lounge they were sitting in was a
shrine to the detective. Every book written about
Sherlock Holmes lined the walls, neatly arranged
in order of size and each one labelled with a
code that could be quickly cross-referenced with
the information cards Miss Marchmont had
meticulously drawn up.

Next to the books were large photographs of
Basil Rathbone, the actor who so often portrayed
Sherlock Holmes in the cinema. The shelves
and surfaces of cupboards were covered in
Sherlock Holmes memorabilia, miniature deerstalker hats, large pipes with curling stems and
plaster-cast images of characters and scenes from
his many adventures.

When confronted with a problem she could
not solve, she frequently contemplated whilst
surrounded by her artefacts, hoping for inspira-
tion. As Sherlock Holmes would discuss matters
of criminal importance with Dr Watson, so

Miss Marchmont would probe the problem via her globular four-legged companion.

Watson sat opposite his mistress, sprawled on his favourite armchair in a state of semi-somnolence. His head lay on his paws, his one ear raised listening to the reasoning coming forth from the human being sitting opposite him.

Watson never knew what any of these ramblings meant; all he could perceive was that somehow they were nothing to do with food. Knowing full well that when these sessions occurred nothing was ever required of him other than to sit there, his mind wandered to his favourite images of meat. Occasionally he would move an oversized limb into a new position and the chair would creak loudly in protest. Within a few seconds his state of somnolence was complete and even his sensitive hearing became totally oblivious to the conundrum now being expounded.

'So, Watson,' intoned Miss Marchmont, and drawing small quantities of pure air through the dark brown briar pipe, she gave Watson a summation of the events of the past few days.

'Mr Knowles dies of a so-called heart attack and yet no one suspects anything. Most strange, don't you agree? He is found semi-naked in the china department tied in his wheelchair and no foul play is suspected. Yet we know, don't we, Watson, that at his birthday party, Mr Knowles and Mr Dunnet had as much love for each other as holiday makers do for French air traffic control? From the noise and actions that

I saw in Mr Knowles's office I would say, Watson, Dunnet was trying to end the life of Mr Knowles, but why would he attempt to do it then and there when everybody could hear what was going on? Mr Dunnet may be many things, but he is not stupid, so what is it all about? There is nothing elementary about this, my dear Watson. This could be the most interesting case we have had since the Vinzenti affair.'

She was referring to the incident several years previously when the entire stock of Union Jacks had disappeared from the linen department. The flags were discovered three days later cut and torn into small shredded pieces, blocking up every toilet pan situated within the Beehive. By patient research, Miss Marchmont discovered that the linen buyer, Anagomi Vinzenti, was of Argentinian descent and the whole exercise was to protest at the British government's reluctance to hand over the Malvinas to his mother country.

There was more to the mysterious passing of Alfred Knowles than met the eye, and Miss Marchmont was determined to get to the bottom of it . . .

9

Gloria Beresford was thirty-eight, unmarried, a native New Yorker, with an apartment on Riverside Drive, a BMW in a garage on Long Island and charge accounts at Saks, Bergdorf, Bloomies and Henri Bendel. She played a mean game of tennis on the Island at Southampton in the summer and an even meaner game of backgammon at the Raquets Club in the winter. She played golf off the men's tees and had a handicap of four. Like everything else about her, her swing was a thing of beauty, a model of how to have everything in the right place at the right time, and though she never lifted her head she turned everybody else's. Particularly men's.

As her old Granny had said to her when she was taken back to the sharecroppers' hut in Alabama where her mother had been born: 'Don't you give them men no mind, little Gloria. Ain't a man born who it was worth burning a pan of grits for.' Granny Beulah was full of cotton-picking wisdom. One of her favourites was, 'A good man is like a parking meter — you can never find one that's free, and when you do there's usually something wrong with it.'

Gloria Beresford had joined Schwartz & Schwartz as a full partner some five years earlier. Before that she had worked for ten years from a store-front office on 125th Street as a public defender. It had been her way of paying some dues. Her own childhood had been happy and comfortable. Her parents were black middle-class, her mother was a teacher and her father was an architect. When she had returned to New York after taking her master's degree at Boston Law School, she preferred to work as a public defender rather than take up one of the nine offers she received from Wall Street firms where they thought a legal pad was the partner's apartment in the Trump Tower. She thought there was something intrinsically glamorous about being a public defender, and if they ever made a film of her life, what a great part it would be for Cher.

Unfortunately, life rarely copies art and up there on 125th Street, Hill Street Blues quickly became millstone blues. But she stuck it out. She dealt with muggers, armed robbers, pimps, pushers, dealers and protection mobs – though she didn't spend all her time with cops. It toughened her up. She learned the language of the streets – all five words of it – funny how those words seem to be the same in every language in the world and certainly in the Spanish, Yiddish, Chinese, Greek and West Indian she heard all day. She got a lot of men off and a lot of men tried to get off with Gloria Beresford, or Glory B as she became known on the streets, but she easily turned away their advances with a kind word, a gentle 'No' and just occasionally a clout with the baseball bat she carried in her car at all times.

As the years passed Glory B became a heroine in the sub-culture of 125th Street and when it came time for her to move downtown, all her old 'clients' got together and stole her a silver tea service.

Now she had an office that was bigger than most people's apartments. It was close-carpeted in the finest woven wool, and not a sign of a cockroach. She still remembered the first time she walked into this office at Schwartz & Schwartz and couldn't work out what was wrong. Then she realized there was nothing crunching underfoot.

The offices were light-years removed from the Dickensian cramp of British chambers. Air-conditioned, open-plan humming with disc-drives and multi-line telephones, the New York office was a throbbing hub of litigation, the place where the tangled knots of legal problems were untied, sorted out, and massively charged for.

Litigation being something of an American hobby, the funds for the refurbishment of the offices had come directly from the pockets of clients from all over New York who had used the services of Schwartz & Schwartz to represent them in the cause of justice. They had won half a million dollars in damages for a man who had walked straight in front of a bus, on the grounds that the bus manufacturers had made no provision on the front of their bus for this eventuality. There was now an action before the High Court to force all bus manufacturers to fit all buses on urban routes with a large cow-catcher on the front, like the old Mid-Western trains. Schwartz & Schwartz had also secured substantial damages for a would-be burglar who had broken his wrist trying to force a lock; the lock manufacturers had to pay out twenty thousand dollars. Schwartz & Schwartz had also won the unconditional discharge of a crazed homicidal maniac who had sliced up his own mother with a meat-cleaver. The homicidal maniac was living quietly in Brooklyn while the directors of the McClusky Cutlery Co. N.J. were facing prosecution for failing to fit appropriate warning notices on their meat-cleavers.

Such were the triumphs of American justice that had made Schwartz & Schwartz their fortune. Currently they were defending a Manhattan woman who had pushed her husband out of the window of their forty-sixth-floor apart-ment. Schwartz & Schwartz were suing the architects of the building for negligence in plac-ing so much distance between the forty-sixth floor and the ground. Their success in these and other cases had led to Messrs. Schwartz & Schwartz, fourth generation German immigrants who had arrived in New York with scarcely a pfennig to their name, to take on the new junior partner only a few months before.

By moving to Schwartz & Schwartz she could

now wear the sort of clothes she liked – tight skirts, mini skirts, cotton shirts, business suits with Reeboks. Anything but the trousers and jeans she'd worn every working day for the previous ten years. Baggy trousers and baggy jeans. The baggier the better, a look designed to discourage even the most ardent swain from intimacy. By and large it had worked though occasionally she would have to dissuade other ladies in equally baggy trousers or jeans from pursuing their avowed intent.

The designer clothes, the designer office, the gold credit cards, the expense account lunches, the working breakfasts and the working workouts, the private jets and the corporate hideaways were all very glamorous and exciting, but they were only a veneer. She still worked in a jungle, and it was just as vicious as the jungle she'd left behind on 125th Street. There were just as many junkies downtown as there were uptown, and even though the addiction wasn't always cocaine – though you wouldn't be surprised how often it was – there were other addictions that were just as evil – power, sex and money – and just as a freaked-out coke head would beg, steal and kill to get another nose full of happy dust, so those pillars of rectitude and circumspection, those guardians of the nation's economic welfare would do just the same – or get somebody to do it for them – to satisfy their cravings. Coming from where she had, Glory B felt nothing but contempt for it all.

In the sixties she would probably have joined the Weathermen, become an urban terrorist, kidnapping rich folks' poodles, but this was the eighties and Glory B wasn't politically aligned with anybody. She had no time for the extremists on either the right or the left – the people who gave a dogma a bad name. There was no denying at times, as she watched some fat cat arbitrageur skim twenty million off the top of a deal merely by threatening to take over some chicken shit company, that she felt like an infiltrator who was sitting down to eat with the enemy.

It was all those years of fighting for the people who were trying to survive on society's under-belly. They had conditioned her. What Gloria Beresford needed, she said to herself in the mirror of her private bathroom attached to her office at Schwartz and Schwartz, was a campaign, something to fight for.

It was closer than she knew.

Her secretary, Philip, who was blond, had blue eyes and 'a great ass' as she had gleefully reported to her mother, had sorted her mail. Invitations to join an exclusive day at the races with one hundred and fifty thousand other privileged holders of the Gold American Express Card, and the like, were in one pile which was invariably consigned, unread, to the shredder. Correspondence concerning on-going cases was in another pile and in a third pile was 'every-thing else'.

On this particular morning there wasn't a lot of 'everything else'. A card from a private investigation agency, the Busy Buggers, touting for business, and a letter from the manager of Irving Manufacturers Trust, the Broadway and 38th Branch, with a note attached from Milton Schwartz, the son of one of the original partners: 'Glory B. Does this mean anything to you?' She read the letter:

Dear Sirs,
I see from my records that you act on behalf of a Ronald Knowles in whose name we hold a deposit account with monies now totalling $1,623,816. My reason for writing is that I have just received the enclosed letter from London announcing that all further payments into this account would now cease. I leave you to take any further action you deem necessary.
Yours faithfully,
J. F. Trublock
Vice President, Dead Accounts.

Attached to the letter from the bank was a copy of a letter from Knowles department store. She read:

Dear Sirs,
I write to you regarding the monthly payment made to Ronald Knowles Esq., Account No. 612 87114, and beg to inform you that following the recent demise of Mr Alfred Knowles, these payments will cease forthwith.
Yours faithfully,
Peregrine Hacket.

Glory B called for Philip to come in. He entered, Dictaphone at the ready, and for not the first time Gloria wondered if she should push her chair back from the desk, smooth her skirt over her thighs and say, 'I've got some dictation, I'll give it to you here.' She thought he'd probably squirm in embarrassment, more at the line than at the suggestion.

'Can you see if we have a file on a Ronald Ringwood Knowles, English. Probably a divorce with alimony from the ex-wife, regular payments into a current account at Irving Manufacturers,' she said instead.

Philip took the letter Gloria was holding. 'Any idea how far back?'

'None, you'll just have to keep looking, pretty thing, and if he hasn't shown by the time you get to George III and the gang bang with Lord North and the Daughters of the American Revolution, you can forget it. Oh, and Philip?'

'Yes?'

'Oh, never mind.'

The phone on Gloria's desk rang. Philip picked it up. 'Ms Beresford's office. If you'll hang on I'll just see if she's here. What do you mean you know she's here? Well, she may well be, but it doesn't mean to say she's here for you. Hold on.' Philip put his hand over the mouthpiece.

'Somebody called the Busy Buggers, said they wrote to you?'

Gloria picked up the card. 'Yeah, some private dick touting for work. You can tell the shamus from me to start making with the feet.'

Philip had noticed Gloria's way of saying things could be influenced by whatever book she happened to be reading. There'd be a period of infinite gloom and boredom when she had been reading Chekov; a bizarre fortnight when she'd been reading P. G. Wodehouse and Amos 'n' Andy at the same time and would come into the office saying things like, 'What-ho y'all.' At the moment it was obviously Mickey Spillane.

Gloria took the phone. 'Who is this? Well, Ms Busy Buggers, or can I call you Silly, I don't need a private dick right now – or a private dickess for that matter.' Gloria listened to the voice at the other end of the line and then nervously turned to look out of the window behind her. 'How do you know all this stuff? State of the art laser technology, and astrology? Now come on, don't give me that crap. So Ronald Reagan did use an astrologer – as I said don't give me that crap. It really is lasers? And where are you? You're not telling. I see. So this is a scam. What the English call a rip awf. Some people would say this was blackmail, Ms Busy Buggers. You would say it was just the American way. OK. I tell you what, the next time I need a private dick, dickess, I'll call you. Meanwhile you switch off the lasers, right? Just one thing – how will I know you've done that?' She listened. 'Really? OK, I'll be in touch.'

Gloria handed the phone back to Philip. 'Go out and buy a parrot, a parrot that talks. It seems that birds are allergic to lasers, and whatever they do, they do more in the presence of a laser. I suppose we could use a pigeon but I suspect we'd be happier with a parrot. While you're working on tracing Ronald Ringwood Knowles, I'll write to this Hacket character and see if he can tell us what we need to know.'

The Hacket character sat in his cubby hole at the Beehive. It was possibly the smallest office in London. It was accommodated under a flight of stairs that led to the cashier's office. Over the years Hacket had learned to fit his movements to his surroundings, but if somebody flustered him – that somebody invariably meaning Eric Dunnet – then he would sit down without thinking and bark his shins on the hot water pipe that ran horizontally through his desk, or get up too quickly and crack his head on the stairs. Mrs Hacket always knew when Mr Hacket had had a hard day at the office: when he took his clothes off for evening cocoa he looked as though he'd spent his day in a scrum with Hull Kingston Rovers.

At the moment he was bent over the letter that had just arrived from Schwartz & Schwartz. It was requesting more information about Mr Ronald.

Hacket reached into the bottom left-hand drawer of the desk and opened a fresh packet of Polo mints. It was his second packet that day, and it was still only 10 am. He was under pressure and he knew he had to watch himself. He'd always promised himself that if he ever got up to three packets of Polos a day he'd just quit and take up smoking, even if it did mean that he'd end up losing a lot of weight.

I'm in a jam, he thought, in a pickle, in the soup. I could get the chop, run out of bread, end up not taking home any bacon and worst of all Dunnet's going to beef. Hacket enjoyed thinking like that. He didn't stammer when he thought.

In a moment of rare bravado he had taken an executive decision. The sort of thing other chief accountants did without thinking, but other chief accountants didn't have Eric Dunnet breathing down their necks every second hour of the day. Hacket so wished he wouldn't; some mornings his breath came straight from the grave, on others it reminded him of an open drain in Cairo.

Hacket had been at the Beehive all his working life. He had started as a cash checker on the ground floor tills in the days when customers still spent white fivers – Hacket, in common with everybody else who'd ever handled one, looked back to the white fiver with an aching nostalgia. Magnificent, oversized, brilliant white rectangles with copperplate black writing, they really felt like money. Breaking into a white fiver was an event. These days if you went into a shop and proffered a fiver, the shopkeeper would say, 'Haven't you got anything larger?' Over the years he had gradually moved up the corporate ladder. He was taken off the tills and put on the arrears ledger where he began to show the first glimmerings of the animal cunning that was to serve him well in later years in his dealings with Dunnet.

Hacket would write to each of his errant customers, and if that failed to produce a response or more importantly, money, he would make an appointment to see them, asking for five minutes of their time. Well, of course, it took Hacket five minutes just to say good morning. By the time he'd actually got round to asking when they were going to settle their outstanding accounts, an hour would have passed with no sign of the meeting ending and usually they were only too pleased to pay up to get rid of him; But if the old stammer ploy failed, Hacket had one last routine. He would tell them that this stammer was the result of stress brought on by being a debt collector, for if he failed to persuade people to pay their bills, then the outstanding amounts would be docked from his pay packet every week for the rest of his life. He'd had to use this last gambit only twice. Most people found the stammer sufficient persuasion.

After his success on the arrears ledger, he had been put in charge of outgoing payments and that was the genesis of the jam he was in today. One summer morning just after the war had ended, Mr Alfred had told him that Mr Ronald would be taking no further part in the running of the store — which would be, thought Mr Hacket, a great relief to all the young girls in lingerie and make-up, but something of a disappointment to all the old girls in corsetry and hardware. Mr Ronald had emigrated to the United States with a possible view to extending the store's activities in that country. The control of the Beehive in London was solely in Mr Alfred's hands. Because of this Mr Ronald received a regular fixed payment of two hundred and fifty pounds a month, to be paid into an account at the Irving Manufacturers Trust on 38th and Broadway, and Mr Alfred would be grateful if no mention of this was made anywhere in the accounts, a task he was sure Mr Hacket could manage in his new job of deputy chief accountant.

Hacket did as he was asked. Each month he drew out as petty cash, for miscellaneous entertaining and gifts for privileged customers, two hundred and fifty pounds which was paid, via their London West End branch, into Mr Ronald's account in New York, and he'd gone on doing so for forty years. Whenever a keen young auditor had questioned the withdrawals Hacket merely produced a slew of receipts from the cache of restaurant bills he had stolen over the years.

Then Mr Alfred had died. Hacket's automatic response was to take his hat off and cancel all the old boy's standing orders – including his membership of Exit, his subscription to *What Necrophilia*, and of course the payments to Mr Ronald's account with the Irving Manufacturers Trust.

Occasionally it had crossed his mind to tell D...D...D...D...D...D...Dunnet – it was the one word that could even make him stutter in his sleep — what he was doing, but then he realized that he'd also have to explain why he hadn't told him before.

But this letter from New York had changed all of that. Somebody wanted information. What was he going to do? He did what he always did in situations like this. He got down on his knees and tossed a coin. It came down heads. Best of three he thought. It came down heads again. He wouldn't show the letter to Dunnet. Best to forget it, he thought. He got up and banged his head.

10

In her office on West 57th Street, Glory B was calling out for lunch. From the Good Earth Place she ordered tofu curds and mung beans on a vege bagel with a side order of sagmush and a carton of dandelion coffee stuff. Like every other citizen of Manhattan, or at least those who could afford to be, Glory B was a health freak. There were so many of them in the city now that Colonel Sanders had opened his first Kentucky Boiled Bean Sprout, and burger houses now sold pulseburgers with soya cheese. They were known as a Big Muck. After lunch she would jog for ten minutes on her porcupine pad — a two-foot-square foam rubber cushion which was thickly covered in one-inch wooden spikes which delivered in six minutes the equivalent of three and a half hours uninterrupted massage by an aromatherapist of the eighth dan. There was a knock on the door.

It was Philip. He carried a dusty cardboard file held closed by a faded pink ribbon tied in a neat bow. 'The Ronald Knowles file, we acted for him back in the late forties. It was one of the last cases old Mr Schwartz handled before he died.'

Glory B undid the bow and pulled out half a dozen yellowing letters. The first two were standard letters – one asking for representation, the reply accepting it. Apparently Knowles had been recommended to the firm by a Mr Giuseppe Ferrari. She made a note on a yellow legal pad – mob connections? Then there were some letters about fees and next of kin. She wrote N. O. K., Alfred Knowles, the Knowles department store, London. The next letter was handwritten.

Dear Mr Schwartz,
I have reason to believe that certain business associates of Mr Ferrari, who as you will recall kindly recommended me to your good self, are about to offer me a permanent position: a block of cement in the New Jersey Turnpike. With this in mind, I enclose my last Will and Testament, properly signed and witnessed. I am writing to you on my honeymoon having married a lady who I now discover was the aforementioned Mr Ferrari's mistress, which explains his interest in my welfare. She is with child and I have made provisions in my will for my offspring's welfare, which I would like you to attend to. In the event of anything happening to me I have written to the Manager of the Irving Manufacturers Trust at 38th and Broadway giving you full power of attorney.
Yours sincerely,
Ronald Knowles.

'That's dated March 1958 and somebody's been paying money into that account ever since. No wonder it's nearly a million dollars.'

There was a knock at the door, and before she could say anything it was pushed open by the roller-skate delivery boy from the Good Earth Place in biodegradable T-shirt and recycled shorts. He swooped across the room on his environmentally correct skates, placed the tray on Glory B's desk, turned in a balletic spin that skimmed a couple of thousand dollars' worth of pile off the shag carpet, and swooped out again.

Gloria picked up the mung beans. 'What do you suppose happened to the wife and kid?'

Philip said, 'I dunno, and do we care?'

'I do. There's a million and a half dollars sitting in that bank and those cats have enough cream without us just handing them more. Let's find them.'

'How?'

'We could start with the Busy Buggers.'

At that moment the entire staff of Busy Buggers was on the phone trying to get the Pope's rising sign, but the man in the Vatican was not being very helpful.

'His Holiness isn't into astrology — the only sign he believes in involves a lot of white smoke going up a chimney.'

She replaced the phone and wondered whether she was doing the right thing. Her real name was Tiffany Holder — actually that wasn't her real name at all. Her real name was Sadie

129

Harpowitz which was a kosher name if you were Jewish which Sadie had decided she no longer was. She was now a lapsed Jew. Why not? If you could have lapsed Catholics, why not lapsed Jews. When she told her mother, Senior Sadie, all she said was 'that's no way to catch a doctor'.

Senior Sadie was desperate for daughter Sadie to meet a doctor and settle down and give her grandchildren and free medical attention for the rest of her days. The doctor she wanted her most to meet was a plastic surgeon – someone who could see further than the end of Sadie's nose. Someone who could take a long view, so to speak.

But until the good doctor came along, Tiffany/Sadie was in need of a job. The slot in the Busy Buggers reawakened a childhood fascination with electronics – hence the lasers – and snooping. She'd sent out four hundred letters touting for business, and then started cold-calling. This Beresford dame was the first lawyer who'd actually deigned to speak to her.

The phone rang. 'Hi, this is the Busy Buggers. Can we keep an eye open for you?'

It was the same Gloria Beresford dame and she was saying, 'I wonder if you could do a job for me?'

'I get two hundred dollars a day plus expenses, and I don't take the subway.'

Gloria said, 'Don't you want to know what the job is?'

'Yeah, well, OK.'

'I want you to find a member of the Mafia.'

'My rate just went up to four hundred dollars per day, plus funeral expenses.'

'All I can tell you is his name is Ferrari and he was pretty active about forty years ago.'

'Let's hope he's given up being active.'

'Plus anything you can find on a store in London called Knowles. And a guy called . . . uh . . . Hacket.'

'I'll get back to you.'

That's what they always said in the movies, Sadie thought, as she put the receiver back. Then she leapt straight up in the air and whooped.

'A job, a job, I've got my first job!' Then she panicked. 'It's the Mafia, so it could be my last job.'

Gloria Beresford put her phone down. Mr Schwartz, the son of the senior founding partner, came in with his timer hanging round his neck. Young Mr Schwartz never went anywhere without his timer. As he never tired of explaining, 'If somebody came up to me in the street, on an elevator or in the men's room and wanted some information, how would I know how much to charge without my timer?' Gloria once asked him, 'Suppose it's just somebody wanting to know the time, would you charge them for that?'

'Of course,' said young Mr Schwartz. 'Time's money, ain't it?'

Today he opened with, 'How did you make out with that letter from Irving Manufacturers?'

'I was going to ask you about that. Do we have any connections with the Mafia?'

Young Mr Schwartz quickly closed the door behind him.

'Ms Beresford, there is no such thing as the Mafia.'

Gloria said, 'No, and God didn't make little green apples and it don't snow in Indianapolis in the winter time. Just assuming there's no such thing as the Mafia, do we ever act for gentlemen with Italian names who like a lot of respect?'

'Like who for instance?'

'Does the name Ferrari mean anything to you?'

'I think there used to be a Ferrari who was with one of the Five Families.'

'Was he the Godfather?'

'Actually Mr Ferrari was a friend of my father's. My mother didn't want us to know it, but this Italian guy was always coming round the house with little presents – a pot of spaghetti sauce, some Sicilian meatballs, some tortellini al pesto. Then he stopped coming.'

'How could I find him?'

'Try my father's old secretary. She runs a dating agency for senior citizens in New Jersey – "Don't be Old, be Bold". Try her.'

Gloria did and when she finally convinced the old lady she wasn't interested in a seventy-nine-year-old stud, own home and teeth, she learned that the best place to find out about Ferrari was Tony's Clam Bar on Thomson Street in Little Italy. 'Mr Ferrari was like a bitch in heat for Tony's hot clam sauce,' she said.

Tony's clam bar was no more than a hole in the wall, a counter, four tables, a lot of white formica and a dozen or so plastic stacking chairs. Tony stood behind the counter with the pans in which he deep fried his clams and mixed his famous clam sauce. The sauce came in three strengths – mild, medium and hot. There were half a dozen men sitting at the tables when Gloria made her entrance. Not one of them had a neck size under twenty-three. Those that had a neck. Gloria was wearing a black leather mini skirt, a white T-shirt, a black leather bomber jacket, opaque black tights and white reeboks. A pair of Raybans were pushed back on her forehead. It was a look that stopped traffic. In Tony's Clam Bar it stopped conversation – or what passed for conversation.

As she crossed the threshold thirteen eyes swung to greet her. It would have been fourteen but Mario had left one of his on a cue in a pool room during a little skirmish with the opposition. Tony tossed a handful of clams into the hot oil. They hissed like a crowd of drunks at a bad strip show. He shifted a toothpick from one side of his mouth to another – he'd seen Kojak do it with a lollipop.

'What can I get you, lady?'

'I'd like some information.'

'You want information dial 911, me, I sell clams.'

'OK. I'll take some clams.'

'What sauce you want?'

'I'll have the hot.'

There was a rumbling sound that could have been a subway train passing underneath the clam bar or the guys at the tables laughing.

Tony said, 'You want hot, right?'

'Right, hot!' If some Mafia godfather could eat it hot she was sure as hell that she could. Besides she had an asbestos tongue. Years of smothering fast food with chilli sauce, the only thing that was guaranteed to kill any of the original taste.

'You ever had Tony's hot sauce, lady?' grunted one of the goons at the nearest table. Gloria said she hadn't. ''Cos I should warn you that Tony's hot gives you a breath you could strip chrome from brass with.'

Gloria said, 'I'll take hot.' Tony ladled a portion of fried clams on to a paper plate and then gently spooned some hot sauce into a polystyrene tub. He did it with such care that it could have been nitro-glycerine.

'Have to take it real slow,' said Tony. 'This stuff has been known to spontaneously combust.' He laughed but Gloria wasn't sure whether he was joking or not.

She took her clams and hot sauce to an empty table and thirteen eyes swivelled after her. It was too late to chicken out. She speared a clam with a fork, plunged it deep into the hot sauce and put the lot in her mouth. For approximately three-quarters of a second nothing happened. Then it was as though her tongue had exploded and was trying to escape through every available orifice and one or two that weren't — if it could make a hole, it would be moving through the top of her skull. There was a ringing in her ears — she hoped it was a fire engine. As the tears poured on to her cheeks they changed into steam immediately. Her fillings (she had two) felt as though they were shrinking in their cavities. Sweat cascaded from every pore. At least, she thought, I'm losing weight. She became aware of a blurry figure standing in front of her holding a glass of water. It was Tony.

'Here,' he said, 'drink this, it's your only hope. That was a very brave thing to do, lady. Me and the boys didn't think you'd go through with it, but as a quid pro quo — don't laugh, I've got Latin blood — what was the information you was wanting?'

Gloria removed the clam with a paper tissue. 'That was *hot*,' she said. 'I thought I knew hot, but that was seriously hot. Is that really Don Ferrari's favourite clam sauce?'

She heard the rumble again. Tony looked suddenly unsure of himself.

'Why didn't you say you was a friend of Don Ferrari? We wouldn't have played such a trick on a friend of Don Ferrari.'

'Trick? What trick?'

'The hot sauce. That's not my real hot sauce — that's just a joke I play on people who come in here for the first time doing a big number about how they can handle hot sauce.'

135

Gloria said, 'I'm sure Don Ferrari will laugh till he has an accident when I tell him. Or laugh until somebody else has an accident.'

Tony now looked like a man who'd eaten too much hot sauce. 'Please, lady, a joke eh? Now what was it you wanted to know?'

'Well, I know that Don Ferrari liked your hot sauce, but what about his mistress?'

One of the goons asked, 'What's a mistress?'

Tony said, 'A broad, the piece that goes between the Mr and the mattress. I don't remember no mistress – and besides it could be distinctly harmful to a man's life to be in possession of such knowledge.'

'But didn't you ever take sauce and clams out to Don Ferrari's house?'

'What, the estate at Lobster Bay? Never. But I tell you who could answer your question. Try the Ferrari Olive Oil and Parmigiana Company on Canal Street and ask for No-nose Louis.'

'No-nose Louis?'

There was a rumble again. 'He fell over in the snow one day.'

'And that cost him a nose?'

'Sure, he done about twenty-three grams of the stuff before anybody found him.'

No-nose Louis couldn't have been more helpful. Well, when you don't have a thing to blow in the morning or a ridge to put your glasses on, you don't get to have cosy conversations with too many angels in leather mini skirts and white T-shirts.

With cartons of clams and Tony's hot sauce, Gloria drove out over the TriBoro Bridge to Long Island and Lobster Bay and played over what No-nose had said.

The old man now lived in isolation on an estate protected day and night by two teams of guards. One team was male and they wore silk and satin versions of the uniforms of the Vatican Swiss Guard. They were very chic. Ferrari called them the Swish Guard. The other team was female. Six former sergeants from the Israeli army, all of whom had also been finalists in the Miss Israel contest. It was a corny idea but it made an old man very happy.

After forty-five minutes' driving Gloria braked her BMW outside imposing gates set in high walls, which went off in either direction for as far as the eye could see. Before she even switched her engine off a voice squawked out of a small loudspeaker set high up on the right-hand gate post.

'What do you want? If you're selling we already got it and if we haven't already got it we don't want it.'

'My name's Gloria Beresford and I'm one of the regulars at Tony's Clam Bar in the City, and knowing how much Mr Ferrari enjoys a plate of clams with Tony's hot sauce, and as I was coming out to Long Island anyway, I thought I'd bring Mr Ferrari some clams and hot sauce.'

The box squawked, 'Wait.'

Gloria's attention was attracted by the

137

gardener working on the lawns of the house opposite. She was walking towards her. She carried a trowel in one hand and what looked like fresh horse manure in the other.

'Don't worry,' said the gardener, 'I'll cover you.'

'Not with that I hope,' said Gloria.

'No, that's just a fake, Miss Beresford, to hide the laser.'

'You're Busy Buggers,' said Gloria.

'Right,' said Tiffany/Sadie, 'nice to meet you.'

'Nice to meet you, but how did you get here?'

'Easy – the City fathers publish a map of the mobsters' homes – you know, like the stars' homes in Beverley Hills. They had more Dons in Lobster Bay than they do in term time at Oxford University.'

The squawk box spoke again. 'Drive slowly up to the front of the house and park to the left of the front steps. Whatever you do, don't try to befriend the dalmations. They may look harmless but they have been trained to lick intruders to death.'

The gates swung open, playing the first eight bars of *The Impossible Dream* as they did so. Gloria drove slowly towards a large house that stood on a small hill overlooking Long Island Sound. It was set amongst beautifully manicured lawns – indeed, as she looked she saw a family of illegal Mexican immigrants manicuring them with nail scissors and cuticle pushers.

The house itself was a cross between a Roman temple and a pizza parlour, and sitting on the porch attended by a Swish Guard and two Israeli sergeants in full combat bikinis was Don Ferrari. Gloria approached the group carrying her clams and hot sauce in clear view of everybody. One of the Goddaughters, as Ferrari called them, took the package and placed it on a table alongside the old man. He looked up from the little plaster horse he was playing with – he was sawing its head off – and gave Gloria a slow gummy smile. If he'd had teeth it would have looked mischievous.

'Sit down, my dear. Such a beautiful delivery girl, you want a glass of lemonade, made twenty minutes ago with lemons from the Old Country?'

'Ah,' said Gloria, 'Sicily?'

'No,' said Ferrari, 'the Old Country's the name of my fruit store in Brooklyn. Anyway, thanks for the clams. What do you really want, Ms Beresford?'

'How do you know my name?'

'Checked it against your car registration – we still got friends in low places. So?'

'Well, I wanted to ask you about somebody called Ronald Knowles.'

Lemonade exploded from Don Ferrari's mouth in a huge arc which drenched the Swish Guard and thoroughly soaked three tubs of geraniums at the top of the steps. The old man's face contorted until it looked like a Jerusalem artichoke. Thirty-two blood vessels in his nose spontaneously ruptured as his eyes fought to push themselves out of the fleshy wallets that surrounded them and he was screaming what sounded like terrible curses in Italian.

Gloria said, 'What's he saying?'

One of the Goddaughters replied, 'You want simultaneous translation, go to the United Nations.'

The old man stopped screaming as suddenly as he had begun. Slowly the blood began to drain back from his head to those parts of the body whose need was greater. He looked at Gloria.

'You are the first person who has dared to mention that name in my hearing in thirty years.'

'I'm sorry. I didn't mean to upset you – but do you know what happened to him?'

'The last I heard he was holding up the traffic on the New Jersey Turnpike.'

'How was he doing that?'

'They built him into a bridge, I heard.'

'What about the child?'

'What child?'

'I heard there was a child.'

'What else did you hear?'

'That Ronald Knowles ran off with a lady friend of yours, got her pregnant, they married, maybe he disappeared.'

Gloria thought there were tears in the old man's eyes. Either that or his contacts were playing up.

'That lady friend of which you speak was the dearest, sweetest, most beautiful creature who ever wore rubber underwear. I could have given her anyone money could buy, but she ran off with this English bum. Then I hear the

English bum has an accident — that's what I hear — and she comes crawling back begging for forgiveness.'

'Did you forgive her?'

The old man sighed. 'Yes, but things weren't the same. She'd picked up strange habits like eating with a knife and fork at the same time. At dinner time she insisted I put on a shirt. We drifted apart.'

'But what happened to the baby?'

'We took care of the baby.'

'You killed a baby?'

The old man looked offended. 'Hey, what do you think I am, some sort of gangster or something? The baby was fostered. My good friend Mike the Meat Cleaver in Denver owed me a favour, so I sent the kid to him.'

'And how,' asked Gloria, 'do I get in touch with Mike the Meat Cleaver?'

'You don't, he ended up frozen on the end of a meat hook. But I unnerstan' they gave the kid to one of the soldiers in the Fusilli Mob, Buster Ringwood, as a recompense for a couple of things he'd had taken away from him. He'd always wanted a son, so they gave him a son.'

Had one of Don Ferrari's Swish Guard or Goddaughters looked through the gates to the lawns across the road, they would have seen a Jewish gardener holding a pile of horse manure to her ear. They would also have seen her suddenly stand up, put the manure in her pocket and race to a red Toyota that was parked thirty yards along the road.

Gloria was in her office the next day regretting, as she was saying to Philip, that she hadn't gone to her favourite shop on 5th Avenue and bought the old man a silver clam spoon. The good news was that Tiffany/Sadie had found the whereabouts of Buster Ringwood, and through him, his adoptive son.

Gloria had a heavy day. She got back to her apartment that night at 11.45 pm, nearly an hour after getting into a cab four blocks away. She'd had dinner with an ex who kept asking why, and so anxious was she to escape that she had failed to check out her cab driver before getting into the cab. Rule number two in the Manhattan Guide to Survival. Avoid any cab driver who looks as though he just got off the beach in Acapulco. He probably did. He set off briskly in precisely the wrong direction, then said to her at the first stop light, 'You speak Inglees?'

'Of course.'

'Good, you ask way when we get lost.'

But the evening didn't turn out so bad after all. There, winking away on her answering machine, was Tiffany/Sadie's request that she call her. And when she immediately did, Tiffany/Sadie had been proving her smarts. She'd talked to that guy at the department store in London — well, talked wasn't quite the right word since he seemed incapable of conveying anything unless he sang her the *Stars And Stripes* – and let her know something very interesting about an old guy who owned that store. Or used to.

Gloria rented a car at LAX and headed into the city on the Santa Monica Freeway. It was the usual Californian motorway madness. Drivers kept shooting past her. She couldn't see what they were shooting, but they sounded like .38 magnums. As she got closer to the city her air conditioner went on the blink and she opened a window. Almost a fatal error. Within seconds there was so much smog in the car she could hardly see the windscreen, never mind the road ahead. She should have realized the danger when she heard the announcer on station WNQU coughing as he gave out the day's pollution levels. She turned off the freeway at the exit beside the world's first drive-in massage parlour – a free oil change with every fifth massage – and headed down town on Wilshire Boulevard to the Fairbanks Building. She parked across the street from the building and set the car's burglar alarm. The latest in a long line of electronic deterrents, this one made a noise like a baby crying when the car was tampered with. The idea was it not only drove the thief away, it would also make him – or her – feel guilty.

She pressed the button for apartment 32. The spotlights came on and two TV cameras swung towards her. Only in California, she thought,

would you get a choice of camera angles on a
security device. A voice said, 'Yes?'

'Is that Buster Ringwood's son?'

'Who wants to know?'

'It could be your fairy godmother,' said Gloria.

'Well, you sure look like a fairy godmother
to me. Come on up.'

Jake was standing at the open door when,
in a state of considerable shock, she stumbled
out of the elevator.

'There are people cooking in your elevator,'
she cried.

'I'm sorry,' said Jake, 'I should have told you.
That's no longer an elevator, it's apartment 46A.
Come in. Kelsey isn't here right now, but you
can tell me all about it. I'm Jake.'

Gloria poked her head into the driver's window
of the black cab on the rank outside Terminal
4 at London Heathrow and said loudly, 'Do you
speak English?'

For a moment the driver, who'd been having
a nap, thought he was on the Esther Rantzen
Show.

'Course I speak bloody English, and take your
'ead out of my cab.'

'Just checking,' said Gloria. 'In New York you
can never be sure.'

'Well I hate to surprise you but this ain't New
York. This is bloody London. Now where to?'

Gloria, Kelsey and Jake climbed into the back
of the cab.

'Do you know a shop called Knowles?'

'You don't want to go there, you want to go to Harrods.'

'We *don't* want to go to Harrods, we want to go to the Beehive.'

'Please yourself. But it won't be open yet.'

'Then we'll just stand and look at it.'

'Most Americans prefer to stand and look at the Tower of London.'

'I'm not most Americans,' said Gloria, 'just drive.'

11

As Eric Dunnet walked to work, he noticed three
people staring at the store. This in itself was
unusual because nobody stared at the Beehive.
Most people hurried past it in case it was har-
bouring some terrible disease. But there was
something about their appearance and intensity
of gaze that disturbed him. The one doing most
of the talking was a very attractive woman in
her late thirties — far too young for him, of
course. Her companions were two younger men.
One was good-looking in that healthy, toothy,
vapid all-American way and the other looked
like a small gorilla in jeans and a baseball cap.
Around them on the pavement was an assort-
ment of luggage which indicated to his razor-
sharp mind that either they had just arrived
or they were just leaving. Either way, thought
Dunnet, it's a bit odd.

Five minutes later he thought it was even
odder when he looked down from his office
window to see the odd trio still standing there,
gazing at the store. They looked up to where
Dunnet was standing and even though they
couldn't possibly see him, he pulled back. Now,

now, he said to himself. Don't start getting paranoid. They're just tourists, probably think this is the V and A. He went back to the window and looked down. Gone, nobody there. Can't think why I was getting so uptight. He sat down at his desk for a quick ten minutes with the latest batch of replies to his advertisment in the Saga Holidays newsletter.

Had he but known, Eric had every reason to be uptight. The trio had suddenly disappeared because their next port of call was the all-important visit to Lawrence Chadwick & Peck to inform them that the new heir to the Knowles empire had just hit town.

The Most Reverend Montague Stelling, High Bishop of Lambeth, hurried from his car in through the front door of the Beehive. He was a familiar figure, having been one of its most regular and revered customers. To Alfred Knowles he was the epitome of the clientele the store liked to service. A man of great standing in the high church, an impeccable pedigree of ancestry and dedication to the Christian ethics – or so it would appear to the outside world.

His penchant for comfortable living and quality surroundings was little known to those outside his immediate circle. His pious and ascetic appearances to the public at large belied many a moral fissure that would mean instant defrocking if his superiors knew of them.

Indeed his excesses were such that many a

time he would overstep his means and run up an account at the Beehive that, were it not for Alfred's fawning dismissal of his attempts to pay, would have caused the Bishop severe financial problems.

Eric Dunnet had been aware of this situation for many a long year and had kept a careful record of all the monies owed by the Bishop to the store. From time to time he took the opportunity of informing the Bishop of his extremely large debts. Eric, knowing full well that one lapse of morals led to another, had had the Bishop followed and checked out several times as to his extracurricular social activities.

He had discovered the Bishop was a frequent visitor to a discreet yet well-known brothel situated in Streatham, and over the years Eric's dossier contained many a damning indictment of sexual profligacy. Furthermore, Eric had encouraged the Bishop to indulge his spending sprees increasingly, and had at times even procured for him certain accommodating young ladies to visit his own personal residence. The Bishop, surprised at first, had willingly followed Eric's encouragement, and so by a slow process of spinning inducements, Eric had ensnared the Bishop in his devious web.

It was a hesitant Most Reverend Bishop that sat in front of Eric that afternoon. Eric spidered his fingers together and, focusing the Bishop with a careful stare, said, 'You know why you're here, don't you?'

The Bishop nodded solemnly. 'I presume it's to do with the death of Alfred Knowles and the future of the store we are now sitting in.'

'Correct,' said Dunnet. 'You'll be pleased to know that the solicitors Lawrence Chadwick & Peck have finally sorted out Alfred's Will. There being no heir, the Beehive will become the property of the Church within the next few months. I think our pay day is not far away.'

'Am I right in saying, Mr Dunnet, that the only people who know the conditions of the inheritance are yourself and the solicitors?'

'And Mr Big and his friends of course,' said Dunnet.

'Quite, the Church of England is no problem,' stated the Bishop. 'Being in full control of the diocese my colleagues in the Church will know as much as I want them to know. The problem, it would appear, is how do we get round the solicitors. Surely with such large amounts involved they're going to suspect something is wrong if they only deal with me.'

'I have been thinking about that,' said Dunnet. 'I am going to set up a meeting between yourself and the Executors and you will explain that due to the very sensitive nature of financing within the Church and the publicity resulting from such a large windfall, the utmost discretion must be exercised. You will point out to the solicitors that if the donation becomes public knowledge, the Church is open to criticism from all sides as to what to do with the money, and therefore it is the wish of the Church

Council that you deal with all arrangements personally and the utmost security must be observed.'

The Bishop looked doubtful. 'Will my sole involvement be sufficient for the Executors; do you think someone may suspect something untoward?'

'The Executors, thank God – and you know more about that than I –' said Dunnet almost apologetically, 'would not smell a rat if it had been dead for six months behind their own skirting board. The fact that they deal with the Bishop himself will allay anything untoward that they may feel, and as long as they get a suitable commission from the sale you need have no fear from them.'

The Bishop just murmured in agreement, knowing full well the predicament he was in.

'Besides which,' Dunnet continued, 'you're not going to be alone when you deal with the solicitor.'

'What do you mean, not alone?'

'What I mean is, Mr Big would like to be in on the meetings, to oversee his interests, shall we say. No worry, they will be perfectly discreet.'

'They?' The Bishop was puzzled.

'Mr Big and his aquaintances, Rupert and Mangle. No doubt you have clerical garb, vestments, dog collars, that sort of thing, that they could borrow?'

'You mean you want them to look like the clergy?' asked the startled Bishop.

'Well it would add some credence to you. You could say they were the Church's financial advisors, accountants, anything! You'll think of something.'

The Bishop was now most concerned. How anyone could mistake the yeti Mangle for an accountant was stretching incredulity. However, his avarice overcame his caution.

'Very well, if Mr Big has a certain amount of mistrust in our dealings, then let him attend. But do emphasize to him that I shall do the talking. I would be grateful for minimum contribution to the proceedings from him and his compatriots.'

'Ah, good morning my lord Bishop, welcome to our most humble surroundings,' Peck's voice shrilled close to the ears of the Bishop, making him shudder as one does when hearing dry hard chalk on a blackboard.

The Bishop gave Peck a wincing smile. 'Thank you Mr Peck, charming offices, such a change not to be surrounded by computers and teletexes and the modern technology one is unfortunately subjected to in this micro-chip infested age.'

'I'm so pleased you feel the same way as we do,' said an obviously delighted Peck, 'it is our policy to eschew such devices, preferring to rely upon the written word in the main, although we do have a typewriter of course!' Peck thought this last remark hysterical and his laughter was so high-pitched the Bishop was forced to put fingers in his ear. Peck was interrupted by his phone ringing many octaves lower than his laughter.

'Excuse me, my lord.' Peck picked up the black
GPO 1930s' issue phone. 'Yes? Oh good, send
them up right away. Your people have arrived,
sir,' Peck informed the Bishop. 'Shall I have
some tea sent up for everyone?'

'That would be most welcome,' said the Bishop,
fascinated by the bobbing epiglottis.

Peck walked out of the room to instruct someone to make the tea. By the time he returned
Mr Big, Mangle and Rupert were already there.

Mr Peck was quite taken aback by the appearance of these representatives of the Church of
England. Mr Big was quite the smallest vicar
he had seen and he obviously had difficulty
finding dog collars that fitted him. The one he
was wearing now fitted extremely well, even
though it covered his entire mouth. Mr Big's
nose poked over the top of the collar.

Rupert did at least have the correct black
sombre vestments, including smart calf-hugging
black gaiters. Although his shoes were not
standard ecclesiastical issue, they were jet-black
Nike trainers with Gary Linnaker's signature
imprinted upon the side.

Mangle, it had to be said, had surpassed
himself. He had been along to a theatrical
costumier and had hired a Friar Tuck outfit.
Dangling from his neck was a full six-foot 150lb
crucifix. Swinging from his right hand was a
thurible which he swung periodically to release
the perfume trapped within the toilet block
rattling inside the ball.

If Peck's astonishment and surprise was

noticeable it was nothing compared with the Bishop's utter disbelief. Almost at a loss for words, he turned to Peck and attempted to introduce the three imposters before him.

'Mr Peck, may I introduce three of the Church's business executives. The Reverend Sly, pastor of, er . . . Hillingdon.'

'Bless you, my son,' said Mr Big.

'Cannon Cutler, who has special responsibilities for regional Church finance.'

'Good morning,' said Rupert.

'And this,' said the Bishop, having to force the words through a drained white face, 'is Father Desmond Ackrill, head of Hampstead Monastery.'

Mangle, ever keen to impress, held up the crucifix and started reciting the Lord's Prayer.

Peck, worried that Father Ackrill might drop the giant crucifix, scampered round and sat behind the safety of his desk. After four words of the Lord's Prayer, Mangle could not remember any more and Peck took the opportunity to remove from a drawer in his desk a large sheaf of papers and documents relating to the Knowles empire.

'My lord Bishop,' trilled Peck, 'you will no doubt be aware that the department store known as the Beehive is very likely to fall under the control of the Church of England within the very near future.'

'Apparently so,' said the Bishop, 'something to do with wills and inheritances, I believe?'

'Quite,' said Peck, 'the original wills and

153

testaments of the founding brothers stipulated that if there were to be no succeeding male heirs, all monies and properties thereof should be bequeathed to the Church of England, and in particular the diocese where the store is situated – in this case, your own, Lord Bishop.

'The original conditions are far-reaching, many of them stipulating the type of goods for sale, the need for thrift and economy and other restrictions, which has meant that in general the Beehive has traded most unprofitably for the last several years.'

'Tell me, Mr Peck, if the Church of England was to take on the store, what conditions would apply to the Church?'

'A debatable point,' said Peck.

'Shit,' said Mr Big.

'I beg your pardon?' said Peck, taken aback by what he thought was an extremely unlikely expletive to come from the lips of a reverend.

Mr Big, trying to retrieve the situation, shouted 'Bishop,' with a mouth full of dog collar.

Ah, that's what he said, thought Peck.

'Yes, Reverend?' said the Bishop.

'Won't the Church leaders be delighted at such good fortune,' said Mr Big, making sure the dog collar got in the way so that it distorted syllables and vowels to the point where his speech was almost unintelligible.

'Er . . . Yes, quite,' answered the Bishop, wondering how on earth he had ever agreed to this ridiculous charade in the first place. 'Please carry on, Mr Peck.'

'Thank you, Lord Bishop. Of course, as and when the property reverts to the Church, there is nothing in the original agreements to say that you have to carry on trading as a department store. You may wish to trade in another business, or in fact sell the whole building and land per se.'

Mr Big's eyes lit up in unison with the Bishop's. Rupert gave a slow inward smile and Mangle, blissfully unaware of the ramifications of the last statement, swung the thurible around his head with great vigour, only to clonk Jesus Christ on the nose.

It split open and showered the immediate surroundings with smouldering pieces of toilet block. Several pieces dropped on the carpet, a couple in the waste bin, and one slipped down the front of Mr Big's dog collar.

Mr Big leapt from his seat and jumped up and down yelling with pain, imploring Rupert to put his hand down the front of his vestments and retrieve the smouldering lump. Mangle, realizing that he had made another one of his foopahs, immediately got down on his knees to pick up the smouldering pieces of toilet block, forgetting to unhook the crucifix around his neck and thereby half hanging himself from the upright cross.

The Bishop realized there was every chance of the crucifix, now toppling forward, acting as a mallet on Peck's forehead. He grabbed hold of it.

At that point Peck's secretary entered the

room with a tray of tea for five and beheld the scene before her. A bishop supporting a large crucifix with a friar dangling at the end; a gaitered man of the Church with his arm down a choirboy's trousers and a flaming wastepaper bin that was in great danger of setting fire to the oak panelling behind her boss's desk; her boss was seemingly transfixed and mesmerized in his chair, eyes riveted to a precarious crucifix about to deal him a death blow.

The Bishop, now in a state of harassed shock, let go of the crucifix. Mangle's weight toppled it to send the edge of the horizontal beam hurtling towards a Peck transfixed like a rabbit on the motorway. The edge of the cross missed his nose by a good nine inches; it crashed instead into his epiglottis.

It is understandable in such circumstances that the secretary dropped the tray and fled from the room screaming for help. This arrived in the form of an over-enthusiastic articled clerk with a fire extinguisher pouring out white stuff at a violent rate of knots. Pointing the nozzle at the wastepaper bin he extinguished the flames and then, to be on the safe side, pointed the nozzle at anything else he felt could be a danger. This included the smouldering bits beneath the dangling Friar.

He was relieved of the fire extinguisher by Mr Big, who promptly shoved the nozzle down the front of his choirboy uniform and gave a sigh of relief as the liquid foam extinguished the burning sensation in his loins. The nozzle somehow got caught in his clothing and continued to pour forth on to the floor via his ankles.

The rescue attempt by the articled clerk, while heroic and swift, was too late to stop the sprinkler system being activated by the smoke now filling the room. As the torrents of water were released from the sprinklers, everyone in the room thought it advisable to leave as rapidly and with as much dignity as possible.

12

Striding out of the Piccadilly Hotel, Gloria
Beresford looked round for a taxi cab. Hard on
her heels were Kelsey and Jake. There was a
slight drizzle in London that morning and as
any Londoner will tell you, a taxi cab for hire
in the drizzle is harder to find than an Irish
joke on Channel Four.

After thirty seconds of waiting Gloria's
patience ran out. She stepped into the middle
of Piccadilly and stopped the very next taxi.
The driver screeched to a halt and in bold
cockney terms enquired as to why she was
obstructing his progress. Ignoring the foul-
mouthed expletives, she opened the back door
of the cab where an elderly gentleman with a
briefcase and umbrella was fully expecting to
arrive at Waterloo Station within the next few
minutes.

Gloria informed him that if he did not move
his 'white middle-aged arse out of the cab pronto,
immediatement, now', she would rip off her
clothes, throw herself over him and accuse him
of rape. The passenger was dumbstruck, and
not a teeny bit terrified. It is difficult to gather

your inner suburban composure when confronted by such an unexpected demand. Gloria was already unhitching her skirt and preparing to throw herself on him. Rational thinking departs in such circumstances, and knowing full well the consequences of being thus accused, no matter how little truth there was in it, he scurried from the cab ignoring the polite demands of the taxi driver to reimburse him for the fare on the meter.

Turning her attention to the driver, Gloria now informed him that if he drove a New York taxi cab, he'd soon recognize perverted pimps such as that he had been carrying and think himself lucky she was not going to report him for being an accessory after the fact, and anyway, 'Here's a bunch of your goddamn stupid money, so why don't you shove that down your fat face and take me and my companions to where we want to go.'

The driver looked at the forty-three pence in two-penny and one-penny pieces thrust into his hand, and in disbelief realized he had no option but to comply.

Once the journey was underway, Gloria looked at Kelsey and said, 'Now, leave all the talking to me. This Dunnet sounds like a squawk box from Queens. We've got him over a barrel and if I read it right, we could make this short-arsed town jump like a bare-arsed honky on a hotplate.'

Jake began to enthuse about what he could do with the communication system in the store, obviously having little idea of the antiquated methods conveying cash documents between the departments.

Kelsey, not really listening, was trying to figure out how he could possibly have bought twenty tickets for *No Sex Please, We're British* from the commissionaire when, after all, he had been trying to sell him an automatic umbrella that opened when the first spot of rain was detected.

As the taxi made its way up to Kensington High Street, Gloria kept up a running one-way conversation with the driver through the glass partition.

'No long-cuts, honey, I might not know this town but I can smell a fare-rigger quicker than a rutting skunk in a shoe-box.'

Whether or not a taxi journey in London has ever been undertaken with complete silence from the driver is not known, but Gloria Beresford's trip came very close to it.

As the bemused taxi driver pulled up outside the Beehive, Gloria and her entourage bounced from the cab and swept in through the front revolving doors. Jim the commissionaire, a rabid glint in his eye, bore down on her. She simply shoved him sprawling to the gutter.

Once in the store, noticing the lift, she commanded the attendant to take them to the M.D.'s office. Fortunately for Jacko's sake, it was one of his better days and he closed the lift gate without the aid of the stool, and propelled the trio to the second floor. Jacko sensed that here was someone who would not tolerate incompetence and so was extra careful to make sure the lift stopped precisely level with floor two. This necessitated several movements of the lever into the up and down position. After a minute or so of these manoeuvres, Gloria bellowed in his ear, 'Open the goddam gates, dimble brain, I'm not a goddamn milkshake!'

Jacko, unused to such forthright demands, opened the gates immediately and, trembling somewhat, allowed his passengers out.

Eric, unsuspecting the onslaught fast approaching his office, was interviewing a prospective new employee for the cashier's department. He had instructed the personnel agency that he wanted someone of very mature years and it was therefore with some surprise that a Mrs Mildred Ashford had received a call from the agency to attend the interview. Being seventy-three years old, she had retired some thirteen years previously and could not understand why someone younger and more attuned to present-day needs was not asked for. Eric, of course, spent the first ten minutes of the interview consumed with passion for Mildred.

He helped her to the chair and as she sat down, left his hands briefly pinioned to the seat by her backside. Eric sat close to Mildred, holding her hand with a firmness that was beyond that of a concerned employer. His questions as to her background and in particular her present social habits were perhaps more intimate than was the norm on these occasions. She informed him that she had been widowed eight years ago and that she led quite an active life with regular whist drives and outings with the local Darby and Joan Club.

Eric's eyes roved up and down Mrs Ashford with barely disguised desire. For forty-five years, Mrs Ashford had been secretary and cashier for many bosses of many firms but had never before been interviewed in such close proximity. In fact, as the interview progressed so the distance between herself and Eric became almost non-existent. If she did not know better she would say that here was a gentleman who had more than an employment proposition on his mind. She was fairly certain it was more than an employment proposition Eric had to offer and she found herself not a little flattered by this lecherous attention. Not that she encouraged him, not at all, but there again as Eric's hand dropped seemingly innocently on to her knee she made no effort to remove it, or indeed stop its progress on to her inner thigh.

A hot flush searing within her loins coincided exactly with the arrival of three Americans bursting through the door into the office. Eric leapt like a branded piglet to stare incredulously at this apparition standing before him.

'Are you Dunnet?' asked Gloria Beresford.

'Who the hell are you?' gasped Dunnet.

'You will find out soon enough,' screeched Gloria, and turning to Mrs Ashford said, 'OK Mae West, beat it.'

Mrs Ashford hurriedly gathered her things

together and with a glance at Eric, walked out of the room.

Eric, still agog at what was before him, watched as all three took up what seating there was in the room. Composing himself a little, he walked round behind his desk and with as much authority as he could muster asked Gloria for some explanation for this unacceptable intrusion.

'OK,' said Gloria, 'Kelsey, stand up.'

Kelsey did so, eyeing Eric up and down and taking in the surroundings of this strange yet somehow very English set-up.

'Good morning,' said Kelsey, 'I'm the new owner.'

'You're what?' stammered Eric.

'I'm the new owner of the Beehive,' said Kelsey. 'Pleased to meet you,' and with that he put his hand out to shake Eric's.

Eric sat limply back in his chair, totally confused and not understanding at all what was going on.

'I think some coffee would be in order,' said Gloria, 'or maybe you would prefer tea. Both taste the same in this hellhole of a town.'

Eric nodded doubtfully and pressed the intercom to instruct his secretary to bring the necessary beverages.

Over the next forty minutes Gloria painstakingly filled Eric in on all the details. Eric sat bemused and stiff, not wanting to believe what was being said, but he knew all too well something familiar was being stated here and several things that Alfred had said over the years were starting to fall painfully into place.

After seven pots of coffee Gloria got down to the nitty-gritty. 'So, Mr Dunnet, what we have here is a clear line of descent. Kelsey Ringwood's name is Kelsey Knowles. His father married his mother, and therefore Kelsey is a direct descendant in name and blood and thus the heir to the Knowles empire.'

Eric's mouth moved, but no sound came out. His carefully laid plans were threatened if not ruined by these preposterous people before him.

'Kelsey, my client, gets control, he's how we say head honcho, numero uno; quite frankly, Mr Dunnet, he now calls the shots. You have twenty-four hours to vacate this office and we will return tomorrow to take control. In the meantime, perhaps you would study the documents I have here. You will find all the necessary details and legals to confirm every word that I have said. We are all looking forward immensely to your co-operation in running the place. Now we would like to look around our new store.'

With that Gloria, Jake and Kelsey left the office to take stock of their new acquisition.

Eric reached for the Scotch bottle he kept handy for special occasions and emergencies. As every day was special to Eric and most days had two or three emergencies, the Scotch had to be replenished frequently. Pouring himself half a tumbler, he cracked it down in an attempt to clear a head that was reeling with waves of fear and confusion.

He looked at the documents the frightening woman had left for him on the desk. As he flicked his way through them it would indeed appear as if Ms Beresford was telling the truth. There was Kelsey Knowles' birth certificate; his father was Ronald Knowles, profession 'Entrepreneur'. There was a copy of Ronald's Will signed, sealed and dated in the Schwartz & Schwartz offices. There was even a death certificate for Ronald Knowles with a coroner's verdict of 'Death by misadventure'.

His thoughts slid into a deep depression, but were interrupted by the phone ringing on his desk. Eric picked up the receiver to hear his secretary's voice. 'There's a Mr Big for you on the line, Mr Dunnet.'

'Tell him I'm out,' he panicked.

'I have done that already,' said Melissa. 'He said he knows you're out but would like to speak to you all the same.'

The last person Dunnet wanted to speak to right now was Mr Big. 'Tell him anything, Melissa, tell him the store's had a bomb through it, there's Legionnaires' disease in the canteen, anything, I just don't want to speak to him!'

'I'll try, Mr Dunnet, but he's very insistent.'

'Do the best you can,' and with that Eric replaced the receiver. What would he tell Mr Big, that he couldn't have the store, the deal was off? Some bastard he had never known existed suddenly turned up with a black sharp-tongued lawyer from New York and they were going to take over the Beehive. He would send Mangle round with a chainsaw and Eric would be sold as dog food within three days. What a nightmare.

Eric cursed Ronald, and wondered how widespread and how extensive his wild oat sowing programme had been. Could it be a vast horde of Knowles bastards were even now on a flock of 747s descending on Heathrow to lay claim to the Beehive? He paced round Alfred's old office in a state of considerable agitation. So many of Alfred's odd remarks and curious habits came flooding back to Eric. He remembered particularly, 'There is more than one plum duff in the oven when the chef's a keen baker.'

Suddenly the telephone rang. Dunnet scooped up the receiver. Melissa again. 'It's Mr Big on the line yet again Mr Dunnet; he insists that you answer his call, he knows very well you're not in but wants to speak to you all the same.'

There was nothing else for it. 'OK. Put him through.'

'Hullo Dunnet,' said the capital's most diminutive gangster, and Eric twitched with fright.

'Good morning. How nice to hear from you.'

'Well, well, enough of the pleasantries. When are we going to get the deeds to your little shop?'

Dunnet giggled hysterically.

'I said something humorous?' asked Mr Big.

'No, no you didn't say anything funny.'

'Then why are you laughing?'

'I'm just thinking of all the money you're going to make, Mr Big; it makes me happy.'

'Good,' replied Mr Big, 'so when will we get the deeds?'

'Well, there has been a slight technical hitch,' said Dunnet, 'nothing too important, certainly nothing that will hold up the proceedings more than a month or two.'

'What's the hitch?' said Mr Big.

'A technical point, lawyers' jargon, that sort of thing.'

The tone of Mr Big's voice changed. 'Mr Dunnet,' he said, 'I am not accustomed to playing games with the possible exception of pinning the axe on the defaulter's head. A small technical hitch does not take two months to sort out, even with that firm of mouldering geriatrics that call themselves solicitors.'

Calmly Eric placed his hand over the receiver and screamed hysterically. Scream over, he returned to the call.

'It really is a minor legal complication. It should be sorted out very shortly, don't worry.'

'Oh, I don't worry,' said Mr Big, 'worrying's not my game, other people worry. For instance, *you* should be worried, Mr Dunnet, lest I decide to give you a free course of lessons in skydiving down a mine shaft.'

There was a click and the phone went dead.

Eric gulped down more Scotch. Things were getting serious. At that moment Melissa entered the room.

'Mr Dunnet,' she began and then, noticing the

half-empty bottle on the table, 'drinking at work? Tut tut,' she chided.

'I wonder if Americans like skydiving down mine shafts?' said Eric out loud.

Melissa understandably was a bit lost as to the logic of this question.

'You can't just let three strangers run the store, can you?' sobbed Dunnet.

Looking at Dunnet and the whisky bottle she said, 'I'll come back later,' and turned to leave.

Dunnet's eyes fastened on her bottom as she turned. Yes, he thought, in about thirty years time when it's a bit less pert and shapely and a bit more flabby and drooping, who knows. At which point he fell back into his chair and thought it best to get anaesthetized as quickly as possible.

13

Much as Dunnet was perturbed and irritated by the arrival of this American interloper, after a short while he wasn't unduly worried. Blithely, he assured a suspicious Mr Big that this was a mere unforeseen delay to their plans.

Mr Big gruffly assented to this. He was busy with another scheme, which involved turning an NCP multi-storey car park into a drive-in wine bar called 'Spaces'. The scheme was meeting with stiff opposition from Westminster Council, who had raised a number of technical and legal objections, chief amongst which was that it was the 'most bloody stupid idea we've ever heard'.

Dunnet was quietly confident that Kelsey Ringwood would not possess even an ounce of enthusiasm for running the store once he actually saw it. Dunnet knew very little of Americans or America. He was not a well-travelled man. A few years previously he had persuaded himself to go on a holiday abroad for the first time ever.

The Costa Del Sol had come as a shock, His chief reason for venturing there had been the lure of readily available women. The 'Young at Heart' brochure had offered tantalizing photographs of retired and widowed ladies who every year swallowed five stiff gins and boarded a 737 for Malaga. Dunnet visualized the beaches, the sun-browned flesh and himself as the Don Juan of Torremolinos. Like most English people on their first trip abroad, he somehow thought that foreign parts meant exotica and mystery. He was rudely awakened when he discovered that southern Spain was just as noisy, drunken and unpleasant as most of Britain. The only difference was that it was also intolerably hot. Dunnet had spent a miserable two weeks watching his skin growing puce and downing gallon after gallon of Sangria. His one near-conquest was a spinster librarian from Droitwich who Dunnet patiently followed around countless examples of interesting medieval Andalusian church architecture in a vain attempt to have his evil way. Finally, on the last night, he plied her with so much Rioja that when he removed his clothes she laughed non-stop and with such gusto that the hotel security thought he must be molesting her, and ejected him from the hotel. The next day he sat miserably on the plane, feeling thoroughly sick, until turbulence over the Bay of Biscay put him out of his misery. Since then, he had never been abroad again.

He distrusted foreigners. This quality was not a particularly good thing in the manager of a department store in one of the most popular tourist areas of London. Dunnet was totally oblivious to the benefits of encouraging tourists to visit the store. Many a bemused French or Japanese tourist had left in disgust on hearing Dunnet cry, 'Mary! Serve this slimy frog,' or 'We've got nothing small enough to fit you, custard face.' This overt hostility to foreigners had brought Dunnet to the attention of the Race Relations Board on one occasion, but it had done no good. He didn't like foreigners and that was that. They didn't want to buy proper things. All they wanted was souvenirs, appalling tea towels and brass clocks in the shape of the Houses of Parliament.

Apart from affecting the balance sheet of the store, this xenophobia also affected Dunnet's view of Kelsey Ringwood. Americans were the worst of all: loud-mouthed and with a totally different concept of service from the British. Americans actually expected service. The British just counted themselves fortunate and privileged if they got it.

Americans, Dunnet knew, were retailing whizz-kids, into high-pressure selling and that kind of guff. That was not the way of the Beehive. Ringwood would soon realize that, and once he had, he'd be on the first plane home.

On the Monday morning, Ringwood officially took over. Dunnet drove in as usual, whistling softly to himself as he threaded his way through the mismanaged mayhem of London traffic. At five to nine, he parked in the staff car park, noting with distaste that Ringwood had hired

a Mercedes. Bloody German car, fumed Dunnet.
He peered in through the tinted glass. Jake had
left sweet wrappers and cassettes lying all over
the interior. There was chewing gum stuck on
the carphone and, Dunnet noted with disgust,
lying on the rear seat was a paperback called
'SELL! How to Go For It and Win Win Win
EVERY TIME!' by Hiram J. Strangleheimer III.
He tut-tutted at the foreignness of it, and made
his way into the store.

Eric Dunnet faced the employees of the Beehive
across the check table-cloths of the staff canteen
on the top floor of the building, immediately
below Alfred Knowles' penthouse. The canteen
was one of the few places in the Beehive in
which the twentieth century had been allowed
to intrude, and with predictably dire results.
In the centre of each table was a Lazy Susan
upon which were stacked what Jacko insisted
on calling the 'condomments'. There was one
large red plastic tomato and two long narrow
plastic tubes, one a pale vomit yellow, the other
dung brown, which looked as though they might
at one time have been containers for Duckham's
Multi Grade. Certainly the three sauces they
now held bore a startling resemblance to motor
oil, if not in colour then certainly in consistency.
Though the oil probably had a little more
flavour. Three large fans suspended from the
ceiling provided the only form of ventilation.
All they achieved was to shift the dead fumes
of all the years – the cabbages and leeks, the

172

long-gone faggots and reconstituted fish cakes of another age — from one end of the room to the other. That was why so many of the older employees still talked fondly of World War II — they'd been allowed to wear their gas masks in the canteen.

The staff had wondered why Dunnet wanted to see them. It could only be bad news, they were sure. Dunnet was not a man for pleasantries with the staff. Indeed, the only time he ever talked to them was if he passed when they were serving an old lady. Then he would pounce, take over the sale and try to lure the old lady to his upstairs office on some manufactured pretext — she'd won the Old Lady of the Month award, or somesuch.

The staff of the Beehive were not exactly the crème de la crème. They weren't even the skimmed milk de la skimmed milk.

Dunnet cleared his throat, a noise that always reminded Miss Marchmont of a duet between a stuck pig and a chain saw. 'Now you're probably wondering why I've called you here this afternoon — and though it's during working hours, I know you'll be delighted to know I will not be deducting a single penny from your pay packets.'

If Dunnet was expecting a standing ovation he was disappointed. He didn't even get a squatting ovation.

'The reason I have asked you all here today is that I shall be relinquishing absolute control of the store forthwith.'

The noise Dunnet could not identify was the sound of a small cheer being suppressed.

'As you know, it had been my hope — some might even say it was my just entitlement — to assume the position of chairman, as well as managing director, upon the demise of Mr Alfred. But, as the poet Nobbie Burns once said, "The best laid plans of a nice men aft gang a bang."'

Jacko whispered to Hacket, who was standing alongside him, 'I can't hear what he's saying.'

Hacket said, 'W. . .W. . .W. . .'

'It's therefore my pleasure to tell you that you have a new chairman. He's an American but I don't think we should hold that against him.' Only Dunnet laughed. 'His name is Kelsey Ringwood and he is a grandson of the founder. I therefore hope that you will all show him the respect and affection that you show me.'

Elsie, who had been a cleaner at the Beehive for forty-three years, said to her neighbour, 'Oh I couldn't treat anyone that badly.'

'Mr Ringwood, or Mr Kelsey as I know we shall all come to call him, will be taking up his duties on Monday. And I'm sure we all wish him well.'

I'm sure you don't wish him well at all, thought Miss Marchmont as she went off to find Watson, wondering whether the Beehive would soon be seeing another death from 'unnatural causes'.

In her room on the eighteenth floor of the Hilton,

Gloria Beresford was holding a council of war.

'Well, what do we think, people?' said Gloria, sounding a little like that nice sergeant who used to start *Hill Street Blues*.

'When Napoleon said England was a nation of shopkeepers, he clearly hadn't seen the Beehive. It makes the average five-and-ten back home look like Nieman Marcus. I don't know whether it could ever make money. And what do we know about shop keeping, anyway?'

'I think it has possibilities,' said Kelsey, standing by the window and watching as twilight settled over Hyde Park and swards of police beat the bushes for bonkers.

'As what,' said Gloria, 'a garage?'

'I think it has a certain charm,' he said.

'So do enemas, if you happen to have the blocks,' said Gloria.

'Hey, lighten up, you guys,' said Jake. 'What do you mean charm, Kel? A lot of the stuff in the Beehive – and for that matter a lot of the staff – look as though they could have been around when Queen Victoria was on the throne.'

Gloria said, 'It was and they almost were.'

Kelsey said, 'Junk happens to be my field.'

'That's right,' replied Jake. 'Back home he's got fields full of junk – and Victoriana is the new thing in the States. It started during the Reagan years – people wanted things the same age as the President.'

'If they had an inkling,' said Kelsey, 'that all this was just seven hours away by plane,

175

Richard Branson would be turning Virgins round faster than an Armenian marriage broker.'

Jake looked up from the TV remote control he was rearranging. Some people when they stay in hotels have a compulsion to fill in other guests' breakfast menus hanging from their doorknobs, or, in days of yore, exchange the shoes they'd left out to be cleaned. Jake liked to rearrange the TV remote. By the time he was finished with it every command was reversed. On one memorable occasion he had succeeded in rigging a control so that it operated the set four rooms away.

'I thought,' he said, 'we were going to drag this place into the twentieth century.'

'No,' replied Kelsey. 'I think we should drag it further back into the nineteenth century. We'll clean up!'

'Well, I was going back to New York, but I think I'll stay for the fun,' said Gloria. She picked up the phone and dialled the hotel operator.

'Could you give me the names of half a dozen good real estate people? Thank you. If we're going to be here for a while,' she said, putting the phone down, 'I'm going to get us a place to live. I am to hotels what Jackie Collins is to convents.'

Kelsey, Glory B and Jake emerged from Jacko's lift looking like an overwrought martini – shaken *and* stirred. Glory B looked back at the rickety iron cage with the sort of wonder and sense of achievement Blériot or the brothers Wright must have felt after their first flights.

'Did we really travel in that thing?' she said. 'In New York that would be a litigant's dream. I mean, in the twenty minutes we were in there—'

Jake interrupted, '—we were lucky. Some poor guy's been stuck in there for two and a half hours or more.'

'But we were only going one floor,' said Glory B. 'I counted at least a dozen cases of malpractice, negligence, physical damage, psychological damage.'

'What psychological damage?' said Kelsey, who was just taking it all in, wondering whether he was going to wake up and find himself in a warehouse in Bakersfield, California, surrounded by fourteen thousand winking plastic Jesuses, or whether he really did own this crazy shop.

'Elevator trauma,' said Glory B.

'I haven't heard of that before,' said Jake.

'That's because I just invented it. That's known as creative law. The greatest example of creative law was the genius who invented whiplash. There he was, going to his office in a cab in mid-town Manhattan. The cabbie stopped suddenly, the lawyer's head snapped forward and back and before you could say "That's gonna cost you a million bucks, buddy", whiplash was born. For the American legal industry it really was the greatest thing since alimony. I could name you half a dozen highly respected New

York firms who started out chasing whiplash cases. One of them even employed indigents to drive cabs badly and create whiplash cases. But everybody's wised up to whiplash, we need something new, so I just invented elevator trauma.'

Jake said, 'What are the effects of elevator trauma?'

'Well, apart from a fear of elevators and the resulting inconvenience and serious likelihood of heart failure brought on by having to climb hundreds of flights of stairs a day, for women there's also the aversion to shopping. Traumatized by the experience in the elevator taking them to the designer gown floor or wherever, some women will find it impossible to even look at a designer gown again, thereby finding themselves with a seriously reduced life-style and ability to enjoy life, and total loss of social libido and desire for social intercourse. Now that's got to be worth millions. I think elevator trauma could be the whiplash of the nineties. What do you think, K?'

K. wasn't paying attention, which was why Glory B had asked the question. 'Sorry,' he said.

'You probably can't hear with that thing on your head. What do they call that? Is that an English bowler hat?'

'No, this is a deerstalker.'

'The idea is,' explained Jake, 'that when you go out hunting deer you put one of these on your head and when the deer sees you he laughs so much that he forgets to run away and that's when you bag him.'

'What sort of bag do you use?' said Glory B, whose understanding of the verb 'to bag' was limited to groceries at the checkout of her local Gristedes. 'Elastic or re-cycled brown paper?'

'No, Gloria, when the English say they bagged something they mean they shot it. They get together in groups and go up on the moors and bang away in the heather for hours.'

'And who are they banging away with? The peasants?'

'No, they bang away at the pheasants. Banging also means shooting.'

'They're very fond of shooting at things, aren't they? I thought the English were supposed to love animals.'

'Oh, they do — roasted!'

14

For over a century, the Beehive had conducted its business around the assumption that shoplifting wasn't done. True, a lot of the clientele were of fairly advanced years, and incapable of lifting anything but the lightest item, let alone the shop. Also true, the younger and fitter offender was not particularly likely to find much to pilfer amongst the merchandise arrayed at the Beehive. The average street-cred young criminal wouldn't be interested in hoop-supported crinolines or phonograph cylinders. Until snuff boxes became required accessories of the shoplifting set, the Beehive had acquired a certain degree of immunity from such tiring blemishes of the twentieth century as petty theft.

The provisions department possessed jars of jam whose origin was lost in the mists of time. Labels had become illegible with age, and the jars were simply stacked according to colour: 'Red flavour, green flavour, mauve flavour', and so on. The age of this confiture for the cognoscenti was uncertain. Estimates varied from mid-nineteenth century to early Georgian. Until the introduction of radiocarbon dating, there was no certain way of knowing. The majority of purchasers avoided Beehive jam like most people now avoid a Pot Noodle. A few hardy regular customers, however, swore by the stuff, claiming that not only did it cure gout (smothered over the ankles, rather than consumed orally), but it also served admirably for keeping cats out of a vegetable patch.

The jam, however, was fit for a king compared with the biscuits. The Beehive had bought in a job-lot of biscuits in 1900 which were specially baked to commemorate the turn of the century. Whereas jam, theoretically, keeps for a long time, the ability of biscuits to retain their full freshness for four decades was rather an unknown quantity. Every now and then a packet would be sold; no one knew for what purpose, since any attempt to consume the biscuits would almost certainly leave the would-be biscuit-eater in need of major dental repair. It was always assumed that there were Beehive biscuits in service across the country as clay-pigeon targets, and possibly the British ice hockey squad used them as pucks.

It was Hitler, however, who provided a new lease of life for these ageing foodstuffs. As the black market flourished in the early forties, desperation forced uneasy consumers to consider the Beehive's biscuits and jam as an alternative to no biscuits and jam at all. It was at this point that the Beehive suddenly found itself with a shoplifting problem on its hands for the first time in its history. Housewives would attempt to leave the shop with enormous numbers of biscuits stuffed into their clothing. Most of them were caught, principally through hernias. Mr Knowles was alarmed and dismayed that such a ghastly, plebeian crime as shoplifting could have penetrated the hallowed walls of the Beehive. And so it was that, reluctantly, he had engaged a store detective for the first time.

After the war, however, the shoplifting subsided and the security staff were dropped. It wasn't until the sixties that they were needed again. This time, the fatal moment had occurred in late 1965 when Andy Spangle, the guitarist of hit sixties band The Vibrators, had wandered into the Beehive thinking it was a club that was actually two hundred yards down the road. This drug-induced disorientation, however, produced one of the greatest sales booms the store had ever experienced, for the good Mr Spangle, who later described his visit to the store as 'a bad trip', discovered en route that one particular brand of snuff which the shop had stocked since the 1870s had acquired over the years certain qualities not normally associated with that gentlemanly pastime. Amongst these qualities, the snuff, which came supplied in an elegant Victorian box, had the ability to convince the taker that he was a fish, or occasionally to provide a sense of deep inner peace and a consequent hit song. Pop stars from all over the place converged on the Beehive and for a while hip parties world-wide were not really hip unless one of the guests had some Dorcheson and Maltravers' Premium Gentleman's Snuff to hand around.

This sales boom lasted for about a year, until finally the police realized that certain types of snuff had qualities not found in the original article. A raid by the drug squad removed every remaining box of Dorcheson and Maltravers from the premises, and disappointed musicians, writers and dropouts the world over had to turn to LSD instead.

After this, the store had decided to employ a security guard full-time. Initially Alfred Knowles had brought in a friend of his. The friend was almost the same age. A seventy-three-year-old store detective was less than effective when it came to dealing with the determined shoplifter, and for several years the Beehive rang with the sound of running feet as miscreants escaped with their booty, pursued by an old man shouting, 'Bring back National Service, that's what I say.' Finally, a particularly arduous pursuit across the fourth floor had ended in coronary thrombosis and a job vacancy.

The gap was filled by Miss Marchmont, then fresh from college and looking for a challenge. She was also on the rebound from a broken engagement – her fiancé, the Viscount Hotherington-Fotherington of Dodderington, had fallen into a combine harvester while studying agricultural land economy at Cirencester College for the Rich but Thick. Miss Marchmont had no previous experience in store security work. What she did have experience of, however, was dog training, amateur theatricals and reading. Her one principal hero in life was, of course, Sherlock Holmes; it was more than possible that she had rather misunderstood what the term 'store detective' actually meant . . . A hearty, outdoor type, she prowled the store in a tweed skirt, cape and deerstalker, pouncing on shoplifters and frogmarching them to Mr Knowles' office, where they would remain until they had written out 'I must not purloin that for which I have not rightfully paid' one hundred times. She also possessed Watson, whose viciousness was out of all proportion to his size. A bloodthirsty creature, he would be brought into action against any offender who slipped from Miss Marchmont's grasp. As the thief fled, he would be felled by Watson, who would then sink his small but effective fangs into the miscreant's lower limbs until his mistress would reward him with a small saucer of raw flesh.

The combination of Miss Marchmont roaming the store with hockey stick ready to apply to the seat of any wrongdoer, and Watson, who slavered and growled his way around the sales floors, frequently attacking the staff if deprived of other human blood, quickly made the Beehive's security some of the tightest in London. Word went round the organized shoplifting gangs: Marks and Spencers, Debenhams, Selfridges – fine, but for God's sake don't tangle with the Beehive. Miss Marchmont's zeal was formidable. A man who made the mistake of hiding a pair of plain grey socks in his coat pocket when he realized he'd left his cheque book at home, found himself in Mr Knowles' office till nine that evening, translating Latin prose until Miss Marchmont finally let him go with a warning that if he set foot in the store again she'd box his ears. Offers came in for Watson from the Bank of England, the Tower of London, and even one from an American Mafia boss; but Miss Marchmont turned them all down, and her faithful bulldog stayed with her, quite happy to spend his life scouting round the Beehive biting people.

On Kelsey's first morning in the store, he was astonished by the lack of security systems. Rather than closed circuit TV cameras, two-way mirrors or uniformed guards on the door, a young horsey woman carrying a shooting stick, striding around the sales floors, followed at a distance by a fat yapping bundle, was all he saw.

He went over to Miss Marchmont and introduced himself. 'Good morning,' he said politely, 'I'm the new owner of—'

At that moment he felt a sharp, stabbing pain in his calf. He looked down to see the flabby bulldog, driven into a psychotic frenzy by the sight and smell of a stranger, had sunk his fangs through his expensive 5th Avenue trousers.

'WATSON!' shouted Miss Marchmont.

'Is this your mutt, lady?' said Kelsey, through gritted teeth.

'Yes, and before you complain, he knows a shoplifter from fifty paces. Marchmont's the name, and you're under arrest.'

'Ringwood's my name, and I'm your new boss.'

'Oh dear!' said Miss Marchmont. 'He doesn't like strangers, you see,' she explained.

'Miss Marchmont,' replied Ringwood. 'Er . . . I don't wish to appear churlish, but . . . well, it occurs to me that a dog which doesn't like strangers is . . . well . . .'

'Well? Well what?' replied Miss Marchmont.

'Well, it's just that a major department store is, at any time, likely to be filled with ninety-nine per cent strangers. A dog, therefore, which will readily attack any and every customer in the store is . . . well, a bit of a liability.'

'Mr Ringwood,' said the store detective, chewing on her unlit pipe. 'Allow me to bring you a few home truths. Sad as it may seem, there are a lot of villains abroad. My task here is to catch them to the best of my ability. If that entails inflicting minor flesh wounds on the innocent at times, then that is the price that must be paid. I am sure that our customers appreciate that it is for their benefit. The honest shopper loses out if the wrongdoers are allowed to escape.'

'I absolutely agree, Miss Marchmont, but all I am saying is that unprovoked canine attacks on honest shoppers are not calculated to win customers back. After all, if they drop into the Beehive to browse and end up in the local casualty unit being inoculated for tetanus, they are not over-likely to wish to return and continue their purchase.'

'I have a sixth sense, Mr Ringwood. In most cases, I am correct when I instruct Watson to attack.'

'But he just attacked me, and I own the shop.'

'But he doesn't know you, you see.'

'Exactly! He attacks at random. I really don't think we can continue in this way.'

Miss Marchmont harrumphed contemptuously.

'You Americans,' she said, 'you're all so feeble. No spunk.'

'Pardon?'

'No spunk, no balls.'

'The one as a result of the other, presumably.'

Miss Marchmont looked at Ringwood, much as Mary Whitehouse might view Paul Raymond.

'I am speaking figuratively, Mr Ringwood. Doubtless your obviously disgusting mind would not appreciate that. May I ask what you intend to do with security arrangements here?'

Ringwood looked around him. The aisle was empty apart from an old man examining some bottles of denture cleanser. Watson was eyeing him suspiciously.

'Well,' replied Kelsey, 'I was thinking maybe of updating a little. Installing some closed-circuit TV cameras, so you could watch each floor . . .'

'Mr Ringwood,' replied Miss Marchmont. 'I do not come to work to watch the television. Do you think that Sherlock solved his cases by switching the telly on? I think not. Where is the skill in that? Where is the thrill of the chase?'

Watson was slowly moving towards the old man, his jaws dripping with anticipatory slaver as he contemplated a nice mid-morning snack of octogenarian's calf.

Kelsey turned away for a moment to survey the floor for a likely spot to mount a closed-circuit TV camera. As he did so, his profile caught the light and Miss Marchmont suddenly noticed something about him which . . . She looked closer, her eyes shining. It couldn't be. Surely . . . it was! Kelsey Ringwood was younger but that profile under the deerstalker was unmistakably . . . yes!

Her heart leapt. Her new boss bore a startling resemblance to Basil Rathbone.

'I think over there,' said Kelsey, pointing to a spot on the ceiling.

'Oh yes,' said Marchmont. 'You're quite right.'

Ringwood stared at her, open-mouthed. Miss Marchmont stared back at him, flushed with embarrassment at his resemblance to the celluloid Holmes.

At that second there came a shriek from the old man as Watson's jaws clamped round his leg. Ringwood and Marchmont's eyes separated. But both of them knew that neither would ever be quite the same again.

Kelsey and Gloria next visited Hacket's office, where Hacket sang the entire last five years' company accounts to them, a feat which entailed using the whole of the first act of *The Mikado*. *Three Little Maids From School Are We* became

Three Years Behind On V.A.T. while the finale, *For He's Gone And Married Yum Yum,* turned into *For We've Gone And Made a Huge Loss.*

After an hour and a half of this, Kelsey and Beresford staggered out, wondering whether Hacket needed lessons in accountancy, singing or indeed a course in speech therapy, more urgently.

Kelsey then made the decision to stop deliveries. This was a total self-indulgence on behalf of the store, perpetuated by Alfred Knowles under the mistaken impression that anything Harrods could do, he could do better. Customer deliveries were a thing of the past for most stores, but even those who had continued them had generally swapped to motor transport. The Beehive possessed an ancient delivery van which regularly wended its way around west London, drawn by a horse whose ability to withstand carbon monoxide poisoning was nothing short of extraordinary. Albert – such was the name of this venerable beast – also possessed a knowledge of the local streets to rival that of any taxi driver. In some bizarre, unfathomable fashion the animal seemed to have a kind of equine A–Z stored in its brain. It knew every short cut, alleyway and mews, and would frequently have twenty-ton juggernauts swerving with a shriek of airbrakes as it tugged the Beehive cart across the main A4, scattering cars, motorcycle messengers and bemused Japanese tourists in all directions.

Despite its navigational skills, however, the

horse was past its prime and no longer capable
of any velocity above a slow plod. Scores of
orders had been cancelled as days on end would
pass with no sign of the Beehive van arriving.
When Kelsey arrived, the van was due back
from a delivery made in Notting Hill several
days earlier. As the horse lurched through the
rear gates of the store, wheezing slightly,
Ringwood's heart melted. This poor creature
obviously had no business still to be working.
The poor creature then loosed off a venomous
fart, which somewhat diminished Kelsey's sympathy. He phoned for a vet, who promptly pronounced the horse as having an equivalent
human age of a hundred and fourteen years,
and therefore well due for retirement.

Having pepped up store security and retired
the flatulent horse, Kelsey could then turn his
attention to the most important aspect of the
store. The selling. To this end, he summoned
the manager to his office.

The summons came at a welcome time for
Eric. He was just fending off yet another enquiry
from Mr Big about what was going on. He made
his way to Kelsey's office. Maybe, he thought,
this is it. Ringwood's finished surveying the
place and decided to pack up and go home. As
Eric made his way upstairs, the hypothesis took
root in his brain until by the time he'd reached
Ringwood's office he made up his mind that this
would be certain.

He tapped on the door and went in. Ringwood
was seated at Alfred Knowles' desk. Gloria

Beresford was biting the cap off a bottle of Perrier in the corner.

'Ah, Eric, come in,' said Kelsey.

Eric sat down in one of the wingbacked leather chairs.

'Have you finished looking round the store?' he asked.

'We have indeed. And let me tell you, Eric, we got a bit of a shock.'

I bet you did, thought Dunnet.

'In fact,' went on Ringwood, offering Dunnet a cigar, 'I have to tell you that this place is the most old-fashioned, decrepit, unprofitable, run-down store I've ever seen in my life. The goods are out of date, staff morale is zero, the whole place is a zilch from start to finish.'

'Nice otherwise, though,' said Dunnet. Involuntarily, he couldn't suppress the grin of glee that was oozing across the lower part of his face.

'Basically, it's a no-no,' chimed in Beresford, pouring a glass of Perrier.

'She's got it,' said Ringwood. 'My inheritance has turned out to be run-down, out of date and not worth a bean . . .'

He paused and Eric smiled broadly.

'. . . and I LOVE IT!'

Eric's smile collapsed.

'You *what*?' he gurgled.

'I love it!' repeated Ringwood, jumping up and skipping round the office like a child in a play-pen. 'It's great, it's fabulous, it's everything I love about the English. It's slow, it's old-time, it's . . . it's . . .'

'It's crap,' said Dunnet. 'It's stuck in a time-warp. Knowles have only just allowed electric kettles.'

'Exactly!' said Kelsey happily. 'It's every American's picture of what Britain is like. All those weird wires and pulleys and that elevator . . . wow! It's like something from the medieval times. It's fantastic.'

Dunnet was dumbfounded. All his mistrust of Americans was obviously not misplaced. They were quite clearly a breed of half-wits.

'What I don't understand,' said Ringwood, 'is why it's not successful.'

Dunnet could only gape, open-mouthed.

Kelsey took a deep drag of his cigar — an enormous Havana which made him look as if he had a small tree trunk between his teeth.

'How do you advertise?' he said.

'Pardon?' replied Eric.

'How do you advertise? How does the Beehive advertise?'

'It doesn't,' replied Eric.

Both Kelsey and Gloria's respective jaws dropped.

'You don't advertise?' said Beresford. 'What kind of assholes are you here?'

'Alfred Knowles didn't approve of advertising,' explained Eric. 'He thought it was vulgar. A store for the gentry didn't need to advertise.'

'Strikes me that this Knowles dude was a pretty strong contender in the airhead stakes,' said Beresford.

'Well, with a change of owner, we can have

a change of policy,' said Ringwood, jumping back into Knowles' old chair with boyish enthusiasm. Enthusiasm was a quality not seen in the Beehive for a century or more. Eric thought it was disgustingly American.

'This afternoon I'm gonna call some ad agencies and get them to pitch for the Beehive account,' he said. 'We'll book TV time, radio time, newspaper and magazine space.'

Eric began to panic. The man was serious. Clearly demented, but serious.

'If you ring any major advertising agency and say you want them to pitch for the Beehive, they'll probably actually die laughing,' he said. 'I'm serious. They'll . . . wee themselves.'

'Great publicity,' cried Ringwood, beginning to dial.

Publicity! The word struck into Eric's soul. Mr Big's men would be looking for a mine shaft the moment any of this got out.

'May I ask,' said Dunnet, trying to sound calm, 'how you propose to pay for all this?'

'Same way I propose to pay for the closed-circuit TV, in-store refurbishment and staff wage rises,' said Ringwood, as he listened to a voice telling him thank you for calling Directory Enquiries, you are held in queue and will be answered shortly.

'And what way is that?'

'Eric, surely you of all people must realize how much equity there is tied up in this store,' said Ringwood.

'Equity? Isn't that some trade union?' replied

Dunnet, utterly and totally confused. Staff wage rises? TV advertising spots? What on earth was going on? His best-laid plans were not only being thrown out of the window, but trampled on the pavement and the window shut and locked behind them.

Glory B came over behind the desk.

'A very simple calculation shows that between the year in which this store was purchased and the present time, the price differential has become considerable,' she said. 'To be precise, its market value when the Knowles brothers bought it was approximately £9,500. It is currently worth £25,000,000. We propose to realize a small proportion of that equity value for the purpose of reinvestment in the store's future.'

Eric's eyes glazed. He might just as well resign himself to a course of underwater aerobics in concrete legwarmers right now. He tottered from Ringwood's office in a stupor, leaving Kelsey still waiting for Directory Enquiries.

15

A few weeks later, Eric was driving to work as usual, his mind in turmoil. Mr Big was growing increasingly threatening over the delay and Eric was uncertain as to whether to tell him or not. He was still confident that Kelsey would see some sense over the store.

Eric was just negotiating a particularly difficult multi-lane junction. One set of lights wasn't working. He had a bus in front of him and a huge Belgian artic. full of live chickens on his right. One lane was blocked off with cones and there was a psychopathic motorcycle courier weaving his way perilously past on the left. It was at this moment that the car radio, which was tuned to a commercial station, blared out a jingle which went roughly, 'The Be. . .eee . . .eehive, good old-fashioned bargains.' Eric screamed and swerved, ploughing into a row of cones and causing a string of obscenities from the motorcyclist. As the bonnet of his car, only a matter of months old, nose-dived into a trench left by a pneumatic drill, Eric looked up to see a huge poster on the back of a bus in front of him. It read: 'The Beehive. A Return to

Victorian Value.' Dunnet screamed again. Extricating the car from the roadworks, he rapidly changed direction. Stopping at a call box, he phoned in sick, telling Melissa he was in bed with a temperature of a hundred and one. Melissa was left with the impression that Eric had finally made it with a lady who'd received her telegram from the Queen.

Eric drove swiftly to Mr Big's. His decision had been made for him. When he arrived, the Bishop was already there.

'Ah, my son,' said the Bishop when he saw Eric. 'Verily, thou art up to thy neck in it and no mistake.'

'Very droll,' replied Eric, looking around him with distaste. The club looked even seedier in broad daylight than it did in the evening. A cleaner was picking assorted debris off the threadbare carpet, debris which included numerous corks, cigarette ends and what looked like a large pair of old Y-fronts. There were also a number of burst balloons.

'No, seriously,' said the Bishop. 'Mr Big's not in a good mood with you. He had a rather nasty shock this morning when he turned the radio on.'

'Yes, I heard the Test result as well,' replied Eric, attempting jocularity which seemed entirely out of place.

'I think we all know what we're talking about,' said the Bishop sharply. 'I needn't tell you, Eric, that if this Yank starts making a success of the Beehive, then you are headed for the high jump.'

196

Eric shrugged and made his way up to Mr Big's room. The man himself was sitting at a table, listening intently to a small transistor radio. Rupert was flicking idly through *Fowlers Guide To English Usage* while Mangle was watching a video. On the TV screen a man appeared to be being dismembered by an alligator. On the floor was an opened video tape case. The label read *Attack Of The Nazi Death Reptiles*. Mangle seemed to be enjoying himself thoroughly.

Mr Big noticed Eric, and jumped up to meet him. Jumping up didn't mean much in Mr Big's case, but he jumped up anyway.

'Ah, Dunnet,' he said, warmly. 'Come in, sit down.'

Eric complied. Rupert looked at him dispassionately, while Mangle enjoyed the sight of a giant lizard biting someone's head off.

'Now Eric, I have a little poser for you. A little conundrum which has been exercising my mind all morning. The question, your starter for ten, is this. If Kelsey Ringwood is about to pack up and go home and leave the store to the good Bishop here, why is every radio station, TV station, bus, train and hoarding in London informing the world about the Beehive and how marvellous it is?'

'You've got me there,' replied Eric.

Mr Big grabbed a remote-control and, much to Mangle's annoyance, flicked the TV on to a normal channel. A jolly man in a Victorian frock coat was telling people to come on down to the Beehive for real old-fashioned value.

'What do you see?' said Mr Big.

'A commercial for the Beehive,' replied Eric.

'Shall I tell you what I see? I see twenty-five million quid vanishing up the Swanee. I also see your head stuck on a spike.'

'Look,' said Eric. 'This Ringwood character is bonkers. He's fallen in love with the place. He thinks it's the sort of thing that made Britain great. It won't last. All he's doing with this advertising is wasting money. I promise you, the place is still ours. We've just got to wait a bit longer.'

'Mmmm,' replied Mr Big, deep in thought, 'I hope so for your sake, Dunnet. I don't like waiting. What we need to do is to definitely make sure he . . .'

'You've split your infinitive again,' chided Rupert gently.

'Sorry,' said Mr Big. 'What we need to do is definitely to make sure he isn't successful.'

'That's better,' said Rupert.

'Just leave him to it,' said Eric. 'Believe me, Ringwood's not going to be able to turn a century of commercial failure round in a couple of weeks.'

Mr Big looked sceptical.

'I'm beginning to doubt your powers of prognostication, Dunnet,' he said, and gained an admiring glance from Rupert for using such a long word. 'You told me he wouldn't stay five minutes. Here we are, several weeks later, and the whole of London is plastered with advertising for the place. The Bishop here is very anxious for the Beehive to be passed to him, so that he can pass it on to us. Otherwise . . . well, far be it from me to denigrate a man of the cloth but otherwise, some of the Polaroids featuring the Right Rev, Mandy and the melon might have to make their way to certain tabloids.'

This man is completely ruthless, thought Eric.

'Now,' went on Mr Big. 'What could we use against this Ringwood chap.'

'He's American.'

'Not everyone has your level of xenophobia. I'm afraid the fact that he's American is not likely to be considered to be particularly scandalous. What else?'

Mr Big probed Eric for twenty minutes in an attempt to elicit information on Kelsey which might be of use to him in smearing Ringwood, but rack his brains though he might, he was unable to come up with anything particularly juicy. Mr Big was just about to give up in despair at a suggested smear based round Ringwood's taste in ties when Eric happened to mention that Kelsey had put the store's horse out to grass.

'Ah ha!' cried Mr Big triumphantly. 'I knew it. Animals are always good for a bit of sympathy. What's this horse?'

'It used to pull the store delivery van. It was old and knackered.'

'And what's happened to it now? Glue factory?'

'No, no – Sunnylea Rest Home for Retired Workhorses in Kent.'

'That's a shame,' said Mr Big. 'Still, it's a nice story. Strong tabloid angle on this one – YANK STORE BOSS KO'S OAP DOBBIN. I'll phone up my contacts in the media at once.'

It sounded promising to Eric. Sadly, Mr Big's delusions of grandeur had led 'contacts in the media' to sound rather more impressive than it actually was. YANK STORE BOSS KO'S OAP DOBBIN indeed ran as a story in the press, but its appearance in the *Leytonstone Weekly Courier and Gazette* did not have quite the effect on the Beehive that Dunnet hoped.

Kelsey and Gloria had noticed another aspect of the Beehive which cried out for change. It struck Gloria first. She had been to London before, unlike Kelsey, and she had immediately noticed something strange about the Beehive compared with other big British department stores. For a few days she couldn't quite put her finger on what it was. Then, one day as they were going through the sports department trying to figure out what half the stock was, it came to her.

'Kelsey,' she announced, 'do you realize that I haven't heard a single American voice in this store?'

'Huh?' said Kelsey. He wasn't really listening. He was trying to figure out just what on earth the bizarre weighted chain he was holding in his hand was.

'There's no Americans in here,' went on Gloria.

Kelsey had discovered a box which explained the identity of the chain arrangement.

'Croquet Hoop Plumbline,' he mused. 'Ensure your hoops are at ninety degrees no matter what the angle of your lawn. Wow . . . I wonder how I haven't come across these before. I'd have bought twenty gross. You never know when you might need to check your croquet hoops are perpendicular.'

'Will you listen to me and cut the crap about hoops?' cried Gloria, almost knocking over a lacrosse stick-cover in her frustration.

'Sure, sure, there's no Americans in here,' mused Kelsey.

'Well, don't you see?' said Gloria, as if addressing a retarded two-year-old. 'This place is full of hundred-year-old garbage. London is full of American tourists. Put American tourists and hundred-year-old garbage together and what do you get? Money!'

A smile dawned on Kelsey's face. Of course! This ancient, obsolescent Victoriana was custom-built for American tourists. He kicked himself for not having seen it before.

A few weeks later, Eric Dunnet was sitting in his office, flicking through a surgical appliances brochure. He was a worried man. All the increased media awareness of the Beehive was having an effect. There were quite definitely more customers in the store than before. Kelsey showed no signs of wanting to pack up and go home. In fact, he had gone round giving the place a spruce-up, polishing the old weighing machines and giving the huge old Victorian tills a good rub-down with Brasso. The commercials were obviously having an effect; Eric had noticed, with horror, that the average age of the customers was getting younger. No longer were the sales floors filled with meandering senior citizens. At weekends now the place was slowly but surely filling up with ghastly yuppie couples who thought that the old nineteenth-century oil lamps were just *briii*lliant, and the croquet hoop plumblines were going like hotcakes to the gormless Sloanes who had started popping in. The Beehive was becoming trendy. Dunnet was a worried man.

He was reflecting on all this when he heard the loud roar of an engine from outside. Moving to the window, he saw that a vast coach had parked right outside the store. The front door opened, and a uniformed guide got out. Dunnet assumed they must be going to the Natural History Museum and hadn't been able to find anywhere closer to park. He was utterly amazed when the coach began to disgorge a stream of what were obviously foreigners, all of whom headed straight into the Beehive.

What on earth was going on? Dunnet rushed out of his office. Jack the commissionaire was coming the other way, his face white with distress.

'Mr Dunnet sir!' he cried. 'Bleedin' foreigners! A whole load of them!'

'I know,' said Eric. 'Don't worry, I'll get rid of them.'

He stomped off towards the entrance, wondering

what breed of foreigner these were. Maybe Japanese, with their video cameras and interchangeable lens-mountings . . . Or ghastly Germans tramping about the place . . . Or Scandinavians, with their huge rucksacks and Inter-Rail cards. But it was none of these. As Dunnet approached the front door of the store, he could hear whoops and hollers of delight which could only issue from the throats of one nation – the USA.

'Will you look at this, Abner?'

'Have you seen these? They're so CUTE!'

'Look at this old hat . . . Isn't that just like the one Charles Dickens wore in *All's Well That's In A Bleak House?'*

Dunnet gurgled in horror. He raced over to the scene of the invasion, but found Kelsey and Gloria already there, chatting to the guide.

'Er . . .' said Dunnet nonchalantly. 'What's . . . er . . . going on?'

'It's worked!' said Gloria brightly, handing Dunnet a copy of the *New Yorker* magazine.

Dunnet looked at it. It was open to reveal a half-page advert for the Beehive.

'I'm amazed you never realized what you've got here, Eric,' said Kelsey, warmly. 'This place is like a magnet for Americans. It's so old and genuine and just plain great. It worked for me and it'll work for my fellow Americans. All summer long we're gonna be packed from morning to night. Together, you and me are going to make this old place the most successful store in Britain.'

You speak for yourself, thought Dunnet. If this becomes the most successful store in Britain I'm a goner.

But Kelsey was oblivious to Dunnet's panic. He was, for the first time in his life, a success. This store was going to take off.

Take off it did. In a very short time, the combination of the marketing, the word-of-mouth, the prices, the old-fashioned style and the amazing genuine old products brought in thousands of customers who had previously only been able to buy such items in expensive facsimile form.

Eric Dunnet was in a foul mood.

Not just a paddy, or a bit of an off-day. This was a real Stygian blackness of a mood, a profound pit of depression into which no psychiatrist's rope ladder could hope to come anywhere near the bottom.

Kelsey Ringwood was making a success of the Beehive. That slimy, sharp-suited American git was proving a massive hit. The trouble with the British, mused Dunnet bitterly, is that they were the only people in the world who didn't appreciate the value of Britishness. The British spent their time wishing they weren't British, wishing they had a different climate, watching American television programmes on Japanese televisions and then driving in their German cars to eat American food in characterless shopping precincts designed by multinational conglomerates. The British happily drove motorways and housing estates through their countryside, and positively revelled in destroying every last vestige of the culture that made them so attractive to foreigners in the first place. Very few of their qualities indicated any degree of international success; insular, xenophobic, only venturing abroad if their brochure promised readily available fish and chips and lager, most of them would never go beyond Dover if the weather in August wasn't so bloody awful.

But this Ringwood character – he'd sussed exactly what people loved about the British and played on it shamelessly. And the Beehive was a roaring success. Only an American could have done it, for, as Dunnet was well aware, the one thing the British hate more than anything else is success. Every true British hero, from King Harold to Sir Clive Sinclair, was famous for failure. Was Sir Francis Drake famous for defeating the Spanish Armada? No, he was famous for playing bowls while it approached. It was the bloody British weather that defeated the Spanish Armada. Sir Francis Drake was busy playing bowls. *Bowls* . . . of all the tedious, dull, godawful games to be playing while a gang of swarthy foreigners invade your motherland, bowls was just about as tedious, dull, godawful and thoroughly British as you could get. Would Richard Branson be famous if he was just a highly successful businessman? No, it was only his rubber-band powered boats and deflating balloons and condoms with a silly name that ensured *him* a place in the pantheon of British heroes. Only the British would regard Dunkirk and the Charge of the Light Brigade as on a par with the Battle of Britain and Waterloo. The British specialized in self-flagellation on a grand scale.

The Americans, on the other hand, had their innate marketing man's sense of Britishness as a Unique Selling Point par excellence. Kelsey Ringwood had taken a hopeless, antiquated Victorian monstrosity of a shop and converted it, in a matter of months, into a roaring, raving success. And how had he done it? By changing it? No . . . by exaggerating what Dunnet perceived as its worst qualities − its slowness, its outdatedness and its non-existent commercial acumen. Its slowness, outdatedness and non-existent commercial acumen had turned it into the fastest-growing, most fashionable and commercially successful store in the country.

Hardly a day went by when some star or other was not photographed shopping at the Beehive, and featured in the national tabloids. In the slack newstime of the summer silly season, the Beehive had become a national obsession, with its 'Victorian Value' slogan on every bus, poster-hoarding and railway station in the land. Eric had been persistently pestered by the *Sun*, who had been constantly phoning in order to compile Twenty Things You Never Knew About The Beehive. Features on the Beehive had been published in *Tatler, Harpers*, and even *Cosmopolitan* ('Crinolines And The Modern Woman − Read Our New Survey'). *The Face, Blitz, Arena* − all had featured the store ('The

206

Buzz On The Beehive' 'The Beehive – Other Stores Face The Sting'). The Sunday colour supplements, from the *Observer* to the *News of the World*, featured gooey eulogies to the Beehive, with big colour pictures of Kelsey Ringwood posing by the authentic mid-nineteenth-century bacon slicer, which had been carving up pigs for a hundred years before the Common Market was a gleam in some bureaucrat's eye. There was even a rumour that Ringwood might be invited to appear on *Wogan*, a rumour which left Dunnet green with unadulterated envy. A long-time devotee of Radio 2, his life was left with a big hole in it the day Terry had left the breakfast show.

One of the papers speculated that Kelsey might win an award for services to British industry, or the Business Development award from the DTI. Jacko was replaced for a day by a seven-year-old who had written to *Jim'll Fix It* wanting to be the lift operator at the Beehive. BBC Radio 4 came round interviewing for a programme they were making called *Success In The Eighties*. Janet Street-Porter made a feature on the store for a BBC youth programme, under the title 'The Beehive; Retro Takes Off'.

The shop was thronged with customers from nine in the morning till five-thirty at night. In fact, to everyone's horror, Ringwood, with his alien American zeal, had suggested that they should open at eight-thirty in the morning and not close until twelve hours later. Gavin O'Connell, the store's union leader, had (with

Dunnet's full backing) opposed this vigorously, but Ringwood had offered temptingly high rates of overtime and almost all the staff had accepted immediately. All except Mrs Oliver on the haberdashery counter, who had objected to closing at eight-thirty in the evening on the grounds that it would disrupt her rehearsal schedule with the Barnes and Twickenham Amateur Dramatic Society.

Mr Big was getting more and more impatient. With every day that passed, the Beehive slipped further and further out of his grasp. He and Eric tried to spoil the success. Eric released rats in the food department in an attempt to get some bad publicity, but the rats had made the mistake of eating some of the one-hundred-year-old Camembert on the top shelf, and had retired to the sewers to die. Eric had seized the opportunity to get in some old women and had set up a crack squad of blue-rinse floorwalkers, who had prowled the store arresting customers at random and generally making life unpleasant. And he had tried to engineer a special sale in which all prices would be considerably raised. But none of it had any real effect. The Beehive's success, solidly founded on kitsch and rendered invincible by publicity, steamrollered any obstacle that Eric and Mr Big could put in its way.

Then, one day, came the news to cap it all. Kelsey ran into Eric's office holding a very posh-looking envelope. Buckingham Palace had been in touch. Princess Diana, a keen shopper, desired to visit the famous Beehive, and Prince Charles was very interested to see this store whose massive success was very largely based on its traditional Britishness.

Eric read the letter four times over. Much as he was frightened of Mr Big, a royal visit was something he couldn't resist. He puffed up with pride and looked at Kelsey.

'We've done it,' he said.

Kelsey, little suspecting that Eric had spent the previous few months trying to undo everything he'd done, nodded.

'Yup,' he said. 'We sure have.'

16

Overnight, silently and efficiently, the Metropolitan Police had done their work. Long lines of yellow parking cones had materialized all along the surrounding streets. Subtle, unobtrusive checks had been made in neighbouring buildings. Plain-clothes officers would check local buildings for bombs with the aid of highly trained dogs. In order not to arouse suspicion, it was essential not to use alsatians, so a whole squad of highly trained chihuahuas and Yorkshire terriers had been brought in. These carefully disguised personnel – the disguised dogs and incognito humans – were all bussed into Knightsbridge in huge transit vans marked METROPOLITAN POLICE BOMB DISPOSAL SQUAD.

Highly trained police marksmen were positioned on rooftops all over the surrounding area. In order to confuse any terrorists in helicopters, all such personnel were disguised as sunbathers, with regulation sunlounger, infra-red sighted rifle disguised as an Argos parasol, and standard issue Jackie Collins novel. For a whole square mile around the Beehive, hundreds of police and army experts costing thousands of pounds in taxes were busy making sure that it was safe for Princess Diana to go shopping.

Eric Dunnet surveyed the scene with satisfaction. A royal visit appealed to the snob in him. Much as he loathed Kelsey Ringwood, he couldn't but feel a certain smug satisfaction. He, Eric Dunnet, was to shake the hand of his future monarch. As manager of the Beehive, he was at last going up in the world.

A policeman was wandering up and down in front of the store. Preparations were well advanced now. The sniffer dogs had finished their work. It now remained to examine the more inaccessible places. It was quite possible to hide explosives in nooks and crannies where no canine, no matter how highly trained, could ever reach. Scotland Yard, therefore, had begun a secret scheme to train other animals to sniff for bombs. A cageful of sniffer hamsters were being despatched down the drainpipes at each corner of the store, while sniffer otters were busy exploring the sewerage channels that ran beneath the streets.

The staff, meanwhile, were busy spring-cleaning the place. Layers of dust were gradually being removed from shelves and the sales floors were looking almost as spruce as the day the shop had opened in 1888. Eric wandered up and down, a smile of glutinous, snobbish pride on his face. For a brief few hours all his troubles seemed behind him. For a brief few hours, Mr Big and his developers could wait. Eric Dunnet was dreaming of royalty. Who knows? If Princess Di likes the place . . . she could pass the word on . . . Maybe H.M. herself might pop in . . . a few new leads for the corgis — some nice fishing tackle upstairs. The Beehive had always supplied live worm for the gentry. In Victoria's time no gentleman would contemplate a visit to Balmoral without first popping into the Beehive for a box of worms. All that could start again after today. Who knows, thought Dunnet . . . If I play my cards right, I might even get invited to a royal garden party. Cucumber sandwiches and Darjeeling up at Buck House with all the nobs. Chatting over the drop scones with all the other successful British businessmen. Dunnet's greedy little eyes gleamed. There he'd be, up the Palace talking about banging the drum for Britain with Dickie Branson, Alan Sugar and that woman who started the Sock Shop.

For a time, Dunnet almost forgot his main task in life at that moment was to ruin the store as fast as possible. But if he had forgotten, others hadn't.

In a seedy, run-down room above The Bowler Hat A-Go-Go in one of the less salubrious streets of Soho, Mr Big had called a meeting of his confederates.

The Bowler Hat A-Go-Go was run along Mr Big's normal business lines. Entrance was two pounds but membership was fifty pounds. Once this had been paid it was explained that membership was renewable weekly. If the punter objected, it would be pointed out to him that a hidden camera in the wall had already taken a polaroid of him paying his entrance fee. Since this photograph was against a backdrop of a large sign saying 'Topless Service', the punter would normally acquiesce quietly and enter the club.

Once inside, the rip-off proper would begin. Customers had been known to remortgage their homes in order to meet the bar tariff. Furthermore, the 'Topless Service' sign outside the club neglected to mention that most of the waiters were male. The 'top-quality entertainment' however, was indeed top-quality. Customers at the Bowler Hat A-Go-Go could watch some of the most famous names in the business. The top bands, the top comedians, Frank Sinatra, Liza Minelli, and the James Last Orchestra were all acts that had appeared on the video machine at the Bowler. Some of the live acts were less well-known, but a typical night might feature Dhana, the Exotic Eastern Chanteuse from Plaistow, and the Amazing Little, a man who tied balloons into the shape of genital organs. For his finale, he tied his genital organs into the shape of a balloon.

Mr Big also ran, in conjunction with the club, an Escort Agency. This was a mini-cab firm who used exclusively old Ford Escorts, a job-lot of which Mr Big had bought in 1975. In these vehicles, the punter would be ferried home, charged fifty pounds, and left to explain his late arrival to his wife with only the threat of the polaroid to help him invent a believable story. The club's clientele frequently consisted solely of parties of tabloid journalists, but no one knew whether they were on a mission to stake out any unsuspecting celebrity punters, or whether it was simply the sort of place where tabloid journalists like to spend an evening off.

In the room above this establishment, on the night before the royal visit to the Beehive, sat Mr Big. Downstairs, the night's entertainment was just beginning, a video of last week's *Top of the Pops*. In the corner of the room, an employee was busy scraping 'Fine Fare British Sparkling Vin Mousseux' labels off bottles. Beside him sat a bottle of glue and a pile of labels reading 'Moët et Chandon Premier Cuvée'.

'All right boys,' said Mr Big, by way of commencing proceedings. There was silence, apart from the lackey in the corner scraping the labels off the glass. He was steaming them from a kettle and then using a stolen American Express card as a scraper. It was doing nicely.

'Give it a rest, Nobby,' said Mr Big.

'Got to do a new lot of bottles,' replied Nobby, without looking up from his scraping. 'They've run out down there.'

'All right, but make it a bit quieter, there's a good lad. Sorry about the din, gentlemen,' he explained to his assembled thugs, 'but punters want their shampoo, and who am I to deprive them?'

214

There were murmurs of assent all round.

'Now,' went on Mr Big. 'To business. First of all, a little bird has told me that Alfie the Flea has skipped off down the Costa Del Sol with most of the profits accruing from the activities of Sun-U-Quik Timeshare Apartments Limited, one of my little business ventures which, as you will remember, regrettably had to be wound up following some unwelcome attention from Roger Cook.'

'You mean Alfie's got the moolah?' said Mangle.

'As usual,' continued Mr Big, 'Mangle has summed it up in a nutshell, in his inimitably precise way.'

Mangle grinned, although he didn't understand the sentence.

'Now,' said Mr Big, 'I propose that we despatch Mr Mangle and Rupert to the sunny climes of the Andalusian coastline, with the objective of locating Alfie and turning his knackers into paella.'

This suggestion was met with enthusiastic approval, notably from Mangle.

'Very well,' said Mr Big. 'Also, of course, the money must be recovered. It will be ploughed into my next little venture. What with all this glasnost stuff I think it's about time someone started offering timeshare apartments in the Soviet Union. I have recently concluded a deal which should enable me to do exactly that. I have also to report that, regrettably, the tickets for the Wimbledon men's singles final which

215

were offered to me the other day have proved to be clever forgeries. On close inspection, we realized that such tickets are not normally handwritten in biro. The forger, however, is a very lucky man. After all, there's a nine-month waiting list for leg amputations on the NHS. We carried out the operation within five minutes of locating him.'

He paused to sip some Appletize, while his confederates watched in awe. This was not a man to mess with.

'But now,' announced Mr Big, 'we've come to the main business of the evening, and once again, I regret to say, it's the little matter of the Beehive department store. I'm afraid that, despite our warnings, Mr Dunnet has not yet been able to persuade Mr Ringwood to sell the place. Indeed, Mr Ringwood is proving to be positively tenacious in his intransigence.'

Mangle looked totally bewildered. There were far too many syllables in this conversation for his liking.

Mr Big paused to light a cigar. It was a very large cigar, of the type much beloved by gangsters. Such was the diminutive nature of Mr Big's physical stature that the cigar almost dwarfed him. In relative terms, Mr Big smoking an ordinary Havana cigar looked like an ordinary-sized man smoking a toilet roll tube.

'However,' went on Mr Big, exhaling a large cloud of cigar smoke, 'I have a piece of information which I believe should enable us to . . . take a major step forward in obtaining the deeds to the store. It appears, thanks to an observant colleague of mine in High Street Ken, that we may have an ideal opportunity tomorrow to ensure that this Ringwood sells the place to us as quickly as possible.'

'We gonna do 'im?' said Mangle brightly.

'Really,' muttered Rupert, offended by the dropped aitch.

'No need for violence,' said Mr Big, and Mangle's face fell. 'I have reason to believe that tomorrow, the Beehive is going to get a visit from royalty.'

'How do you know that, boss?'

'I don't for certain. But I've a pretty shrewd idea. According to Crowbar Christie, the Old Bill have been sending sniffer dogs all round the area and no one's been allowed to park near the place for the last twelve hours. Princess Di's known to be a fan of the place. Some sixth sense tells me that her and Charlie are going to be dropping in tomorrow. Also they've put a big sign saying "The Beehive welcomes Charles and Di" over the front door.'

There were widespread murmurs. The evidence sounded pretty conclusive.

'Now,' said Mr Big, 'you may well ask – what use is that to us?'

No one did.

'We,' went on the leader, 'are going to turn this royal shopping trip to our advantage by making sure that the Beehive is firmly taken off the list of royal visiting places. In short, we're going to ruin the thing. The publicity'll be so appalling for Ringwood he won't be able to wait to sell up.'

Evil chortles broke out around the room.

'We're going to make sure that the Beehive gets on to every front page throughout the world . . . but not in the way Ringwood would like!'

'It sounds intriguing,' said Rupert. 'But how are we going to go about it?'

'That's what the rest of this meeting is about,' replied Mr Big. 'You! Stop scraping those bottles, for God's sake. If you've run out of sparkly they'll have to make do with that Paraguayan Liebfraumilch. Shake it up a bit, that'll make it fizzy. Now get out . . . We've got things to discuss . . .'

17

The morning of the royal visit to the Beehive dawned clear and sunny. Eric Dunnet's mood matched it as he dragged himself from his bed, peeling back the duvet like an old bandage. He shaved carefully, lest the royal eyes should notice telltale streaks of stubble where a lazily directed Bic had skated over. He selected his tie with unaccustomed care and ate his Rice Krispies in a strange, legs-akimbo position so as not to spill any milk on his freshly ironed trousers.

He drove carefully to work, constantly checking his tie knot in the mirror. Several cyclists and pedestrians almost ended up in plaster because of Dunnet's tie knot. Dunnet's visibility in the car was severely restricted. He was always one to put things off, and had not yet had the windows properly repaired after an enraged motorist had smashed them in reply to Dunnet's two-finger sign when he was cut up. Most of what should have been toughened Triplex glass was bits of polythene and sellotape. The car looked as if the windows had been installed by the *Blue Peter* team.

As he drove past the Beehive, Dunnet looked proudly at the front of the store. The brass had been polished up, the bulbs in the canopy replaced, and red, white and blue bunting fluttered happily in the breeze. Dunnet grinned and hummed a few bars of *Rule Britannia*.

It was then that he noticed the sign over the front door.

He himself, the previous day, had personally supervised the painting of a nice big banner reading 'The Beehive Welcomes Charles and Di'. He had overseen its installation over the door. He clearly remembered looking at it proudly the previous night before he'd gone home. In which case, he was slightly puzzled as to why the banner now read 'The Beehive Says Bollocks to the Queen'.

The sight of this traitorous message outside his shop caused him to completely abandon any pretence of following the Highway Code. His eyes stayed fixed on the banner while his foot stayed on the accelerator, and the progress of the car was only checked by the tailgate of a large lorry which was waiting at the traffic lights.

It was a huge articulated lorry, and it had a huge lorry driver who articulated his feelings towards Dunnet very clearly. A tirade of abuse poured forth, none of which was disputed by Dunnet, who was accused of being everything under the sun. A policeman arrived and attempted to discover why this nice new Jaguar with polythene windows had just smashed its bonnet into a lorry. Dunnet could offer no explanation, since he didn't really want to admit he'd been staring at a banner, on his property, offering an open insult to his monarch. The policeman warned Dunnet that he would probably face a fine for reckless driving. Dunnet nodded vigorously, thinking that this was light punishment compared with the gallows he would face if he didn't get that banner down.

As soon as the policeman had taken his name, address and insurance details, Dunnet parked what remained of the car and raced round to the front of the store, where he leapt maniacally at the banner, trying desperately to dislodge it. Finally, he managed to grab hold of it and it crashed to the ground, taking with it most of the bunting. The crash brought Kelsey Ringwood running from inside the shop to see what on earth was happening. He found Dunnet, the bunting and a large banner, all lying in a wheezing heap on the pavement.

'What in hell are you doing, Dunnet?' shouted Ringwood angrily. 'What are you doing with the banner?'

'Tearing it down,' replied Dunnet, gurgling with the effort. The mortal remains of thousands of cigarettes were protesting noisily in his lungs at the unaccustomed disturbance.

Ringwood looked bemused.

'Ah,' he said finally, light dawning in his eyes, 'I've got it. You're an anarchist, huh? An anti-royalist type? You should have told me earlier. I'd have given you the day off.'

Dunnet gurgled.

'Tell you what,' said Kelsey generously. 'I don't hold with anarchism and communism myself, but I believe in freedom of thought and you just go home if all this offends your beliefs.'

Dunnet fought to regain his powers of speech before this lunatic American delivered the Gettysburg address and sent him away. Dunnet's chance of shaking hands with Diana was vanishing fast.

'Kelsey,' he spluttered. 'I. . . I. . .'

'Don't trouble yourself,' said Ringwood. 'I can see you're really choked up. I had no idea you felt so strongly.'

Dunnet cursed his own unfitness. He still couldn't persuade his lungs to return to normal. From now on, he vowed, it's muesli and rowing machines for me.

Gloria Beresford strode through the front door. She was dressed in a very smart outfit and a pair of extremely expensive 5th Avenue shoes. In fact, the tastefulness of her whole ensemble was only spoiled by a metal badge reading 'I ♥ Charles and Di'.

'What the hell's going on here?' she demanded discreetly.

Dunnet tried to speak first, but Kelsey was too quick for him.

'Eric is a communist and he hates the royal family,' explained Kelsey. 'He's torn down the banner.'

Beresford looked at Dunnet, still lying in a heap amid the tangled remains of the banner which in turn was made from several of Miss Marchmont's sheets sewn together. (Eric had offered his own sheets for the purpose, but on close inspection these had contained numerous stains which were felt to be too dubious for royal eyes.)

'Republican, huh,' growled Gloria.

'What?' moaned Dunnet. 'You lot are a Republic, aren't you?'

'A Christian Democratic Republic,' replied Beresford. 'Not some goddam atheistic Leninist-Marxist dictatorship. If you don't want to meet your future king and queen, then get the hell outta here, you commie scumbag.'

Clearly the torch of *glasnost* shone strong in the New York legal profession. Dunnet, now recovered from his exertions, began to rise to his feet, noting with embarrassment that a small crowd of passing shoppers and bystanders had gathered, intrigued by the fracas.

'There's been a mistake,' he said, meeting Beresford's and Ringwood's eyes. 'I'm not any sort of anti-monarchist. Not in the slightest. I just wanted to . . .'

As he stood up, he was unravelling the fallen banner from his limbs. As he did so, he inadvertently unfolded it sufficiently for its message to be legible.

'The Beehive says Bollocks to the Queen,' murmured Ringwood. Beresford's eyes flitted from message to Dunnet, and back again.

'I see,' she murmured. 'So you were putting it up, not taking it down.'

'What?' cried Dunnet in horror.

'It's pretty clear. You're a subversive commie anti-monarchist ratfink asshole, you pretend to want to put up a loyal greeting, then when you think we won't notice you try to put up a protest banner.'

Dunnet buried his head in his hands.

'For God's sake,' he moaned. 'Will you just listen? I'm trying to tell you the truth and . . .'

'Truth?' yelled Beresford, and the line of spectators jumped back a foot. 'Your sort don't know the meaning of the word. You've been caught red-handed in the act of traitorous commie treachery, Dunnet. Now you put back the original banner and get off home before I get you arrested for treason.'

'I was not putting this up!!' shrieked Dunnet, jumping up and down in frustration. 'I was tearing it DOWN . . . can't you get that through your heads?'

'Forget it, Dunnet. If you don't like the royal family, you can get back to Russia. I'm sure the rest of the staff will be quite pleased to meet the royal couple without managing director Trotsky.'

'Look at my clothes,' shouted Dunnet. 'I've ironed my trousers. I've used two Bics . . . I bought this tie NEW . . . do I look like an anarchist? I was tearing this banner down because I saw it on the door and I was ashamed . . .'

'For heaven's sake,' said Ringwood, tut-tutting. 'At least have the courage of your convictions. If you want to make anarchist statements then at least have the courage to stand by them and not disown them. This is a free country—'

'Unfortunately,' cut in Beresford. 'Personally, I think a Marxist anarcho-syndicalist revisionist waphead like Mr Workers-of-the-world-unite Dunnet here should be strung-up and shot.'

'Where did you study law, Mussolini College?' muttered Dunnet.

'What?' barked Beresford.

'Nothing,' said Dunnet. 'At least if you ever lose your job as a lawyer you can go and write for the *Daily Mail*. Now, if you'll excuse me, I wish to find the proper banner and replace it.'

'Bravo,' cried Ringwood. 'Eric's seen the light. Another ex-commie saved from the jaws of the devil. Halleluja!'

Too much TV evangelism hath this man consumed, thought Dunnet, bitterly, as he pushed through the door and into the store, with Beresford still complaining outside that no leftist sympathizers should be allowed to meet the royal visitors. Dunnet was almost beside himself with irritation. He, British through and through, was being accused of being a republican, while the two American interlopers, who'd never so much as seen a red bus, a British bobby, or an out-of-order telephone kiosk in their lives until a few short months ago, were presuming to tell him he wasn't patriotic.

He skulked towards the lift. Jacko was pottering round inside, dressed in a Sunday best suit that looked as if its last outing had been the Coronation.

'Morning, Jacko,' said Dunnet, marching into the lift.

'Morning, Mr Dunnet,' replied Jacko, beginning the laborious process of setting the antiquated elevator into motion. Dunnet sniffed and became acutely aware of an overwhelming smell of mothballs, which, as the lift crawled slowly towards the fourth floor, threatened to overcome him with nausea.

'My God, Jacko – how long has that suit been in the wardrobe?'

'Since 1952,' replied Jacko.

So its last outing *had* been the Coronation. Dunnet tried to breathe as shallowly as possible and discreetly hold his nose as the aroma reached a pungency which gave off almost visible fumes. Finally, the lift settled on the fourth floor, and Jacko tugged open the metal doors. Dunnet almost fell out, gasping as if he'd just spent several minutes under water.

Jacko clanked back off towards the ground floor again, while Eric surveyed the fourth floor with satisfaction. All looked spick and span and Miss Marchmont was doing her own bomb detection, using her highly trained explosive sniffing dog (Watson). He stumbled about, wheezing heavily and taking frequent rests.

Dunnet checked his watch nervously. It was nine twenty-five and the royal couple were due at eleven. He went to his office and sat at his desk. Melissa was wearing a Laura Ashley posh frock and a rather strange hat with a broad, lacy brim which she had bought when some young man had taken her to Ascot. Unfortunately, as the champagne had gone down the young man's intentions towards Melissa had become all too apparent. On the first ghastly Sloane grope she had made it quite clear that he was not even going to reach the starting gate. She had, however, determined to get some further use out of the hat. It was a bizarre piece of millinery, looking not unlike a UFO from some particularly naff fifties science fiction film. It was the sort of hat you can really only wear at Ascot, and even then only if you want to be on the *Six O'Clock News* to get laughed at by the rest of the country. In an office on a November morning it looked distinctly out of place.

'What on earth is that hideous hat?' asked Dunnet, displaying all the charm and tact which helped to explain his persistent bachelorhood.

'I bought it for Ascot,' replied Melissa. 'I don't get the chance to wear it very often.'

Dunnet looked bemused.

'I've got a snorkel-mask and a pair of flippers I don't get the chance to use very often. That doesn't mean I put them on to meet Prince Charles,' he said.

Melissa poked her tongue out at him.

Eric decided to break the rule of a lifetime. Half-nine or not, he needed a drink. What with crazed Americans accusing him of being a communist, and secretaries wearing UFOs on their heads, and the future monarch dropping in in ninety minutes. . . .

Dunnet poured himself a small whisky and knocked it back. It cleared his head slightly and he went to the window to get some fresh carbon monoxide.

He looked down on the High Street. Outside the Beehive all was coned off, and policemen were milling around, trying to look busy. Across the road, metal barriers had been erected. All the security measures had had the effect of telling all and sundry exactly what was going on, and a small crowd was beginning to gather on the side of the street, speculating as to who these obviously important visitors to the Beehive might be. Speculation ranged from Joan Collins and Princess Michael of Kent through to Esther Rantzen or the Mallards, the latest teenypop sensation who were currently number one in the charts with their song *Love Goes Round In Circles And Sometimes Falls Over*.

There was also a group of school-children who had been given the morning off. They were all chattering excitedly. Dunnet grimaced. He loathed children. Next to them, however, was a group of old ladies who were much more in Dunnet's line. One of them particularly caught his eye. Her ankles were enticingly wrapped in surgical stockings and the fluttering of her headscarf caused a fluttering in his heart. She also possessed a remarkably large bosom which Dunnet stared at fixedly. However, this staring was not quite as voyeuristic as it might first appear, for Dunnet was staring not so much at the breasts themselves, but at the fact that they appeared to be visibly shrinking. His jaw dropped in astonishment as, from his fourth-floor eyrie, he looked over at the little knot of spectators, one of whom appeared to have deflating mammaries. Within thirty seconds she had shrunk from a forty-two-inch bust to a thirty-four-inch and it was still decreasing.

As Dunnet watched, another old woman next to her appeared to notice her friend's plight. The two of them looked round, slightly flustered, and then, in front of Dunnet's disbelieving eyes, the second old lady dived into the first old lady's coat, undid her blouse, and placed the tip of the first woman's left breast between her lips. What was more, the woman's breasts appeared to be yellow and green respectively. Even Dunnet, with his limited experience of the opposite sex, realized that something was amiss.

He looked again. Beneath the headscarves he recognized two of Mr Big's henchmen, cunningly disguised as old ladies. One of them had two balloons stuffed up his blouse. The other was attempting oral reflation of one of them.

The shock of this realization sent Dunnet's glass slipping from his hand. He recoiled back from the window in horror as the tumbler smashed on the pavement below. Twenty policemen instantly whipped round, staring up. Taking advantage of this, the two henchmen slipped to the back of the crowd to sort out the cleavage problem.

'They're out there,' cried Dunnet.

'What?? They're early!' shrieked Melissa, straightening her hat.

'Not them!' cried Dunnet. 'Mr . . . er . . . I mean . . . no one . . . not them . . . don't you panic.' With this incoherent reassurance he rushed out of the office, wondering what on earth was going on. Why were two of Mr Big's henchmen in the crowd outside? What was the meaning of swapping the two banners over?

'Where is Mr Ringwood?' he demanded of an assistant, who was busy tying little Union Jacks round the edge of a counter.

'In the toy department,' replied the assistant, and Dunnet set off down the stairs, unable to face Jacko and his mothballs for a second time.

As Dunnet ran down he almost crashed into Ringwood coming up.

'I was just looking for you,' they both cried simultaneously.

'Kelsey,' said Dunnet, 'listen to me. I'm not sure quite what's going on, but I have every reason to think that . . .'

He stopped, partly because he realized he couldn't really explain anything to Ringwood without giving himself away, and partly because Ringwood was flushed red with anger and shouting at him.

'Dunnet,' yelled the American. 'Just what the hell are you trying to do to my store?'

'Your st . . .' replied Dunnet, checking himself just in time. 'What's wrong now?'

'Look what I just found in the toy department,' said Ringwood, from between clenched teeth.

He held out an Action Man, which Dunnet examined in astonishment. Not only was it clad in small, replica leather bondage gear, but it had additions to its anatomy which no Action Man is supposed to have.

'We've got special instructions to show Prince William and Prince Harry round the toy department,' cried Ringwood. 'Suppose they'd seen this.'

Dunnet was speechless.

'I don't know just what sort of communist organization it is that you belong to,' growled Ringwood, 'but you sure as hell got some explaining to do. Follow me!'

Dunnet, bemused, followed the irate Ringwood down to the toy department, where he stood and stared in complete astonishment. In front of him, prominent in the display, were two My Little Ponies, engaged in what could only be interpreted as copulatory activity.

'Nice thing for two little princes to have to look at, huh,' said Ringwood.

Dunnet could only gape and nod.

'Surely,' he said, 'you don't think I've got anything to do with this?'

'Miss Marchmont!' called Ringwood.

On the far side of the toy department, Miss Marchmont was inspecting goods with her magnifying glass. She moved back towards Ringwood and Dunnet. As she moved there was a strange clattering noise.

'What's that noise?' asked Dunnet as she approached.

Miss Marchmont motioned Dunnet towards

a handsome pedal car, sitting on the floor near him. 'Sniff the seat,' she said.

Dunnet, thinking this sounded vaguely perverted, complied anyway.

'Superglue!'

'Correct,' said Miss Marchmont. 'Poor Watson had the misfortune to jump in there earlier. Before I realized what had happened he had jumped up on to the model railway display and . . .'

As she spoke Watson lurched round the corner of the counter and stumbled towards them. His familiar lumbering gait was now hampered even further by the Hornby locomotive which had attached itself immovably to his tail. As he bumbled along, he banged and thumped. The engine was leaving a little trail of funnels, buffers and small wheels all over the floor as it gradually disintegrated.

'Look,' said Dunnet. 'You surely don't think I had anything to do with this? I went home last night and didn't come back here until twenty minutes ago.'

'That does not prove anything,' replied Marchmont. 'The store was broken into last night.'

Dunnet's jaw dropped. 'Broken into!'

'That's what the lady said,' barked Ringwood.

'Would I break into my own shop?'

'Who knows what sort of commie perversions you might get up to?'

'I have reason to believe that it was not Mr Dunnet,' said Miss Marchmont, and Eric breathed a sigh of relief. 'I have reason to believe that the break-in was carried out by two men. One of them was quite exceptionally large and stupid, and the other has a passionate interest in correct grammar.'

Dunnet gave a start. Miss Marchmont's abilities appeared to be approaching those of her hero. She had described Rupert and Mangle exactly, but what on earth were Rupert and Mangle doing breaking into the store? Eric's mind whirled.

'How on earth do you make that out?' he laughed dismissively. Any suggestion that he knew the two men, and was in close league with their boss, and he would be in deeper water than he cared to contemplate.

Miss Marchmont sat down on a rocking-horse which appeared to have had its head removed, and began her explanation of the night's events.

'The two men broke in through the window of the small office adjoining the main delivery bay,' said Miss Marchmont. 'The large size of one of them can be deduced from the fact that the entire window, frame and part of the wall had to be removed before he could get through it. In going through, small threads of his suit got caught on the jagged glass. The threads correspond exactly with a suit available only from L'Homme Gros, a tailor in South Molton Street specializing in outsize wear. The two men then broke the lock on the door of the office, and made their way swiftly on to the ground floor sales department. On inspecting the food hall I discovered these.'

She held out a handful of price notices from the food department. They had read 'Biscuit's', Best Banana'S' and Potatoe's', but the superfluous apostrophes and misspellings had been meticulously corrected.

'This can only be the work of a man obsessed by grammatical mistakes,' said Miss Marchmont.

Eric nodded.

'But why do you think the other man was stupid?' asked Ringwood.

'Because,' said Miss Marchmont, pointing across the room, 'the astute criminal is not in the habit of signing his name at the scene of the crime.'

Eric's heart sank. A child's blackboard was on display, and scrawled on it in different coloured chalks was the legend – MANGLE WOZ ERE. Evidently the lure of showing off his progress in his literacy classes had proved too strong.

So it was Mangle and Rupert. There could be no doubt about it. But why? Why had Mr Big taken things into his own hands? Why hadn't he consulted Dunnet? And why do these absurd things to the store in the first place? Eric glanced at his watch. The royal couple were due in one hour.

'Surely,' he said, looking in despair at the blackboard, 'surely this name must be an attempt to trick us. The criminal has done it to try and throw us on a false trail.'

'On the contrary,' said Miss Marchmont confidently, 'I am certain that the opposite is the case. Surely no criminal with any brain at all could possibly think that we would ever fall for such a simple ruse. I think we are dealing with a genuine lumbering cretin.'

Dunnet jumped. 'Genuine lumbering cretin' was such an accurate description of Mangle that he began to wonder if Miss Marchmont possessed psychic powers.

'Anyway,' announced Dunnet brightly, 'surely, Kelsey, this ought to convince you that I didn't have anything to do with this. It was these two blokes – the big one and the one keen on grammar. I told you it was nothing to do with me. It was these two men.' He paused. 'Whoever they are,' he added hurriedly.

Ringwood looked unimpressed.

'Tell him,' he said.

'Tell me? Tell me what?' said Dunnet, trying to disguise the dread in his voice.

'The two men knew you, Eric,' announced Miss Marchmont quietly.

Dunnet gave an Oscar-winning performance as Best Actor Pretending To Be Totally Surprised.

'Me . . . but . . . what!. . . no. . . I . . .' he spluttered. 'What on earth makes you think that?'

'Take Mr Dunnet to the bedding department,' said Ringwood, and stomped off, looking at his watch.

Dunnet, dumbfounded and dazed, followed Miss Marchmont towards the bedding department. At a distance followed Watson, the remains of the toy train still superglued to his tail.

In the bedding department, Miss Marchmont picked her way through the iron bedsteads – the Beehive had yet to hear of divans and futons – until she stood by one particular bed. Dunnet looked at it. Miss Marchmont peeled back the display blankets.

Dunnet gasped in horror.

There, nestled against the pillow, was the severed head of the hobby-horse in the toy department. Pinned to it was a note which read, simply, 'Hello Dunnet'.

'It appears that Mangle and his friend are acquainted with you,' said Miss Marchmont.

Dunnet looked nonchalant. He had to brazen it out now.

'I've never heard of either of them,' he said.

'I hope not, for your sake. A few years ago, I stopped Mangle in this very shop. He was attempting to shoplift. His sleeves were quite obviously stuffed with stolen goods. Or so I thought, until I removed his coat and found nothing there except arm.'

Eric gulped.

'After that I did some research on our friend Mangle. It appears he served five years in the Scrubs for accidentally dropping a Ford Cortina on someone's head. He now works for a rather unpleasant character called Mr Big.'

Dunnet panicked internally. Miss Marchmont only had to make one more connection and he would be out in the open. The game would be up. If she should even suspect that he, Eric

Dunnet, her boss, actually owed money to the same Mr Big . . .

'What I can't work out is why Mr Big should want to send two of his men in here just to do such trivial things. Nothing appears to have been stolen. It's almost as if they just wanted to embarrass us all during the royal visit.'

Eric laughed. 'It does look that way, doesn't it?' he said. As he spoke there was a huge clunk as Watson's train crashed into a brass bedpost and shattered in two.

'But why,' asked Dunnet, trying his best not to sound worried, 'would these two ruffians leave a message for me?'

'That I don't know,' replied Miss Marchmont. There was sorrow in her voice at this admission of failure. 'But I think you should be worried. For some reason, two known thugs have left you this awful warning.'

Eric looked at the toy horse's head, lying on the pillow. As warnings go, he thought it could have been worse. This wasn't so much the God-father as the Great-Aunt.

Miss Marchmont looked at her watch.

'Goodness me!' she cried. 'Ten to eleven, they'll be here in forty minutes.'

Dunnet was brought back to earth with a bump. Mangle and Rupert had obviously strewn the store with embarrassing mementoes of their little visit, although quite why, Eric still couldn't figure. It didn't even occur to him that the lack of consultation indicated that Mr Big had decided to act without Dunnet's approval. Eric,

237

thinking that the whole thing must simply show a bizarre sense of humour on Mr Big's part, trotted back to his office. On the way he passed two of the counter staff in haberdashery who were busy erasing graffiti reading 'Down With The Royals' from one of the tills.

As he headed back towards the sanctum of his office and his drinks cupboard, he was confronted by Kelsey and Gloria, both looking none too pleased.

Dunnet grinned at them, in a vain effort to convince them that everything was under control.

'What in hell are you grinning at?' asked Beresford. 'You stand there smiling like some sort of half-assed basket case while these friends of yours have been messing with the store—'

'Friends of mine? They're not friends of mine!' cried Dunnet, and Kelsey looked at him suspiciously. He'd said it just a little too quickly.

'Why did they leave you a note?' he asked. 'Nice thing, some goon squad busting in and trying to spoil our visit.'

'I don't know what you're trying to suggest,' said Dunnet, with as much dignity as his mendacious position would allow him, 'but I have no idea who these men are, or why they have referred to me.'

Beresford eyed him with a glance that could pierce a tank at two miles.

'If I find this is some revolutionary socialist plot,' she said, 'I shall personally strap you to the undercarriage of a 747.'

This friendly banter was interrupted by one of the till girls from the second floor arriving breathlessly.

'Mr Ringwood,' she cried, 'come quickly – in the fishing tackle department . . .'

'What?' cried Kelsey.

'The live bait we'd got for Prince Charles . . .'

'The worms, yes . . .'

'Someone's swapped them.'

'Swapped them?'

'They're still live, but not the same worms . . .'

'How on earth do you know?'

'Because they've eaten all the rods.'

Ringwood, Beresford and Dunnet raced to where a small crowd of terrified onlookers was staring in horror at a writhing, tangled mass of hideous slimy creatures who, with the accompaniment of ghastly slurping noises, were devouring everything in their path. Some were slithering inexorably across towards the cricket bats and golf clubs.

Miss Marchmont stood close by. She had captured one of the fearsome worms, and was busy examining it under her magnifying glass.

'There is no doubt,' she announced, 'that had Prince Charles attempted to fish with these, he would almost certainly have lost several fingers, if not his hand. This, unless I am much mistaken, is the Uruguayan swamp worm, or *Lumbricus voracisis*, one of the most dangerous creatures in the world. It will eat anything. What's more, if you chop it in half it will grow another head and eat anything twice as fast.'

Ringwood looked horrified.

'We might have sold these to the future king!' he screamed at Dunnet, who was transfixed by the sight of the wriggling mass currently devouring the display of anglers' umbrellas.

Dunnet began to panic. There was no telling how many of these little amusements Mangle and Rupert had placed around the store. Mumbling, he ran back to his office where Melissa was putting the finishing touches to her appearance. Dunnet shooed her out and locked the door. A glance across the road told him that the two thugs were still in place, and moreover, the balloons were now back to their previous size. What were they waiting for?

Panic began to rise within him fast. It was all getting out of control. Supergluing Prince William to a toy car was one thing. Lethal worms were another. Furtively, he dialled a secret number he had never written down. The phone rang twice and then the voice of Mr Big came unctuously from the other end.

'Hello, Eric,' he said. 'And how are preparations going for your day with royalty?'

'You know very well,' replied Eric. 'They'll be leaving Kensington Palace about now. For God's sake, tell me what you've done here so I can get rid of it before they arrive.'

'I don't know what you're talking about,' said Mr Big. Eric fumed with frustration.

'Don't give me that,' he said, 'our store detective has worked out exactly who broke in. They've left a message for me and Mangle signed

240

his name at the scene of the crime. The joke's gone far enough.'

Mr Big's voice hardened.

'I paid you a deposit on your little shop,' he said. 'You have not delivered.'

'What's that got to do with it?' cried Eric. 'I've told you. I'll have this store ruined in a matter of months.'

'So you keep saying,' replied the gangster. 'But you see, I have worked out a way of ruining it by mid-afternoon today.'

Dunnet's jaw dropped. Surely, not even Mr Big could sink that low.

'But you didn't tell me,' he moaned.

'Why should I?'

'Because we're partners! That's the way it's always been . . . I get you the store, we split the profit.'

'But you haven't got me the store, and I'm getting impatient.' The phone went down.

So that was it! Dunnet groaned. He'd been double-crossed. Instead of a day of glory and an invitation to the Palace, it was going to be a day of ignominy. Either course of action was going to lead to embarrassment, humiliation and tabloid outrage. He could either cancel the visit, which was at Princess Diana's own request and had been given a blaze of publicity. Or he could go ahead and risk having deadly worms devouring royals or God knows what other booby traps. Mr Big was right. Either course would close down the store in a day, and he was powerless to stop it without revealing his own complicity with the thugs.

He walked, deliberately and slowly, to the wall of the office. Pinned to that wall was a graph, showing the amazing success of the Beehive over the previous three months. Eric, with studied, careful movements of his neck, commenced to bang his head against the wall.

18

At 11.30 am precisely, a large black limousine, flanked by motorcycle outriders and watched over by security police from every surrounding building, drew up outside the Beehive. The crowd cheered. Mr Big's two transvestite henchmen nodded to each other and shuffled forward through the cheering throng, hitting those cheerers who would not move out of their way with tins of Whiskas. Once towards the front they suddenly whipped out, from beneath their coats, large placards displaying anti-royalist slogans, and implying that they represented the Beehive. 'Shop Staff Against Monarchism!' The crowd turned on them angrily, and there was the sound of balloons popping. But it was too late. The TV cameras had already committed the incident to video tape, and Dunnet thought with horror of the publicity they would get on the evening news.

The royal party, surrounded by a scrum of bodyguards, made their way towards the revolving door at the front of the Beehive, which had been oiled for the first time in one hundred and fifty years to ensure that no regal personage got trapped in it. As they did so, a small but lethal dog was unleashed from somewhere in the crowd. It hurtled like a furry bullet across the street and dived into the scrum of security men, a kamikaze hound, evidently trained by Mr Big for the purpose. Fortunately, one burly bodyguard managed to grasp the slavering mutt before it could sink its teeth into the elegant calves so beloved by millions.

From his window, Dunnet watched the whole thing in a daze. Mr Big's treachery had stunned him . . . That, he thought bitterly, was the reason why he was the manager of this terrible old shop, while Mr Big was the powerful crime boss he undoubtedly thought he was. Dunnet lacked that killer instinct. He just didn't have the sort of depraved brain needed to concoct schemes to glue royal princes to toy cars.

He realized, miserably, that once the hand-shaking and smiling was over, he was in for a showdown with Kelsey and Beresford. They now knew – or must have guessed – that he, Dunnet, was in league with these unprincipled thugs to ruin the store. If Ringwood sacked him . . . if he lost his claim . . . if he couldn't repay Mr Big the two hundred thousand . . . it didn't bear thinking about. Which was why he spent the whole of the next hour thinking about it. When the royal personages shook hands with the manager of a uniquely successful British institution, they must have wondered why he was the most utterly miserable recipient of a royal handshake since Anne Boleyn.

When it was all over, the black limousine had pulled away, the crowd had cheered their last cheer and the police were dismantling the metal barriers, Dunnet slunk miserably to his office to ponder his next move. Melissa was already there, seated at her typewriter.

'Kelsey's looking for you,' she said. Her tone was ambiguous. It wasn't quite just informative, but it wasn't quite a fully fledged warning. It was just a trifle ominous.

'Oh?' said Eric.

'And Miss Beresford.'

'Oh?' said Eric again.

Nervously, he clutched up a handful of letters that had arrived in that morning's post. The thought of Gloria Beresford on the warpath unnerved him. He felt angry, betrayed by Mr Big. He wanted to call him right now but he couldn't with Melissa sitting right behind him, calmly clicking away on her typewriter unaware of the seething turmoil in the brain of her boss.

Eric ripped open the first envelope. It was a complaint. It was from a woman in Herne Hill who had bought a tin of beans from the Beehive. On opening them she had found baked beans, a dead cockroach and a large piece of shrapnel, all in a tasty tomato sauce. Eric groaned and put the letter into the 'Complaints' file. This was a huge box-file which was used to record every complaint which arrived concerning goods sold by the Beehive. The letters were assiduously logged, noted, and once a year, burnt as part

245

of the entertainment at the staff party. In one hundred years, not one had ever been replied to.

The second letter was from a ninety-three-year-old in Lyme Regis who was looking for a replacement spindle for her 1907 sewing machine. She had been unable to find one anywhere else and thought the Beehive would be her only hope. Dunnet picked up the phone and called the household goods department.

'Derek . . . we got any sewing machines in?'

'Plenty.'

'Spare spindles?'

'What year?'

'1907.'

There was a pause as Derek checked the stocklist.

'Sorry, Mr Dunnet. Nothing that recent.'

Eric scribbled a reply to the ninety-three-year-old. 'Dear Mrs Hetherington. No we haven't so piss off.' He read it through and decided that his less-than-happy frame of mind had affected the way he'd worded it. After all, there was no need to take out his own problems on this little old lady. He crossed out 'piss off' and wrote 'bog off' instead.

The publicity the Beehive had been receiving of late had not pleased everyone outside of Mr Big, Dunnet and the Bishop. Mr Peck sat in the offices of Lawson, Chaddesley and Peck deciding whether to make an important telephone call or not.

The success at the Beehive had disturbed him

246

greatly, having been achieved by what he felt were 'American practices'. He had once been proud to be associated with the Beehive. Its dealings and principles were much in conjunction with his own. He had toured the store just two days previously and had been horrified as to the changes. The place had been seething with noisy over-priced Americans with check shirts, so loud a Canadian lumberjack would have been embarrassed to wear them. He had taken an instant dislike to the Americans ever since they had burst into his office demanding to see him. Sadly there had been no disputing their claim. It would lead to no good; he was sure he was right.

Upon returning from his visit to the Beehive, he was determined that something should be done. He could not see why this young American upstart should come over and destroy what he felt was a Kensington tradition. If there was any way of stopping him, he would find it and he had set to diligently researching the original manuscripts that referred to the store's regulations. The search had been long and hard but eventually had produced something most worthwhile and now he felt it was just a matter of time as to the best way of making use of what he had discovered.

All his instincts said, 'Trust a man of the cloth', and with that he dialled the Bishop's number.

The phone rang by the side of the bed that contained a naked Bishop of Lambeth seated on top of a large-bosomed lady dressed in a nun's habit, minus the wimple. This the Bishop was wearing back to front to add an air of mystery to that morning's revelries.

He picked up the phone and made a muffled enquiry as to the caller on the other end. It was that solicitor, Peck, the one whose neck, he'd heard, was encompassed in large swathes of bandages protecting his damaged epiglottis. His persistent whining was less shrill than normal due to the restrictions imposed by the first aid covering.

'I'd like to speak to the Bishop of Lambeth,' asked Peck.

'You're speaking to him,' said the Bishop through the wimple.

'When will he be in?'

'I am in,' said the Bishop, 'it's me speaking.'

Peck could hardly distinguish what was being said through his end of the receiver.

The Bishop attempted to pull off the wimple but only managed to tighten it around his neck.

'Damn it,' said the Bishop and attempted to put the phone through the hole in the wimple at the back of his head and force it round to his face, but only succeeded in ramming the speaking bit into his mouth and clamping the listening end firmly over his left eye.

'Hang on,' shouted the Bishop, but the sound was now more unintelligible than before.

The nun whose flight into orgasmic oblivion was reaching peak squeaked long and high. Peck, hearing the noise, assumed he was talking to an answering machine, and cursing modern day technology started to leave the message.

The Bishop meantime, by fiercely wrenching the speaking bit out of his mouth, shoved the earpiece round to the right-hand side of his face, just in time to hear Peck say, 'Would you please instruct the Bishop of Lambeth to attend the offices of Lawson Chaddesley and Peck as soon as possible, it is most urgent.'

The nun, during her bout of ecstasy, opened her eyes to see the head of the Bishop covered in her wimple with the telephone sticking out at the front. She was immediately reminded of the Elephant Man and for some reason this heightened her gratification to its ultimate climax and she screamed with sheer pleasure.

Peck presumed that that was the end of the tape and put the phone down.

The Bishop, becoming exhausted what with the previous physical demands and wrestling with the phone, was trying to suck in great gulp fulls of air to provide the oxygen his body needed. The air was restricted by the wimple, causing a lack of the vital element to his system; whereupon he passed out.

The nun, now fully aware that the wages of sin was death, thought the Bishop had received his pay packet. Managing to rip off the wimple, she gave him mouth to mouth resuscitation, praying fervently for forgiveness and professing life-long devotion and obedience to her order.

By the middle of the afternoon, the Bishop had recovered sufficiently to remember the unexpected telephone call from Peck, and as he had said it was a matter of urgency, he phoned and went straight round to see him in his office.

The Bishop sat in front of Peck in an office that was all the better for having been freshly decorated since the previous time he had visited the solicitor. He enquired as to the progress of Peck's epiglottis.

'It is considerably better than it was,' squeaked Peck, 'but it was a while before I was actually able to talk. Will any of your colleagues be attending this meeting?' asked Peck, with a great deal of understandable trepidation.

'No,' said the Bishop, 'they're all involved with other projects now.'

Peck gave a more than visible sigh of relief.

'Now why have you asked me to attend your offices?'

'Well, it's to do with the Beehive,' said Peck. 'I have come across a piece of information which I feel I should have a discreet word with you about.'

'Ah, the Beehive,' said the Bishop, wishing with all his might he had never heard of the damn store. 'What might the information be?'

'As you know, the early conditions laid down were strange and somewhat complex and I have been studying them in relation to the renaissance the store is now enjoying. We have a very unusual situation here.'

'What might that be?' asked the Bishop.

'Well,' continued Peck, 'having read of the

Beehive's new popularity and its seeming abundance of sales, and I take it therefore, profit, by doing so it would seem to infringe one of the conditions laid down in the original manifesto. Namely, that if the store makes a profit and the proceeds are not distributed to the poor and needy, this is a contravention of the original proviso. Now, in all my dealings with the Beehive, the one problem I have never had is profit, but I could categorically state that if the Beehive continues to make a surplus in its trading accounts by the end of the year, the new-found heir will be in contravention of his forefathers' wishes and frankly, my lord Bishop, the property will revert to the Church.'

The Bishop remained silent, but an inner glow of excitement suffused his body.

'May I enquire, Mr Peck, if you have divulged this information to anyone else?'

'No,' said Peck, 'I thought it best for your ears only and perhaps you may give me your thoughts on the matter.'

'Tell me why you have not informed the heir — a Mr Ringwood?'

'He is an American, my lord Bishop. I loathe and detest them. If it was not for Americans, we would not have this infernal desire for gadgets, for slick, sharp business practices, for all that is ungentlemanly and uncourteous. The thought of the Beehive being turned into something akin to a Las Vegas amusement arcade fills me with dread, and with the present owner, I can't see it ending up as anything else.'

'Oh, I can agree,' enthused the Bishop. 'It would be a tragedy indeed if such circumstances were allowed to happen. What would you feel, Mr Peck, if we were to keep this information to ourselves?'

'I feel it would be, how shall we say, prudent?' said Peck, getting excited and making the stricture around his neck visibly wobble.

'Ah yes, prudent is the word,' said the Bishop, 'but you do realize Mr Dunnet will have to be informed?'

'Yes,' said Peck, 'but I understand Mr Dunnet's loathing of the Americans is similar to mine.'

'I think we can trust him. He's a slippery character, knows which side his bread's buttered.'

'I will leave the matter in your hands, my lord Bishop.' Peck's voice was improving all the time and the octave levels once again irritated the Bishop's nervous system. He rose, grateful for the information but also grateful to leave the premises and the screeching solicitor's voice. As he made his way down the staircase to his waiting car, he mused as to the outcome of this most important piece of information. It changed things considerably. Mr Big would be most interested.

Though he didn't know it, when Kelsey Ringwood was invited by Miss Marchmont to join her in her secret room, he was being accorded a unique privilege. Nobody had ever been invited there. This was the sanctuary, the

252

haven, to which Miss Marchmont fled when she needed to escape from the passing parade of dips, hoovers and peedees. Dips were pickpockets, hoovers were the operators who could clear an entire counter in seconds – Australian gangs specialized in this caper – and peedees were Paul Daniels, the aristocrats of shoplifters who, no matter how closely you watched, could still get away with it.

The walls were decorated with a selection of Holmesian memorabilia which had been brought from her flat in Baker Street. There were embroidered samplers of 'The Wit and Wisdom of Sherlock Holmes' – 'There will never be a perfect crime, because the person who commits it will have to tell somebody.' Kelsey sat in an easy chair that had once belonged to the Upholstery Boys, a firm from Hackney who had masqueraded as delivery men. On the wall above Kelsey's head was an oil painting of the young Sherlock Holmes that had been presented to Miss Marchmont by the National Association of Store Detectives and Floor-walkers on the occasion of her thousandth shoplifter. It was inscribed, 'To Judith Marchmont, who has felt more collars than the Sweeney.'

Again Miss Marchmont was struck by Kelsey's resemblance to the World's Greatest Detective. She just hoped Watson would behave himself. Lately, whenever she had started to think about Mr Ringwood, Watson would growl. Some sort of canine telepathic jealousy. Perhaps she should write to the editor of *Doggy Doos* – the magazine for the dogaholic.

Kelsey asked, 'How did you find this place?'

'I didn't. Watson did.' The dog was lying in a heap in the corner. He growled at the mention of his name. 'There's an old storeroom next door and Watson was rummaging around, probably looking for food, and he fell against a piece of wall. It swung back to reveal this place. It obviously hadn't been used for years. Dust everywhere. There was the chaise longue I'm sitting on, some sort of drinks cabinet and a champagne bucket.'

'Sounds like a waiting room in a bordello.'

Judith Marchmont coloured slightly at the word 'bordello'. 'I must say I wondered to what purpose it might have been put. Whether perhaps old Mr Alfred had used it. Then I deduced from some of the things the older employees told me that it was much more likely to have been Mr Ronald.'

'You mean this is where my father came for his extra-curricular nookie? The naughty old bugger.'

'Would you like some coffee?' When it was made, she served it in mugs in the shape of Sherlock Holmes' head. The handles were his nose. When you tipped the mug towards your mouth, it induced a curious kind of vertigo, as though you were drinking through the top of somebody's head. Kelsey wondered why Miss Marchmont, Judith, had invited him here. Was he supposed to make a pass? Or was she going to make a pass? Women did these days.

'How do you like my secret room?' she asked.

'Very nice,' mumbled Kelsey, who had decided that he should make the pass. He stood up and took a couple of steps towards Miss Marchmont, who also stood up because it seemed like a polite sort of thing to do. Watson watched with interest.

As Kelsey had once read in a book called *To Woo To Win*, a manual for the romantically inept, 'Focus your gaze upon the mouth of your intended. Women find this irresistible.' As he moved towards her and his gaze locked on her mouth, all she could think was, 'Oh God, I think there's a fish finger stuck to my lip.' It was Thursday and it was always fish fingers in the canteen on Thursdays. She turned to check in her Sherlock Holmes mirror — the one with the meerschaum frame, on the wall behind her — at precisely the moment that Kelsey lunged. Instead of planting a kiss upon her cheek, he found himself burying his mouth in her hair at just the point where a hair-clip was working itself free and in some freakish reversal the clip seemed to leap from Miss Marchmont's chestnut brown tresses and attach itself to Kelsey's lower lip.

He backed off, looking like one of those plate-lipped African tribesmen. At the same time Watson launched himself into an attack. He would have sunk his teeth into Kelsey's leg, but, getting on a bit now, his first aim also missed and he only clipped Kelsey's trousers. Judith Marchmont burst out laughing. 'Stop,

Watson,' she said, pulling him away. 'What on earth were you doing!' she said to Kelsey, removing the clip from his lower lip.

'Well, as a matter of fact, I was trying to kiss you.' Miss Marchmont didn't know what to do. She was flustered. All the things those silly magazines said would happen, were happening. Her heart was beating faster, she did feel hot and she didn't know what to say, so she tried. 'Would you like to try again?'

'What about Watson?'

'You can kiss him later.'

Shyly they embraced, and feeling a little self-conscious about it all, Kelsey lowered his mouth towards hers. They were just about to kiss when Miss Marchmont opened her eyes and mouth very wide. Kelsey's eyes were closed (chapter three of *To Woo To Win*), and so the first he knew of this development was when Miss Marchmont's front teeth brushed the tip of his nose as it disappeared into her mouth. 'What the . . .' He pulled back to see Miss Marchmont putting her finger to her lips. They heard a muffled conversation from the storeroom adjacent to Miss Marchmont's secret hiding place.

Peering through a crack in the door, Miss Marchmont recognized the figure of Mr Dunnet and a man in a large purple cassock and gaiters.

'It's the Bishop,' whispered Judith.

'Bishop who?' asked Kelsey.

'Sshh – I'm trying to hear.'

No matter how she strained, she could not

catch any of the hurried but excited conversation. Then she heard a reference to Peck and the research he'd done; as they left, the Bishop said clearly that he'd let the dwarf know.

'What was all that about?' asked Kelsey.

'Blowed if I know,' replied Judith, 'but Dunnet is up to something and I'd like to know what the Bishop's up to as well. Come on, Kelsey; I think we ought to look into this with your lawyer.'

19

Kelsey had moved into Mr Alfred's old apartment on the top floor, and to Eric Dunnet that was a year's supply of Saxo rubbed into the ever growing wound.

More than anything Dunnet coveted that apartment. How often had he imagined the long, languorous, rapturous afternoons there? The place, he would fantasize, would be amok with old ladies, the air heady with the pungent smell of lavender and camphor, not so much careless rapture as careless rupture. He saw himself preening with princesses, dallying with duchesses, meddling with marcheses, lingering with ladyships and humping with hons. And because of some Yank he still found himself having to make do with a quick grope under the dustsheets in the soft furnishings storeroom while the staff were away having tea. He'd only got away with that for as long as he had by explaining to the old duck of the day that he'd had a terrible experience when he was a teenager that had left him emotionally scarred – something to do with a cub mistress, a toadstool and a piece of string – and that he was only capable of physical affection behind a sofa under a dustsheet.

It seemed to work. Mind you, with some of them if you had said that you had to do it wearing plimsolls and a codpiece in the store's main window on a bed of Christmas puddings they'd have said yes.

Kelsey was sitting at Mr Alfred's desk. He liked to imagine that it was here Uncle Alfred, as he had become to Kelsey, had written that last will and testament that had led to this.

Kelsey had called a meeting to discuss what he and Miss Marchmont had or hadn't heard. Glory B was the first to arrive. She was dressed to kill. She was wearing a US Marines combat uniform with an M16 carbine slung round her neck and a string of grenades garlanding her waist. Kelsey was no longer surprised by anything his lawyer wore. He had belts that were wider than some of her mini skirts. When she walked past Italian restaurants in Soho, waiters would emerge and line the streets like soldiers, pepper grinders held in the present-arms position.

'Been shopping at the army surplus store again?' enquired Kelsey.

'No, this is the new look for this season – it's called Urban Guerrilla – not so much Rambeau as Rambelle. The carbine isn't real and neither are the grenades – in fact, if you pull the wrong pin my trousers fall down – but the weirdos don't know that and I can't wait for some kink to try to jump on my bones as I'm walking home one night. If the karate doesn't get him the Mace will, and while he's lying there on the ground wondering if that's what an orgasm is really like, then I'll tie one of my grenades to his zipper and start counting.'

'Maybe you could tie one to Dunnet's zipper.'

'He wouldn't have a zipper, not the type, he'd have flies. All round his head usually. Why, what's he done?'

Kelsey said, 'I dunno,' and then went on to explain about the mysterious meeting between Dunnet and the Bishop.

'I think,' said Glory B, 'that I should call my friend on Long Island.'

'Would that be the friend with a fondness for clams and Tony's special hot sauce?' asked Jake.

'It would,' said Glory B. 'I think he was quietly lusting after me. Kept saying how much he liked my nose – what he called my cosy nostrils – and if ever I wanted anything all I had to do was call.' As she was speaking, Glory B was dialling the number of the house overlooking Lobster Bay. She wondered who would answer – Swish Guard or Israeli sergeant. In the event it was neither. She got the old man himself.

'Hallo,' she heard him say, 'whoever you are I hope for your sake you ain't got a wrong number.'

'Don Ferrari,' said Glory B. 'It's OK. It's me. The clam lady. What are you doing answering you own phone? Not what I'd expect from a man of respect.'

'Hallo, clam lady,' she heard him wheeze back

over 3,500 miles of slight echo from the satellite. 'We have a little trouble here. We're under attack.'

'I thought you guys had given up all that gang warfare stuff.'

'It ain't exactly gang warfare,' said Don Ferrari. 'We got Jehovah's Terrorists – they're like Jehovah's Witnesses but militant. They're all around, throwing lighted *Watchtowers* over the wall. The girls and boys are out there taking care of it. Now what can I do for you?'

Glory B told the old man what had happened since they last met.

'Whadya say this guy's name is, Doughnut?'

'Dunnet.'

'Spell it.'

'D as in Don, U as in Umberto, N as in Napoli, N as in Nostra, E as in Echo, T as in Tagliatelle.'

'Got it. Don't you worry your pretty little tukus, clam lady, I have a friend in London who would be greatly honoured to do me a small service. I will talk to him about your Mr Dinette. Got to go – the Jehovah's Terrorists have broken through – they're all carrying M16 Bibles.' Before he hung up Glory B heard the sporadic rattle of collection boxes. . . .

The friend in London who would 'consider it an honour' to do a 'small favour' for Don Ferrari was known as the Chinaman. He was currently at number six in Scotland Yard's top ten but another good hit would take him to the coveted number one spot and a chance of a video on *Crimewatch*. The Chinaman ran gambling dens, opium dens and dirty dens. It was said no Chinese meal was served in south London unless he had a hand in it.

The Chinaman was not Chinese. He was Australian. A sort of Crocodile Hong Kong. His mother was Chinese and she had met his father, a Melbourne fireman, when he'd come to the restaurant and taken her away. The Chinaman was one of thirty-eight children – apparently once you've had one Chinese child, three months later you have to have another. He was a complex, dangerous man whose favourite torture was to tie victims to a plate of pavlova and play Rolf Harris records very loudly whilst reading from the works of Clive James. It reduced the hardest of men to rubble.

When the Chinaman received his call from Don Ferrari, he was sitting in the back seat of his Rolls-Royce – what his Chinese colleagues called the Loller – MSG 1. He was musing on the possibility of inventing a fax machine that could send Chinese food, thus completely revolutionizing the takeaway business, when the phone rang. The Chinaman didn't at first recognize the voice. When he did he involuntarily sat up a lot straighter, checked to see if his shoes were clean and lowered all the blinds.

'You are a hard man to get hold of,' said the voice of an old colleague.

'A thousand apologies, Don Ferrari,' said the Chinaman, 'these are dangerous times in London.'

'Who's after you – the Greeks?'

'Much worse,' said the Chinaman. 'The Vatmen.'

'Let me tell you why I am calling, Chinaman. There is in London a department store called the Beehive.'

'I just drove past it.'

'There they have a managing director called Dunnet or Dansette or something like that. Now this person is causing a very good friend of mine some discomfiture and I would consider it a mark of our great and considerable friendship if you could see your way to persuading this Punnett that it is less than sensible to cause discomfiture to a very good friend of Don Ferrari, if you get my drift?'

'To perform such a task would be an esteemed honour, Don Ferrari,' said the Chinaman. 'Consider it done.'

Both men hung up. The Chinaman wondered who he could get to dispatch this person to that great takeaway in the sky. A contract had been taken out. Dunnet was living on borrowed time. The car had stopped in Park Lane while the police tried to remove a Mini that was parked illegally in a pot hole. Nobody could understand why the police were bothering – traffic didn't have to drive round it – it was driving over it.

While they waited the Chinaman considered his options. There was Necktie Norman, but the word was that he had arthritis badly in his left hand and recently a couple of his garrottes had slipped badly. There was Basil the Bat – he used to open heads for England – but he was reported to be playing for South Africa these days. Then he remembered the ideal people – the Hare Krishna mob. Born-again hit men. They gave their victims a choice. The choice was becoming a member of Hare Krishna – 'the chants would be a fine thing' – or 'having your karma seriously redirected and your predestination accelerated'. When it was explained that the former would involve spending eternity walking up and down Oxford Street in a silly haircut and saffron knickers most people chose the latter.

The Chinaman leaned forward and tapped on the divider. 'Drive along Oxford Street and pull up as soon as you see some Hare Krishnas rattling bicycle chains.'

The riproaring success of the Beehive was solidly founded on its merchandise – the dilapidated, outmoded Victoriana which had been selling like the very hottest of hot cakes. The dusty antimacassars, the autographed W. G. Grace cricket boxes, the designer gas brackets – all manner of dusty relics were being snapped up, mostly by Americans and one or two Brits, all either very fashion-conscious or extremely un-fashion conscious.

There was one small drawback. Once the Victorian stock ran out there was, by definition, nothing Victorian to replace it with. If the

Beehive replaced it with ordinary eighties goods it would become just another department store; if it restocked with reproduction stuff, it would lose its cachet of authenticity; and if it bought in Victoriana it would become nothing more than a glorified antique shop. It was an insoluble problem. And, as a visit to the basement stockroom proved to Kelsey one morning, it was a problem that very quickly needed solving. The Beehive was running dangerously low on stock.

This fact had not escaped Dunnet. Ever since he had learned of the no-profit clause, it had nagged at the back of his mind. It was utterly essential that from now on the store stayed in profit.

'Getting a bit worried, Eric,' said Ringwood to Dunnet one day, as they watched a jostling scrum of customers rushing to buy the last of the tin baths. 'All this old antique gear has gone over really well with the Americans. Trouble is, we're running out of it.'

'I'm sure you'll think of something,' said Eric. 'Something to keep the profits up.'

Kelsey looked at Dunnet.

'Eric, I think I may have misjudged you,' he said. 'There I was thinking you were a treacherous commie who wanted to ruin the place. Now I see you're a good old boy.'

You Americans make me puke, thought Dunnet.

'Don't you worry. I'll think of something,' said Kelsey, and strode off to his office deep in thought.

A few days later Dunnet was in his own office, using the vantage point of the window to ogle old ladies at the bus stop, when Kelsey, Jake and Gloria burst in.

'Hiya, Eric!' cried Kelsey, with such clean-cut Yankee bonhomie that Eric felt his gorge rise.

Gloria and Jake looked at Dunnet as if to say, don't rely on us being friendly. They both harboured more suspicions of their strange manager than the more *ingénu* Kelsey.

'We've got it,' said Kelsey. 'The solution to our stock problem.'

'Ah,' said Eric, relief spreading over his features.

'We've run out of English junk, yes?'

Eric gave a patriotic 'hmph' at hearing the Beehive's wares described as junk, even though he himself would have chosen a far stronger word.

'So – we'll buy in some American junk.'

'Pardon?' said Eric.

Gloria handed Eric a list of products.

'This is a stock-list of Kelsey's merchandise in the States.' The list read:

3000 pieces of Moses' original cradle
   (blessed by Pope)
Dog exercise cycles (×10,000)
Talking kettles (3 gross)
Underwater shoe-shine kits (5000)
Pen umbrella (quantity uncertain)
Musical golf clubs (2000 sets, +1000
   individual singing putters)

266

In-car sauna (100 for every major car
    model)
Shakespearean door bells (when pressed,
    quote Hamlet)
Heat-seeking soap (subject to licence from
    Pentagon)
Digital toothbrushes (1000)
Biodegradable saucepans (10,000, but
    rapidly decreasing in number for obvious
    reasons)
Calculator cufflinks
Golf-ball warmers (only 30 left)
Luminous toothpaste
Electric nose-hair clippers
Horn-rimmed contact lenses
Taramasalata makers (300)
Sock carousel (2 different brands –
    SelektaSok and Sock-U-Want)
Vibrating bicycle saddle (for reducing fat
    buttocks while-u-pedal)
Dead cat taxidermist kit ('home stuffing
    made simple')
Stale muesli fresheners
Thermal ties (various colours)
Gas-operated bagpipes
Reversible toupees ('dye though bald')
Reusable christmas cards
Pocket chainsaw . . .

Eric looked up from the list.
'Very droll,' he said. 'Not April the first, is it?'
'I'm serious,' said Kelsey. 'Turn over the page,
you missed the personalized inside-leg measurer,

the automatic dandruff shoulder-brush (unfolds from your collar as soon as you reach a certain dandruff-density) and the lapel-mounted halitosis early-warning light.'

Eric gaped.

'This is only the first batch,' said Gloria. 'There's a lot more where this came from. Furniture, records . . . you name it.'

'But no one'll buy this!' cried Eric, in panic. The prospect of plummeting profits was looming large.

'Er . . .' said Kelsey, 'Americans won't, sure. That's why I've got so much of it. But we figure, if Americans'll buy English garbage, then the English will buy American garbage.'

'After all,' added Jake, 'you love our junk food . . . so you'll love our junk.'

'I see,' said Eric. 'You think the English are all crying out for heat-seeking soap, do you?'

'Look, Dunnet,' said Gloria, 'it'll sell. We turned this place round in a month. We know what we're doing.'

'Thermal ties?' gurgled Dunnet by way of reply.

'Sure. The first load'll be shipped in Friday, and in the store Monday. It'll sell, Dunnet, don't you worry.'

Eric didn't share their optimism. On the following Monday he was rapidly proved right. From 9am to 8pm, bemused customers gazed in horror at the ghastly American tat that had appeared on the Beehive's shelves. Hardly a single purchase was made.

Dunnet couldn't believe it. Months earlier he'd been praying for Kelsey to fail. Now he had, and Dunnet was praying for him to succeed again. But no amount of advertising or marketing could persuade the British public that they needed golf-ball warmers.

He wondered how much longer Mr Big would wait.

20

The Isle of Dogs formed a part of London's notorious Docklands history. Once a busy docks where the cargo ships from Europe unloaded and loaded their contents, after the war the decline in trade had been dramatic and the area had become run down and a classified slum. However, with the advent of the Yuppie era, big city money had started to transform the area into a giant commercial project.

Buildings everywhere were being knocked down ready for the onslaught of the architects and builders coming to construct the replacement homes and offices.

In one small area by an old dock pier, a small group of people stood amongst the half-destroyed buildings and the large pieces of plant hire that were responsible for the destruction.

'No one can say I haven't warned you, Eric. The money my consortium has invested in you has been considerable; it would do my reputation, or theirs, no good at all to think that people could take advantage of our generosity and get away with it.'

Dunnet was listening with the intensity one has on these occasions.

Mangle was taking great pains to tie him securely to a demolition ball. This was attached to a metal rope which itself was attached to a large crane. It was apparent to Dunnet that he was to be used as part of the machinery to demolish the brick warehouse perched on the edge of the River Thames, that at one time had been used to store the imports and exports of Britain's overseas trading.

Mangle was delighted with this new idea of disposing of people who displeased his boss, and had got the idea from a video nasty called *I Ate The Surgeon's Remains.*

Eric protested violently that he had nothing to do with the store's sudden loss of trading surplus. The junk that the Americans had imported had remained firmly on the shelves. There was a definite customer resistance, particularly from Americans, as most of them had spent quite a lot of money taking a holiday from the retail system that sold that kind of junk anyway.

Mr Big figured that Eric had done an 'about face', and had made a deal with the Americans to keep the store by engineering a loss for the end of year. Eric protested his innocence most vigorously.

Mangle got behind the controls of the crane and started to swing the ball slightly backwards and forwards.

'Now Eric, fill me in on the details of your arrangements with the Americans?'

Eric, tied securely to the ball, swung backwards and forwards past Mr Big, heading inexorably on each swing closer and closer to the warehouse wall.

'You haven't much time, Eric,' shouted Mr Big.

Eric needed no reminding as the smashed windows of the derelict building revealed for the first time the dark interiors of the warehouse.

Eric's introduction to nineteenth-century brickwork was interrupted by a squeal of brakes. A Daimler Sovereign pulled to a halt as the Bishop of Lambeth leapt out of the car and ran up to Mr Big.

The Bishop was worried. He had had a telephone call from Dunnet's secretary, Melissa, who was equally worried, informing him that Mr Big and his associates had taken Eric forcibly from the Beehive that very morning. She had related to him the heated conversation she'd overheard through the door. The Bishop had put two and two together and realized what Mangle might do to Dunnet.

He had then telephoned the receptionist at the Hamilton Club to find the whereabouts of Mr Big, and received the address of the warehouse on the docks.

'What are you doing? What are you doing?' screamed the Bishop.

'This two-timing evil scumbag has reneged on our deal. No one does that to Mr Big and gets away with it.'

The Bishop, fearful that he might yet become involved with murder, was beside himself.

Mr Big, always a reasonable man, instructed Mangle to keep the ball moving, but not to harm Mr Dunnet until further notice. Mangle was crestfallen but still hopeful that he might yet get the instruction to complete the demise of Eric.

For a further twenty minutes the Bishop argued the case for Dunnet, not sure whether he was in the right or wrong, but the Bishop fervently desired Dunnet to live.

During the Bishop's pleading, Mangle had experimented to see how close he could get Dunnet to the wall without harming him.

Finally Mr Big relented and asked Mangle to bring the ball to a halt. Mangle reluctantly agreed. It took several minutes, during which time Dunnet's hopes rose that his life might yet be spared. As the ball finally came to a halt, Mr Big said to the Bishop, 'Perhaps you could get Dunnet to explain how come a store doing a roaring trade and making a roaring profit can within one month reverse to the point where it is now making a loss. There is something foul here and I want to know what it is.'

'I told you,' said Eric, 'it's that crazy bastard Kelsey, they're all crazy. I told them that the stuff would not sell, they would not believe me, they don't trust me anyhow. They seem to think that Britain is ready for all that gucky American merchandise and that they'll make a fortune.'

The Bishop, well aware of the situation from Dunnet's many heated telephone talks with him over the last few weeks, came to his aid. 'What has Dunnet got to gain by siding with the Americans? He'll make far more money from our arrangement than he ever will from selling dead pet taxidermist kits and reversible toupees!'

'But you have to admit,' said Mr Big, 'that if the situation carries on as it is, the Beehive will make a loss and those damned Americans will still own the store.'

Eric, still intimately acquainted with the ball, said, 'I have an idea.'

'As long as it is not violent,' said the Bishop. 'I can't stand violence.'

'Look, it's simple, I've been thinking about it,' said Eric. 'They are importing all this junk and no one's buying it, so the store's not making a profit. Supposing someone were to buy the goods?'

'Who?' said Mr Big.

'Us!' said Eric. 'We'll buy the goods.'

Mangle moved back behind the controls and started the ball swinging slowly again.

'Stop,' said the Bishop, 'what an idea!'

'Hold it!' Mr Big instructed Mangle, and the ball came to a stop once more.

'You mean to say, if we buy all the goods, the store makes a profit and the Church gets the premises?'

'Exactly,' said Eric. 'There are only a couple of months before the year end, and if we could buy sufficient goods to put the store in the black, we have done it, the problem's solved. I have been working it out,' said Eric, 'with the trading figures necessary, I reckon it would cost us about three-quarters of a million which is peanuts compared with what we all stand to gain.'

Mr Big pondered for a few moments. 'Who do we get to buy the goods?' he said.

'We'll contact as many market research organizations as we can, and tell them we are doing a survey on staff and customer relations. If we tell each company it's highly confidential they will supply a constant stream of customers to purchase the goods.'

'What do we do with the goods when we have purchased them?' asked Mr Big.

'Well, we'll store them somewhere and sell them off as job lots and at least recover some of our money on them. How much you'll get for reversible toupees is beyond me. You could always sell one to Bruce Forsyth!' said Eric, hoping to enliven the situation with a modicum of humour.

'Seems the perfect solution to me,' said the Bishop.

'I will think about it,' said Mr Big, walking towards his psychedelic Daimler. Mangle walked dejectedly behind, disappointed he had not been able to fulfil this unique form of execution.

The Bishop, much relieved, got into his Daimler and sped away back to central London.

Mr Big, deep in thought, felt he had to talk the situation over with Rupert. 'Take us to the Central Library,' he ordered Spinksy, 'I need to find Rupert.'

As both cars sped away, Eric watched them

disappear as he slowly circled round, still attached to the ball.

Mr Big couldn't imagine how he was supposed to make contact with the Chinaman in the crawler lane of the M25 between exits 36 and 37. But this was where the man had told him to come. They were in Mr Big's Jag. Mangle was driving, whilst Rupert amused himself counting the lorry drivers who were eating Yorkies. '46 . . . 47 . . . 48 . . .'

Mangle said, 'Kit Kat.'

'What?'

'Kit Kat. That last one. Don't count.'

Mr Big was feeling nervous. The reason he was meeting the Chinaman was to ask him for some money. Rather a lot of money. What Dunnet and the Bishop had reckoned it would take. Dunnet and the Bishop — it appalled him that he had to mix with those menopausal degenerates. If it wasn't Bible-bondage it was old ladies rattling their Zimmer frames. Still, soon be over. But how could he tell the Chinaman what he wanted the money for — who would lend anybody money to buy fourteen thousand Jesuses with eyes that lit up when you placed them in a car's rear window?

He became aware that Rupert had stopped counting, and looked up and saw why. Ahead of them the crawler lane had been closed. A long line of cones was funnelling traffic into the centre lane. But as they approached, a Chinese waiter suddenly popped up from behind the cones, pulled some to one side, and waved them through. He replaced them and motioned to pull up behind a large green van with the words 'Motorway Maintenance' written on the side. It was less than wholly convincing, because of the signwriter's spelling incompetence. As Mr Big and his companions got out of the car, the rear doors of the van opened and a pair of steps was lowered to the ground. Hands helped them inside, the steps were retracted and the doors closed behind them. The interior of the van had been decorated to resemble a medieval torture chamber — one of the lads from the London Dungeon had done it for cash — and many a night the Chinaman would take a recalcitrant victim out to the nearest motorway roadworks and settle down for an evening of coned-off torture.

'Sorry about the secrecy, sport,' said the Chinaman, sounding like Dame Edna and looking like Madame Mao. 'But I'm having a spot of bother with the Tongs who are trying to run sweets on to my territory. They're after me. And I don't want to get picked up by the sugar Tongs. Now I gather you need some loot, sport. In the words of the good shepherd, don't let's beat around the bush; how much?'

Mr Big took a big breath. 'Three-quarters of a million.'

'What, you want to buy a flat in Peckham?'

'No, it's in the nature of an investment.'

'What sort of investment?'

'I'm afraid I'm unable to indulge that at the moment, Chinaman.'

Rupert whispered in Mr Big's ear. '*Divulge* that at the moment.'

'And when would I get this two million back?'

Mr Big said, 'Who said anything about two million?'

'I did. I have to put on a handling charge. I have overheads. Though to you anything over four feet is an overhead. No offence, short, I mean, sport. When would I get my money back?'

'January,' said Mr Big, somewhat ruffled by the size references. 'Trust me.'

'Mr Big, I can't trust you. That's why I'm lending you the money. If you were a man who could be trusted you'd be going to the Abbey National and not creeping out to the crawler lane on the M25 in the middle of the night.'

There was a tap on the rear of the van. The Chinaman opened the door. It was the Chinese waiter, who gabbled something in Chinese. The Chinaman turned to Mr Big.

'I think you'd better be on your way, sport. It seems the law is taking an interest in our presence.'

'I can't believe it,' said Glory B, studying a digital toothbrush. 'The Limeys are actually buying this shit kicking stuff. If sales continue like they are, this damn store will make megabucks and the whole kit and caboodle will end up in the hands of Dunnet and that overdressed bible thumper.'

Kelsey did not know whether to be delighted or dismayed. His cherished merchandise was appreciated by people at last. For the first time in his life he was successful and yet doomed to failure.

'I can't understand it,' said Jake. 'One minute the stuff's being avoided like anthrax and the next minute it's selling like earplugs at a Meat Loaf concert.' At which point Miss Marchmont entered the room followed by the ever-hungry Watson. She gave Kelsey a shy glance and sat herself down in a chair facing everybody. Watson lay down at her feet, one part devotion and nine parts exhaustion.

Kelsey looked wistfully into Judith's eyes, the spell only broken by Gloria's dissatisfaction at the present situation.

'Don't you think it's strange, Miss Marchmont, that after nearly a month's inactivity the store suddenly bursts into life again?'

'An interesting phenomenon,' Miss Marchmont replied and taking the pipe out of her pocket started to inhale the office air. 'You may be interested in some investigations I have conducted on behalf of the store.'

'Carry on,' said Gloria, leaning slightly closer.

'Well,' continued Miss Marchmont, 'over several days, I have noticed on careful observation of the customers, more than an unusual amount of repeat persons. It would appear that customers are visiting us on a regular basis and purchasing the same extremely unusual items that they had purchased only three or four days before that. I took it upon myself, and Watson of course,' Miss Marchmont petted her faithful companion who raised his head in anticipation of some titbit or morsel, only to be disappointed, 'to follow these customers. Pure instinct of course. Where do you think they all ended up?'

Kelsey looked at Jake who looked at Gloria.

'In a mental institution?' asked Jake.

'Not quite, although there are similarities. A market research company situated in Holborn.'

'All the people you followed ended up at this market research bureau?' said Gloria.

'Not quite,' said Miss Marchmont, enjoying the mystery she was creating. 'Some others went to another market research bureau situated in Paddington, yet others ended up in New Cavendish Square at a similar company.'

'Mmmm . . .' said Gloria, 'the rat is beginning to stench right up my nostrils.'

'In my opinion,' ventured Miss Marchmont, 'the goods in this store are being purchased not for people's personal use, but for some other means, the reason for which I can only guess. My instincts tell me it's something to do with Dunnet and the Bishop.'

Gloria thought long and hard. 'We are dealing with something here bigger than Dunnet and the Bishop. Miss Marchmont, how about earning some overtime, and following a certain man of the Church to discover what he might be up to?'

Judith patted Watson on the head. 'We'd be delighted, wouldn't we, Watson?'

* * *

Miss Marchmont sucked on her dummy pipe, her mind in turmoil beneath her deerstalker. The whole thing was looking deeply suspicious but neither she nor the Americans could quite work out exactly what was going on. Dunnet and the Bishop were both in Dunnet's office again. Urgent mumbles were emerging from within, indicating a heated discussion. Miss Marchmont couldn't for the life of her decide which of the two to follow.

Of course! That was it! Her knowledge of Holmes gave her a brilliant idea. She must do what Sherlock had done in *The Sign of Four,* and Stapleton had done in *The Hound of the Baskervilles.* She must get a dog to do her following for her. While she trailed the Bishop, Watson would trail Dunnet.

She bent down to inform Watson of this important new role he would be playing. Watson seemed singularly unimpressed, and keeled over to sleep, his rolls of fat coiling themselves round his rump as he flopped to the floor of the darkened store.

'Get up, Watson!' hissed Miss Marchmont, as the recumbent animal began his wheezy snoring. 'You've got important work to do.'

She thought quickly. If a dog was to follow a man, then it needed first to be given the scent to follow. Therefore, she had to find some article which would give Eric Dunnet's scent to Watson. She shuddered at the thought of what article would have Eric Dunnet's scent on it. Some item of clothing, perhaps?

Eric and the Bishop left the office and began to make their way downstairs. Miss Marchmont dashed in, and switched on the light. There must be something in here that would give Watson, the magnificent sleuth-hound, the smell of Dunnet to follow. She searched for a jacket, or a jumper he'd maybe thrown off in a hurry during some amorous conquest one lunchtime with one of the old dears from the millinery department. There was none to be seen. Then she noticed a shoe, lying near the desk. Ideal! One of Eric's shoes. That should do. Seizing the shoe, she thrust it under Watson's nose, and he promptly dribbled all over it. She waved it about under the poor, bewildered creature's olfactory orifices for a good ten seconds, then she hissed 'Go!'

Watson, sensing vaguely what he was supposed to do, picked up the scent and scuttled out of the office as fast as his fat little limbs would carry him. Miss Marchmont beamed. Good old Watson! He knew his job! Dunnet couldn't escape her now. He was being tracked by the most tenacious tracker dog in London, who would seek him out whatever sordid destination he had . . .

Her train of thought was rudely interrupted when she noticed that Watson had headed off in completely the wrong direction. He had gone up the stairs, whereas Dunnet had gone down. She looked puzzled, then re-examined the shoe. It was obviously very new . . . in fact, extremely new. It also had no heel. Oh dear, she thought.

More haste less speed. This wasn't Eric's shoe after all. It had obviously been brought to the manager's office in response to a complaint by a customer. In which case, the scent of the shoe could only lead back upstairs to the footwear department.

At that second, there came from upstairs a huge, rumbling crash. Miss Marchmont started and raced up there. The sales floor was in darkness and she groped for the light switch. When illuminated, the scene was a terrible one. Watson, hot on the scent of the shoe, had raced into the shoe department in complete darkness, crashed straight into a large display of shoes and brought the whole lot down on top of him. In the middle of the floor was a vast pile of shoes. Sticking out at the bottom was the tip of Watson's tail.

Miss Marchmont was distressed. Her faithful hound was buried under this mountain of shoes. She scrabbled away, hurling all manner of footwear hither and yon until eventually, at the bottom of the heap, she found the prostrate, concussed form of Watson. He was out cold. Miss Marchmont hesitated. Dunnet and the Bishop would be getting away, but she couldn't leave poor Watson like this. She ran back to Eric's office and phoned for the vet.

The vet arrived promptly. He had met Miss Marchmont before. The last time his services had been required had been an occasion on which Watson was choking to death after Miss Marchmont had tried to teach him to smoke a pipe. Given this case history, he didn't bat an eyelid when Miss Marchmont explained to him that the dog was suffering from concussion sustained by the caving-in of a whole rack of shoes. He took the comatose Watson off to his surgery, and Miss Marchmont was free to get back to more urgent matters.

As it happened, luck was on her side. The ramifications of the junk-buying were so great that Eric and the Bishop had carried on discussing final details of their plan outside the store. They had made their way round to the car park, thus avoiding seeing the 'Vet On Call' car which arrived at the front. Miss Marchmont, adrenalin coursing through every fibre of her body, crouched behind a large crate in the yard as Dunnet and the Bishop exchanged their parting words.

'Don't forget,' Dunnet was saying. 'For God's sake, stress that it's *working*, or I'll end up on the demolition ball again.'

'Of course,' replied the Bishop. 'I'll go and apprise you-know-who of the situation.'

Miss Marchmont clicked her fingers silently. It was obvious that the Bishop and Dunnet were up to something odd. She peered round the crate. To her astonishment, the Bishop was removing his dog collar, and replacing it with another dog collar of a rather different variety. Surely he wasn't in the habit of ascending into the pulpit with a spiked leather choker round his neck! Curiouser and curiouser, reflected Miss Marchmont.

Eric got into his Jaguar and drove off. The

sleek, luxurious car was dented and scratched all over. Eric had previously driven an old Austin Allegro and the handling of a 4.2 litre sports car was still slightly beyond him. The Bishop, on the other hand, drove his Daimler expertly out through the narrow gates and headed towards the main road. Miss Marchmont didn't hesitate for a second. This would have been the point where Sherlock would have leapt into a hansom, and the driver would have whipped up the horses and sped after the fleeing wrongdoer. She rushed round to Kensington High Street and sought the twentieth-century equivalent. A black cab pulled over and the driver's window came down.

'Follow that car!' ordered Miss Marchmont.

'What is this, bleedin' Starsky and Hutch?' replied the helpful cab driver.

'That dark blue Daimler,' went on Miss Marchmont. 'Stick to it like glue.'

'Stick to it your bleedin' self,' said the cabbie. 'Where d'you want to go?'

'I don't want to go anywhere, but I could suggest a very interesting place for *you* to go,' said Miss Marchmont with dignity, and raced away in search of another cab. By the time she'd flagged one down the blue Daimler was almost out of sight at the traffic lights way down the road. The second driver, however, proved more compliant to the wishes of his fare, and sped off down the street, weaving in and out of traffic and jumping lights whilst simultaneously giving Miss Marchmont a cheery lecture about the shortcomings of the government's economic policy.

'You see, what they don't understand is that investment capital is going abroad and . . . Bloody hell, what's his game? . . . Anyway, once North Sea oil runs out the balance of payments deficit will . . . Strike a light, what are you playing at!? . . .' He shot past Knightsbridge and took Hyde Park Corner on two wheels. The episcopal Daimler was headed towards Piccadilly. It dived off to the left just past the Ritz, heading up into Mayfair. The taxi followed. Missing a red light, they carried on just in time to see the Daimler edging into a parking space recently vacated by a Metro. The Bishop's driving skills were evidently formidable.

'Drop me here,' instructed Miss Marchmont, handing the driver some money. He looked rather crestfallen. He'd been quite enjoying himself. Miss Marchmont hid in a shop doorway as the Bishop locked his car, looked about him furtively, and began to walk briskly up the street. At a discreet distance, Marchmont followed. The Bishop's course was strange. He ducked down narrow mews, through alleyways, and along back streets. Finally, with a glance over his shoulder, he headed through a doorway and into what seemed a rather seedy-looking club.

Miss Marchmont glanced up the street. She was sure she recognized one of the large cars parked nearby, but she couldn't quite place it. Somehow, evidently, she had to get into this club and find out what on earth a Bishop was doing going there.

It didn't look like the kind of place a woman could easily get into. Not unless she were some bimbo, on the arm of a rich company director. She looked around for a rich company director, but none was to hand. Reading the notice concerning the Exotic Dancing, she removed her deerstalker and cape, and hid them in a cranny behind a shop doorway. She then marched boldly across the street and up to the doorman, who stopped her with an arm the size of a sewage pipe.

'Where d'you think you're going?'

Miss Marchmont looked at him, straight in the eye.

'I am Olga Volga, the new exotic dancer from Vladivostok,' she breathed, huskily. 'Tonight is my first night. I show you all how we dance in Roooosia.' She wiggled herself, a trifle unconvincingly. It convinced the doorman however.

'Russian, eh?' he said. 'Ain't had any Russian dancers here before. We had a Hungarian, but she actually came from Barnet. In you go.'

'Thank you, handsome Englishman,' said Miss Marchmont, with a suitably Slavonic pout, and descended down the stairs into the club.

As she pushed open the door, an astonishing sight met her eye. The Bishop was in the room, and his dog collar had now been connected to a dog lead, the other end of which was firmly gripped by a woman in fishnet tights and high-heeled leather boots. This, thought Miss

Marchmont, is definitely not standard Church of England ritual.

A suspicious-looking waitress, who appeared to be only wearing half her clothes, approached Marchmont.

'Who are you?' asked the waitress.

'Olga Volga, Rooosian dancer,' replied Marchmont.

'Oh, fine,' said the waitress. 'Sometimes they send policewomen down here in disguise, that's all.'

'That's bad,' said Marchmont. 'They find evidence, yes?

'Not that so much,' went on the waitress, 'as the fact is they might recognize their chief constable. Anyway, go through – the dressing room's in there.'

Marchmont was motioned towards a doorway, hidden by a shabby curtain. She took one last glance around her. Extremely bizarre things were going on, mostly involving women in strange clothing with pieces of fruit. A large number of affluent-looking men were being fed sausages and baked beans from large spoons and several of them were having their hands smacked with rulers. One middle-aged gent – who Miss Marchmont was sure she recognized from a TV programme about gardening – was having yoghurt massaged into his stomach by a woman dressed as Boadicea.

Marchmont went behind the curtain. She was in a narrow corridor. At the end of it was a half-open door, behind which women in various strange costumes were moving about. That, presumably, was the dressing room. Next to her was a flight of stairs leading upwards. She began to ascend when she was stopped in her tracks by the sound of three people coming down the other way. She flattened herself against the wall at the bottom of the stairs and three men went past her. One was very small, one was extremely large and the other was whining about how few of the population knew the correct use of the apostrophe in the word 'its'.

She waited with baited breath. A few seconds later, the three men returned, this time with the Bishop. He followed them back up the stairs. The four figures went into a room off the landing at the top and shut the door. Miss Marchmont placed her ear against the old-peeling-painted surface and caught the words 'Dunnet', 'Isle of Dogs', and 'American junk', and then raucous laughter. The door opened and a noticeably happier-looking Bishop came out and headed back downstairs to join in the fun. The small man shouted after him, 'You'd better be right. Otherwise these little snaps might well end up on the editor's desk at the seamiest newspaper we can think of.'

Marchmont barely dared breathe. The three men returned to the room. The small one tossed the pictures on to a table and then they left, locking the door behind them, and headed off downstairs to watch the cabaret.

Marchmont rushed over and examined the door lock. It was an old type, one she had learned to pick at prep school. It was the same as the one on the tuck-shop door. Taking a hairgrip from her neatly combed head, she deftly manipulated the lock until the door clicked open. She dashed in, and looked at the photos which had been left on the table. As soon as she saw them, she realized she had to get them to Kelsey fast. She thrust them into her pocket and headed back down the stairs and into the club, up the stairs on the other side and back out the way she'd come.

'You done your act already?' said the doorman. 'That was a quick dance.'

'Russian girls do it fast,' said Miss Marchmont, in her best Estonian accent.

The doorman swallowed, and motioned her off into the night.

Marchmont's mind was in a whirl. She collected her deerstalker and cape from where she had left them and tried to get her thoughts in order. Surely Kelsey would be pleased with her for this. She quickly found a cab and headed off for Kelsey's flat in order to discuss the night's events with him, and also admire his Basil Rathbone profile. In the taxi, she began to think it through logically. There was a clear connection between Eric and the strange dwarf. The connection was clearly the Bishop. In her pocket she held evidence that could get the Bishop instantly defrocked, even in the modern Church of England.

Her mind whirled furiously. She couldn't think straight, and the reason was all too clear. She was used to consulting Watson on these occasions. Normally, Watson would frowst in front of the fire with his nose in a bowl of Pedigree Chum while she rehearsed her arguments to him, in the manner of her hero. Many a time, she had caught some unsuspecting gang of shoplifters after a good think-through in the company of her faithful mutt. Talking through a case out loud helped her to think straight, there was no doubt about it. And Watson was a good listener. Sometimes he would growl or make odd rumbling noises, which usually indicated that he agreed with his mistress' hypothesis.

Now Miss Marchmont needed Watson more than ever, but he wasn't there. He was at the vets, being brought round from a state of unconsciousness inflicted on him by an avalanche of shoes. Miss Marchmont paced up and down Piccadilly, trying desperately to think straight, but it was no good. She had to talk to Watson.

She found a public telephone at Green Park tube station, but on picking up the receiver, she was informed that it was '999 calls only'. The next two phones she found also had the same message. The third had no message at all, and also no receiver. Finally, the fourth box she found (by this time she was almost at Marble Arch) was in full working order. For this reason, there was a queue of five people waiting to use it.

The present occupant of the phone booth was a German youth who appeared to be phoning home to his girlfriend. It was an interminable call, and the youth appeared totally oblivious to the seething queue of would-be contributors to Telecom's enormous profits who were waiting outside the booth. The two young German love-birds prattled on and on and on. The youth seemed to have an inexhaustible supply of coins, which he fed continually into the machine to sustain his marathon conversation. Finally the man at the front of the queue leaned forward and with the tact and politeness so beloved of the British, intimated that perhaps the young Germans ought to consider the ramifications of making such a call from a public callbox.

'Get a move on, you bleedin' Kraut, there's other people waiting to use this phone, you know.'

The young man smiled amiably and fed another pound coin into the machine. Evidently he had another few minutes of sweet nothings to say to his *liebchen* in Lenz before acceding to the request. By now the queue was stretching half-way towards Oxford Street and Miss Marchmont was losing patience.

The young German fed in another three pound coins and lit a cigarette. For all anyone knew he was about to start reciting an entire Goethe play. Miss Marchmont snapped and walked firmly to the front of the queue. Seizing the startled young man she thrust him out of the booth, shouting *'Raus! Raus! Schnell, dummkopf!!'* The rest of the queue burst into applause, and Miss Marchmont strode boldly into the booth, picked up the receiver and dialled the number of the vet.

Dr Harrison came to the phone the other end and assured Miss Marchmont that Watson was all right. He had sustained concussion, but had been protected from any severe injury by the enormous layer of blubber around his body. He was sleeping now.

'Wake him up,' ordered Miss Marchmont. 'I've got to talk to him.'

'Talk to him?'

'Yes.'

In her excitement, Miss Marchmont was talking loudly, and the rest of the queue was craning forward, fascinated by what was evidently quite a drama.

'I don't care if he's asleep,' the woman in the booth was saying. 'I need to speak to him now. I've got things to say I can only say to him.'

The people in the queue looked at each other. Evidently, these were exactly the sort of things which they wanted to hear themselves.

There was a short pause, then Miss Marchmont said, 'I know we can't. I've tried to train him to hold a phone, but he can't manage it.'

The people in the queue exchanged glances. Evidently, she needed to talk urgently to an acquaintance who was either educationally deficient or singularly lacking in dexterity.

'What you'll have to do,' went on Miss Marchmont, 'is strap the receiver to his ear.'

The jaws of the queuers dropped.

'He usually lets you if you tickle his tummy first.'

By this time, the rest of the queue was shuffling forward to hear better. What on earth was this attractive young lady in a deerstalker hat doing in such a close relationship with a pervert who couldn't learn how to hold a phone?

'It didn't work?' said Marchmont. 'In that case, slip his collar on and tie him down.'

Broad grins broke out. This was making the *News of the World* look like a church newsletter.

'Speak up,' came a cry from the back of the queue.

'Have you got the phone to his ear? Good. You didn't hurt him, did you? I can hear him whimpering.'

Jaws hit the ground.

At the vet, Dr Harrison had succeeded in sellotaping the phone receiver to Watson's podgy ear. Watson looked as puzzled as any bulldog who has crashed into a rack of shoes, woken up in a vet's surgery, had a nice kip and been rudely awoken only to have a piece of communications equipment sellotaped to his ear.

'Can you hear me, Watson?' said Miss Marchmont.

Watson recognized the voice of his mistress, and barked joyfully. It was a loud bark, and at the other end of the line, Miss Marchmont had to move the phone further from her ear. The sound of the bark carried quite a long way, such was its volume.

'He's barking like a dog,' whispered the queuers to each other. 'It's a real Cynthia Payne job, this one.'

'Listen to me, Watson,' said Miss Marchmont, her voice still far too loud in her excitement. 'I've got photographs of the Bishop.'

This news was relayed down the queue. Somehow, it didn't seem to come as too much of a surprise.

'Dunnet, the Bishop and this strange dwarf person must be in cahoots about something. What shall I do with the photographs, Watson?'

Watson made a few noises, probably indicating that he'd rather go back to sleep.

'. . . Ah-ha! Brilliant, Watson, of course. I've got to get these photographs to Kelsey. But as soon as the dwarf realizes they've gone missing, he'll know that the Bishop is vulnerable. If someone else has got them they could expose him at any time. Therefore, what I've got to do is get these photos copied, and then somehow get them back into the club in such a way that he doesn't suspect they've ever gone missing. Brilliant! Thank you, Watson! You can go back to sleep now!' As the pips went, Miss Marchmont slammed down the phone and raced off to find a taxi to take her to Kelsey's. The people waiting to use the phone stared at her departure in open-mouthed astonishment.

'I think you might be very interested in these,' said Miss Marchmont to Kelsey and Gloria. 'I found them in Mr Big's club.'

She handed out the polaroids. Gloria let out a long, slow whistle.

'Looks like we got ourselves one very silly

Bishop,' she said. 'He really should have thought twice before allowing any women to tie one of those round that. These photographs can get the guy unfrocked faster than you can say Jimmy Swaggart. Whatever this Bishop is up to, we've got a very big lever on him.'

'So, presumably, has someone else – the people who took these,' said Miss Marchmont. 'But I've got an idea . . .'

At the club the next day, a distraught Mr Big was berating his henchmen for the loss of the photographs. Mangle and Rupert were both puzzled. The snaps had been locked in the room the night before. How on earth had they gone missing?

At this point, Mrs Graystone, who had cleaned the club for the previous eight years and who was known to everybody there, hobbled into the room with her ancient vacuum cleaner in tow. In her hand she held a small bundle of photographs.

'I do beg your pardon,' she said to Mr Big. 'Please forgive me, but earlier this mornin' I accidentally put these in with the rubbish. Came in a bit early today you see. Here you are . . . I'm a bit dizzy in the morning.'

'These were still on the table this morning?' said Mr Big.

'Yes, yes.'

'And you thought they were rubbish? No one else has seen them?'

'They were upside-down. I didn't see they was photographs till I emptied the bag out.'

Mr Big jumped up in the air just high enough to kiss the underside of Mrs Graystone's chin.

'Thank you,' he said. 'It's nice to see a bit of honesty round here.'

Mrs Graystone smiled. Mr Big's remark was ironic in a way. Still, if that nice young lady had been prepared to pay her £500 to tell that story to Mr Big, who was she to argue? She went about her vacuuming with a merry whistle for the rest of the morning.

Meanwhile, Miss Marchmont, having successfully bribed the cleaner to return the originals, had had copies of the incriminating photos made by Printz-R-Us. She had got some very funny looks from the staff when they'd handed them over. She'd had to explain, in a rather embarrassed fashion, that they'd been taken at rehearsals for her amateur dramatic society's rather unusual production of *Macbeth*. But that was all in the past now. She'd got the evidence. She'd impressed Kelsey. Happily, she sucked her best pipe and trotted off to the supermarket to buy some biscuits for the convalescing Watson.

Glory B took a break from shaking off the dogs and the flashers on her regular evening run round Battersea to watch some builders defurbishing an early Victorian, four-storied flat-fronted house. It was the construction industry's version of a D and C — everything was being taken out. The builders had come to know Glory B. Not by name. More by "Allo darlin' — fancy a swing on my scaffold?', 'Cor look at the bot'ull

on that' and 'That's prime, that is. Prime.'
'Double prime.' Tonight they were removing
fireplaces, which unlike the lavatories which
were hurled with such accurate abandon from
the highest of floors to the waiting skips below,
were being carefully loaded on to the back of
a lorry by a young man in jeans and a Turnbull
and Asser checked shirt. Gloria had long coveted
an old fireplace.

'Hey,' she called out, 'do you think I could
have one of those, if you're throwing them
away?'

'We're not throwing them away, I'm afraid,'
said the young man in a voice that owed more
to Eton and the Guards than a City and Guilds
at Catford Poly. 'These are worth a fortune.'

'Who buys them?' asked Glory B.

'Oh, people who moved into converted flats
in old houses where the builders took all the
original fireplaces out.'

'You mean like you're doing at the moment.'

'Well, I suppose so, yes.'

'But that's crazy,' said Glory B.

'No,' said the young man, 'that's business.'

Glory B's pager sounded. Like most over-
achievers, she found it impossible to be completely out of touch. She had only her pager,
but some guys, she'd noticed, were now jogging
with a portable phone, a personal computer, and
one guy who did the Embankment ran with
a fax machine on his back. He still hadn't
mastered how to receive and run at the same
time – but he'd got Hitachi working on it, he'd

told Glory B between conference calls. Her message service wanted her to call Don Ferrari.

The old boy was in his bath playing with the heat-seeking soap Glory B had sent him for his birthday. It was one of Kelsey's better junk purchases. The makers claimed it was now impossible to lose the soap in the bath. It was also impossible to put the soap anywhere *near* the bath without it diving back into the water and searching out the hottest spot available. An Israeli sergeant sat at the other end of the bath pretending to be an iceberg – they were playing a game of Ice Station Zebra. She handed Don Ferrari the lobster-shaped designer phone. Don Ferrari was never sure which claw to speak into. 'Who is this?' he said. When he heard Glory B's voice his old villain's heart beat a little faster – though he'd forgotten why it did that – and he dropped the soap, which immediately stabilized itself under the surface and set off to attack the Israeli in the Negev. 'I'm glad you called, clam lady. I have news for you about your Mr Deadnut. I have this friend in London. And this friend tells me that your Mr Deenote is a deeply nefarious individual who is seriously involved in a scam to relieve a group of visiting Americans of a large sum of money.'

Gloria exploded. 'He's what! I'll have that mother's tads for doorstops. What's the scam, what's going down?'

'Calm, clam lady, calm. It seems your man runs a shop called the Wasps' Nest.'

'The Beehive,' corrected Gloria.

'Right, the Beehive. Good name for a sting. Anyway this Behave is one funny shop, I'm telling you. It's the only shop in the world that isn't allowed to make a profit.'

'Wait a minute,' Gloria interrupted. 'Run that past me again. The Beehive can't make a profit?'

'That's what I said, clam lady.'

'Holy shit,' said Gloria. 'This is Peck's doing. I *know* it. Does your friend know what happens if the store makes a profit?'

'You're not gonna believe this,' said the old man.

'I'll believe, I'll believe it,' murmured Gloria.

'If it makes a profit, it all goes to some church.'

'What!' Gloria exploded again. She was going off more times than a firework at Chinese New Year. 'All the profit goes to some crummy church?'

'Not just the profit, pretty clam lady, the whole shebang – the store, the building, the woiks. Crazy, eh? Some one-hundred-year-old law or something. I thought you'd like to know.'

'You bet I like to know. But why would anybody want the Beehive to go to a church?'

'This is the good part,' said the old man. 'The man handling the deal for the church is not a good person. He is a bishop whose sexual appetites would disgrace a politician, never mind a man of God. And because of this certain people have, you should forgive the expression, a hold on him. So when the church takes possession of the Beehold on Jany 1—'

'When?' shouted Gloria.

'—Jany 1, then it will be sold to a small-time London hood called Mr Big for millions of English francs.'

Gloria said, 'Pounds.'

'Okay, for pounds of English francs. Anyway your shop is going to be sold from under you.'

'What a schmuck. And what did you say was going to happen to the profits?'

'According to what my friend hears they will be – what was the word he used – redistributed.'

'In a pig's ass they'll be redistributed. Don Ferrari, I love you. I'll always be in your debt.'

'Glad to hear it,' said Don Ferrari, watching the nine-tenths of iceberg who was now lifting herself out of the bath, 'and as to the debt just bring me some clams and hot sauce and we'll call it quits. Just one thing – my friend in London does not know I'm telling you all this. *Capice?*'

'*Capice,* Don Ferrari.'

21

It had been a while since Gloria B had not had a good night's sleep. Insomnia was not something she was accustomed to, but try as she might she could not get her mind off Don Ferrari's latest telephone call. The long-term prospects were not good for her client and good friend Kelsey. It would be hard breaking the news to him.

The doorbell jolted her out of her thoughts and she crossed the room to answer the door. It was Kelsey and Jake, late as usual. 'Come on in, boys, we have some serious talking to do.'

'Hi Gloria, you OK?' enquired Jake. 'You look as if you've spent most of the night wrestling with Robert Redford.'

'Well thanks Jake, I love you too.'

'So what's the serious bit, Gloria?' asked Kelsey, flopping down in one of the apartment's larger chairs.

'I've been talking to Don Ferrari and the news is not so good,' said Gloria. She sat down next to Kelsey and held his hand.

'What's happened, the mafia have pulled out

of the presidential race?' asked Kelsey in mock horror.

'Both of you cut the sharp lines and listen good,' said Gloria. She then spent the next few minutes giving her client and his friend a breakdown on the information Don Ferrari had passed on to her.

At the finish Kelsey was very silent. A barge making its way down the Thames tooted loudly. The sound broke the concentration in the fourth-floor apartment.

'Can you believe it?' queried Kelsey. 'For once in my life I'm up and then, whammo! back to earth like a penguin without a parachute. What you're telling me is the store can't make a profit because some bible thumping zealot a squillion years ago had a hang-up about getting rich. Are you sure there's no way round it, Gloria?'

'I was on the phone to Peck at the solicitor's for a good two hours yesterday. He's adamant about it, it's one of the original conditions and can't be changed. Besides he hates Americans more than Texans do. Don't expect any help from him. What you've got to ask yourself, Kelsey, is how much do you want to own a store that can't make bagel money. All you'll ever get from the dump now is a "living wage". You might as well shine Hush Puppies in Grand Central!'

'So what's our options, lady with the glad tiding?' Jake was almost as glum as Kelsey.

'Can't say we've got many, but for what it's worth, here are my ideas,' offered Gloria.

The boys looked interested.

'The year ending for the store's accounts is 31 December. Now, if there's a profit showing in the books at that time, according to Peck his company steps in, takes over and starts proceedings to transfer the store to the Church.'

'Unbelievable,' said Jake.

Gloria continued. 'Now when the store gets into the Church's hands, guess who's dealing for the Christians?!'

'The Bishop?' said Kelsey.

'Right!' said Gloria.

'So *that's* what it's all about,' said Jake.

'Not only that but – and don't take this to heart, Kelsey,' said Gloria, trying to soften the blow, 'that's the reason why the junk is selling like it is. Apparently someone called the Chinaman is financing this Mr Big character who's gone out on a limb to buy the stuff to keep the deal going through.'

Kelsey hit the earth again. The *thought* of all his wonderful junk being bought for no purpose except a devious one!

'Still, before you get too downhearted, gents, there's still a chance we can make a few bucks. We've got ten weeks left before the year's end. I suggest, Kelsey, we bring in extra loads of your gaudy goods for the Christmas period and get Dunnet and his cronies to stump up more cash. If we time it right we can withdraw the money at the last minute and skedaddle to the homeland.'

'What do you think we'll make?' asked Jake.

'With what we've got already and from the figures that the Don mentioned . . . Possibly two million bucks.'

The boys brightened up a bit.

'That's not to be sneezed at,' said Kelsey.

'Not unless you intend to buy cocaine,' said Jake. 'But tell me, won't they know that we know about the non-profit clause now? I mean, won't this Peck fellow tell them we've found out?'

'You're smart, Jake,' complimented Gloria, 'but I'm ahead of you. By not telling us Peck committed a serious breach of professional cti-quette. If he so much as breathes anything I've told him to anyone I'll have his epiglottis for meat balls.'

'Can't we do something about those rat finks getting their hands on the store?' said Kelsey. 'I'm no Joan of Arc but I'd hate to think the Church would lose out to these lousy limeys.'

'Oh, I think I can arrange something eventually,' said Gloria confidently, 'in fact I think I'll enjoy that almost as much as making the money. Kelsey, pass the polaroid of the Bishop performing his episcopal duties.'

'Strewth,' said the Chinaman. 'Look at this, sport.'

His confederates looked. The Chinaman was holding up a selection of newspapers with assorted headlines, all conveying the same general gist. SPANKING BISHOP DEFROCKED read one. C OF E BOSS KO'S SEX BISH said the *Sun*.

BISHOP OF LAMBETH IN MAJOR MISDE-
MEANOUR CONTROVERSY was another.

'You realize what this means? I have been
lending my money to a trio of men who have
now been reduced to a duo. And sadly, the duo
now lack the one man who held the key to getting my money back. All is not dinkum.'

The Chinaman pondered for a few moments.
Pondering was difficult – space was severely
limited. He was currently situated in a trackside
hut next to the London-Brighton main line just
north of East Croydon. It was another of his
conveniently out-of-the-way venues for shady
activities.

'This only proves, cobbers, don't mix with
small-fry. If you deal with proper criminals you
don't get this trouble. Harry the Horse or Large
Leonard never gave us this aggro. But I'm afraid
these small-time operators like Mr Big are mere
wallabies up the gum tree of gangland.'

With that, the Chinaman, who obviously felt
he was a far bigger marsupial, picked up his
Vodaphone.

'Get me the Hare Krishnas,' he said. 'They
can do me a nice little double-assignment.'

The Paradise Industrial Estate was situated on
the outskirts of Streatham and was a large area
of land dedicated to warehouses and workshops
built mostly with government grants and tax-
efficient monies supplied by the higher-band tax
payers of the early 1980s.

Warehouse number seven was now on lease

to the Beehive to store the ever-increasing amounts of products purchased by Kelsey in his halcyon buying days in America.

Jake arrived outside warehouse seven in an old MGB Roadster he had hired from a London company called Rent-a-Crate. He had every intention of buying the car and shipping it to America, where he felt certain that with a little bit of attention and one or two innovative technical gismos it would make a perfectly good lawnmower.

He walked agitatedly up and down the front of the warehouse awaiting Kelsey. In his hands he had the keys, but refrained from opening the doors until the arrival of Kelsey.

He had not long to wait. Kelsey came screaming round the corner on a Vespa 125 scooter he had purchased off a mod whilst trying to sell him a portable parka cleaner. Kelsey pulled up, breathless and obviously very proud of his latest purchase. Before he could enthuse about this piece of Italian transport, Jake hauled him by the arm to the door of the warehouse.

'Kelsey, we could be in real trouble.'

'What now? I know the scooter's not insured but Gloria's seeing to that this very minute. By the time we have finished here I will be fully . . .'

'Shut up,' said Jake, 'and get inside.'

With that he unlocked the door and ushered Kelsey in.

'What's the matter?' said Kelsey.

'I will show you what's the matter,' said Jake. 'Come here.'

'OK, what's this?'

Jake was pointing to fifty cartons stacked on the shelves in the middle of the warehouse.

'Well,' said Kelsey, studying the outside of the cartons, 'let me think.'

The lettering on the boxes stated 'Product of the San Fernando Hippie Commune.'

'Ah yes,' said Kelsey, 'it's chewing gum.'

'That I know,' said Jake, 'but what sort of chewing gum?'

'Well, it's just chewing gum,' said Kelsey 'I saw it advertised in a magazine called *Zen And The Art Of Mail Order*. There was a big advert for this chewing gum, it's called if I remember rightly "Acapulco Gold Flavour", there was a discount of a third if you bought two gross.'

'Kelsey, there are times when I wonder what planet you're from,' said Jake, ripping open one of the cartons. 'Do you know what you've bought, do you *know* what you've bought?'

'Chewing gum,' said Kelsey, shrugging his shoulders.

'Yes, Kelsey, marijuana chewing gum. This stuff is impregnated with so much marijuana you could get the entire London Stock Exchange on such a high it would make Lloyds shares appear at sea level.'

Kelsey blinked; in fact, he blinked a lot.

'I've tried this stuff, Kelsey, it's dynamite – have you tried it?'

Kelsey shook his head. 'Can't stand chewing gum, but if that's the case give me a packet.'

'No chance,' said Jake, 'this is London, England,

not California. If the police find this our feet won't touch the floor until we hit Dartmoor; in fact if the police find this their feet won't touch the floor either. We've got to get rid of it.'

'How?' said Kelsey.

'Somehow I have got to find a way of dumping it so no one will know. Until then, I have an idea. We can't just leave this stuff sat here, someone's bound to want to know what it is and we can't take the chance. Here's what we do.'

With that he led Kelsey over to a section of the warehouse that was handling specific goods for the Christmas period.

The main bulk of the area was taken up with the grotto presents. Each year the Beehive would have a Christmas grotto. Its theme would be a fairy tale or Christmas story. Children would pay a fee, choose a gift and walk through the grotto to meet Father Christmas.

This year, the majority of gifts would consist of cheap plastic toy cars, trains, small dolls, and pen and pencil sets that Kelsey had bought job-lots of. They were remnants of promotions by breakfast cereal manufacturers and Kelsey had acquired them several years previously through a magazine that dealt with such goods. Each gift would be sealed in a blue carton for boys, or a pink carton for girls.

It was these cartons that were the key to Jake's idea.

'We will pack these cartons with chewing gum, stack them away from the others and then no one will be inquisitive as to what this stuff is.

Then when I find a suitable site, we'll incinerate the lot and destroy the evidence.'

Kelsey was impressed. 'Great, Jake, it's just a shame we can't sell the stuff. It would be worth a fortune out there on the streets.'

'Listen, Kelsey, unless you want to be eating porridge for the next ten years put that idea right out of your head. Right, we have got work to do. Start packing.'

22

The Saturday before Christmas is regarded in
the retail trade as pay day, the one day
guaranteed that every store and retail establishment in London is packed to the gunwales with
Christmas shoppers buying goods that normally
they would never even consider purchasing,
particularly at the inflated prices charged at
that time of year.

Even the Beehive with its fluctuating popularity was busy. For once, Kelsey's crazy junk
was selling in its own right. The underwater
shoe-shine kits would no doubt end up puzzling
somebody's father-in-law on Christmas morning. And what houseproud mum wouldn't
wonder how she ever got along without
biodegradable saucepans?

The haberdashery department was doing
incongruous but steady trade selling three
thousand pieces of Moses' original cradle,
guaranteed blessed by the Pope. There was a
large crowd gathering in the music section to
view the gas-operated bagpipes. No one had yet
bought a set, but the spectacle of Mr Caffey
walking, if that was the word, up and down

trying to play them had grabbed the attention of the customers. The accompanying wail of the instrument lent a compelling air to the proceedings, and the crowd only dispersed because the gas ran out.

Down in the toy department a small but consistent stream of families was queuing up to enter the grotto. On the Saturday before Christmas every grotto in London would be heaving with parents accompanying children desperate to give Father Christmas their last-minute requests for presents they would hope to receive on Christmas morning.

Busy parents in the know who wanted to avoid the rush and crowds knew that a visit to the Beehive's grotto would be over very quickly. After all, one Father Christmas was as good as another, and although the Beehive's actual grotto was more grotesque than picturesque (children had often been taken away screaming in terror), it got the annual chore of visiting Santa Claus out of the way, leaving the parents plenty of time to concentrate on their own shopping.

This year the theme of the grotto was Snow White and the Seven Dwarfs, one of the four fantasies the Beehive kept in permanent store. Every four years for as long as anyone could remember, the themes were recycled. Snow White would be followed by Pinnochio followed by Rudolph the Red-Nosed Reindeer, then Jack and the Beanstalk back to Snow White. All the figures and props for these fantasy themes were stored in an old dusty warehouse and over the years had become very dilapidated indeed. Recently, however, they had had something of a facelift. Jake had discovered them some weeks previously and been fascinated by the challenge of putting these delightful if a touch jaded figures back into service. It was while he was fixing the limbs and heads back on each respective torso, he had a brainwave as only Jake could have a brainwave. What a perfect place to hide the money when the time came! The cash from the sales of Kelsey's loony stock would soon be over a million pounds – but who would ever think of searching inside Dopey's stomach for it? A perfect plan.

Jake had set to with enthusiasm, equipping the seven dwarfs with movable arms, giving Snow White a voice box and the Wicked Queen a face that glowed green in the dark. Not all of the dwarfs were in a fit state to be reconditioned, so Jake cheated slightly and commandeered several of the characters from the other stories.

Eventually, to display all the characters and scenery a large cave was constructed. Inside the life-size figures of Snow White, her seven dwarfs, the Queen, the Prince and the good fairy stood in animated form to the sound and lights Jake had installed on a computerized system. In the background were pictures depicting the events that lead up to Snow White's demise and her eventual resurrection.

Regular visitors to the normally drab grotto

were pleasantly surprised at the quality of presentation and in particular the animation. True, there were quizzical looks at some of Jake's gerrymandering of the characters. Why Grumpy had a four-foot nose and a cricket on his shoulder no one could give any reasonable explanation, and if the Prince did arrive at the dwarves' cottage on a reindeer with a big red nose, then no visitor owned that particular published version. Still, all in all parents and children were generally impressed with the spectacle and put in a good frame of mind ready to meet Father Christmas.

The only real complaint was about the quality of gifts from the lucky dip barrel. Heaven knows one pound doesn't buy much these days but a plastic whistle shaped like a duck and with the pea missing was just not on.

The customer complaints were all directed to the head of the toy department, Mr Bevan, a strict Welsh Methodist whose two hates in life were drink and children: the former because it led to sinful ways, and the latter because they were sub-human.

Mr Bevan's patience was fast disappearing on this Saturday morning. For the umpteenth time he repaid one pound to the irate parents of a braying brat who was complaining about his wretched dip. Wretched it was, as Mr Bevan had to admit. The boy was clutching a slim plastic transparent case with a picture of Kojak pasted inside on the bottom. The case contained five little metal ballbearings, the idea being to delicately manoeuvre each ball into one of five holes in the detective's face, except that the holes were far too small for the ballbearings. The balls just swirled aimlessly round the case, and understandably the seven-year-old came to the conclusion it was just a baby's rattle. Suitably miffed, he let his parents and the rest of the customers know in no uncertain terms. Mr Bevan couldn't understand why they had to sell this junk. For years they had given out whipping tops for the girls and catapults for the boys — why change things?

In desperation he phoned down to the warehouse to see if there was anything else available for the lucky dips. The storeman who answered the phone didn't know what was in the blue and pink boxes and didn't much care, but if Mr Bevan wanted something else he'd send another load down and hope there would be something more acceptable. He loaded up five hundred each of the blue and pink boxes and sent them round to the store in time for the afternoon rush.

In her office, Glory B put the phone down a definitely worried lady. The value of the lucky dip was not the cause of the deep frown on her face. Don Ferrari had just phoned to wish her a merry Christmas, and during the seasonal greeting he enquired as to whether 'Dimwit, Dunwit, whatever, has been dealt with by his friends yet?' Not sure what he actually meant she was horrified to learn that the Don thought she 'wanted Dunnet scraped off the planet'. Informing him that was not the case, she implored him to contact his Chinaman and call off the contract on Dunnet's life. It was to no avail; the killers were on their way and there was no means of stopping them. She was hoping to find Dunnet and warn him, but Dunnet was nowhere to be found.

With good reason, he was in hiding in the storeroom at the top of the building. He knew full well the Bishop, Mr Big and his gang were on the lookout for him. They were convinced he'd blown the Bishop to the press. He'd tried to convince them that he wasn't in league with the Americans. Trouble was, they thought he'd set them up to buy the junk to share in the money. They were convinced they were victims of a sting.

If only he could get his hands on the store's profits. He'd been to the bank only three days before, and found that over one million pounds had been drawn out in cash. He told Mr Big. Mr Big had his men search all the American's apartments, but they could find nothing.

He knew the American shysters had stacked the money somewhere, but follow and track them as he may he had yet to come up with a clue as to where it was. He was sure they were hiding the money in the store. What Eric could never understand was how they paid for the junk from America when no transactions could be traced through any of the store's bank accounts. He'd known some smart people in his shady time, but these guys were good.

Time was running out. If he didn't find the cash soon the store and the Americans would be gone for ever.

With things unusually busy today, he would take the opportunity to disguise himself and have a good look round the complete floor space to see if anything could give him a clue to the secreted cash. He stuck the beard and moustache on with extra care, making sure the corners wouldn't curl up. Donning a long-haired wig along with jeans and sweatshirt would give him the appearance of a middle-aged hippie.

He peeked out of the storeroom to make sure he could slip into the sales area without anyone noticing. All clear; he walked through the furniture department to the lift. On the way he came face to face with one of the salesmen.

'Good morning, Mr Dunnet, nice to see you into the spirit of Christmas.'

Dunnet hurried by. How did he know? He stopped at the lift where Jacko was just about to descend to the ground floor.

Jacko shouted through the bars. 'Good morning, Mr Dunnet, why are you dressed up, special Christmas idea is it?'

Before Dunnet could reply Jacko had disappeared. 'This calls for a rethink,' thought Dunnet, and made his way back to the storeroom.

Down in the toy department events were taking a turn for the worse. The queue of parents waiting to complain about the lucky-dip prizes was now lengthening. Spurred on by each other and the moans of their children, they were determined to get their money back. Any parents not having time to wait to complain to Mr Bevan took it out instead on Father Christmas himself. The man in the red robe and white beard was getting thoroughly brassed off with these whining kids and whinging parents.

Gerald Dupont, an actor for nearly sixty years, had fallen upon hard times. He had reluctantly accepted the role of Father Christmas at the Beehive to supplement his meagre pension. His temperament was that of the average ex-thespian; patient until over-provoked, and then, geyser-time.

Having lost count of the number of Kojak ballbearing games shoved in his face, he told the queue to 'Bugger off!' and then buggered off himself to the pub for an early lunch. He sat in the Cross and Bowling Green, just round the corner from the store, as bitter as the ale he was now slurping. 'Bleeding Father Christmas, is this what I've come to,' he muttered.

The appearance of Santa Claus in person in the lounge of the Cross and Bowling Green quite amused the Yuppie clientele. As he sat contemplating a whole afternoon of ranting customers, Gerald gratefully accepted offers of drinks from the moneyed youngsters who were showing a rare display of generosity.

Gerald's lunch hour had stretched to two, and

he left the pub in a much better frame of mind but a much worse state of equilibrium. As he weaved his way through the Christmas traffic he paused in the middle of Kensington High Street to deliver a soliloquy on the time he played a very important walk-on part in a production of Shakespeare's *Macbeth*, presented at Norwich. Eventually he returned to his place in the grotto and started once more to receive the children.

Because of Gerald's unexpected early lunch and late return Mr Bevan had had to bring in an emergency temporary replacement. The only person in the store not busy was Hacket. Protesting that he was not the ideal person to interview children, he had been proven correct. In two hours he had managed to interview twelve youngsters and then only by singing his questions to the tune of *Camptown Races*. 'What do you want for Christmas time, doo dah, doo dah, what can I bring you Christmas morn, doo dah, doo dah, day.'

Mr Bevan had taken to cussing in Welsh to relieve the pressure he was under. Not only was he now getting complaints about the length of time the families had to wait to see Father Christmas, but the new load of lucky dip boxes contained something even worse than the load he'd taken away. Pink or blue boxes, it didn't matter — every one was filled with some ridiculous American chewing gum.

In desperation he gave each child waiting a pink or blue box and waived the one pound fee.

At least Gerald was back now and maybe common sense would reign for the rest of the day. How wrong could he be . . .

Outside the main entrance in the high street a pyschedelic Rolls-Royce squealed to a halt. From its interior stepped first the ex-Lord Bishop of Lambeth carrying a wooden cross in one hand, with the T-bar at one end sharpened; then Mangle, who, although he couldn't spell it, had excitement written across his face. He helped Mr Big out and waited for Rupert to hand him his cosh. The four of them wanted blood. Dunnet's blood. They wanted enough to paint the outside of the store red, and in their present frame of mind nothing less than a bathful would do. They entered the store through the revolving doors and started to search.

Jim the commissionaire knew better than to stop their admission, now fully aware who they were. Besides, he had more important things to deal with. Coming down the street he heard the familiar chanting and ball-jingling of the bloody Hare Krishnas. He always looked forward to dealing with these loonies. He could bully and physically attack them in the knowledge that their principles of non-violence would protect him from retaliation. As they neared the store he prepared to enjoy himself.

'Hare krishna, hare krishna, krishna krishna, hare hare!' The four brethren of the strange sect chanted their sacred mantra in union. They jingled little bells to accompany the chant. The passing shoppers gave them scant attention, used to such demonstrations.

As they reached the entrance, they turned to walk past Jim and into the store. Jim couldn't believe his luck – they actually wanted to enter *past* him.

'OK, Sunny Jims, just hold it there, where d'you think you're off to?'

The apparent leader of the four said (in a strong East End accent), 'We are here to spread the teachings of the Lord Krishna to the ladies and gentlemen of your shop. I'm sure you won't mind.'

'I certainly do mind, I'm not having four bald-headed Ghandi Pandy fans let loose in my store. Piss off!' With that Jim gave the leader a smack in the face with his hand and kicked another up the backside.

It is doubtful whether the Lord Krishna would have approved of the retaliation now being exercised on the hapless commissionaire. Jim certainly didn't. The leader had grabbed him between the legs with a grip that would have done a Black and Decker Workmate proud. As Jim screamed with pain, he bent down to relieve the agony only to meet the knee of another devotee coming up in the opposite direction. The leader spun Jim round, releasing the grip on his private parts. Relief was temporary as the leader regained his grip, only this time from behind. Jim, now bent double, nose pouring blood, was propelled forward until his head was resting against the door frame. While the leader held him fixed into position the other three set the revolving door in perpetual motion, pummelling Jim's head until he collapsed senseless into an undignified heap.

Without further ado the band of four started up their chant again and made their way over the slumped body into the store, they too in search of their contract victim.

Miss Marchmont, keeping strict surveillance at all times on the merchandise, was patrolling the ground floor with Watson in tow. She saw the Krishna devotees enter and thought it strange they had got past Jim. 'Ah well,' she said to Watson, ''Tis the season of goodwill.' Watson wasn't so sure; he hadn't been fed for two hours. He looked at the mass of legs and wondered whether to help himself to an early snack.

Miss Marchmont walked over for a closer look at the Krishna disciples. 'On the other hand, one never knows, Watson, they could be shoplifters. Those robes make ideal hiding places for stolen booty.' With that she followed the chanting quartet at a discreet distance.

Mr Bevan once again grabbed an armful of dip boxes and handed them out to the queue of parents and children waiting to see Father Christmas. He was puzzled as to why the queue was longer than ever. Surely Hacket wasn't back on duty?

Hacket was not back on duty. What was holding the queue up was Father Christmas full to the brim with Christmas spirit. Gerald was now sitting each and every child on his lap, breathing great gales of Bells whisky and Canada Dry into their faces. Normally children would recoil in shock at the alcoholic blast, but Kelsey's Acapulco Gold chewing gum was having its effect. The kids had been waiting so long to see Father Christmas that the parents had let them open the present to give them something to do. Each child in the queue, and a few parents too, had great wads of the gum masticating in their mouths.

Gerald was having a whale of a time. His glassy eyes peered into the dilated pupils of the children on his knee and demanded to know what they wanted for Christmas.

Not satisfied with their innermost desires, the old actor wanted to know who their grand-parents were, where did they live, what did Grandpappy do in the war. Where did Mummy and Daddy take them for their holidays? Had they ever been to Norwich? Maybe they saw him in *Macbeth*. As every interview got longer so did the queue. Mr Bevan made his way through the front of the line to see what was happening; as he did so, his hatred of children was enhanced. Some of the little blighters were giggling hysterically at the moving models. He couldn't understand why the parents weren't doing something about it, indeed, they seemed to be joining in. One parent was intent upon finding out what was under Rudolph's tail. 'Disgusting', thought Mr Bevan, and would have remonstrated with the voyeurs had his nostrils not caught the unmistakable smell of the demon liquor. Rushing up to Gerald he found him swaying amongst a group of children asking for their opinion on the effect of censorship in present-day modern theatre.

'What the hell do you think you are doing?' yelled Mr Bevan. Gerald swayed towards him. 'Taffy! Me old mate Taffy, come here and give us a kiss.' Gerald placed one arm around Mr Bevan's waist and pulled him towards him.

Mr Bevan winced as he smelt the stinging breath coming from the middle of the big white beard.

'You're drunk, Gerald!'

'And you're Welsh,' retorted Father Christmas.

Mr Bevan broke free from the amorous advances of his red-robed lush.

'Get out of here and sober up immediately!' instructed Mr Bevan.

'Shan't, you Cardiff coyote!' and with that Father Christmas sat back on his throne and started to lead the children in a chorus of something or other from *Aïda*.

Mr Bevan knew this was serious and rushed off to get help.

'Has anyone seen Mr Dunnet?' he yelled, running through the store.

'Haven't seen him this morning,' replied Mr Caffey, fixing a new bottle of gas on to the bagpipes, preparing another performance for the benefit of the shoppers.

'Jacko, have you seen Mr Dunnet?' asked Mr Bevan breathlessly. Jacko, disgorging a group of people from his left, said, 'Well, I saw him this morning in the storeroom on the fourth.'

'Take me there, will you, and quickly, it's very urgent!' Mr Bevan entered the lift.

Jacko closed the lift gates and ascended to the fourth. It was quite a good day for him, so it only took five attempts to get the lift level with the fourth floor. Mr Bevan got out with much haste, ran to the storeroom door and began banging furiously. 'Mr Dunnet, are you in there? It's Mr Bevan, we have a very serious problem!'

Dunnet opened the door carefully and popped his head out. 'What is it, Mr Bevan?' Mr Bevan wondered why Mr Dunnet was wearing a beard and moustache.

'It's Gerald Dupont, you know, Father Christmas.'

'Yes,' said Eric, looking nervously round.

'Well, he's drunk.'

'Who?'

'Father Christmas!' said Mr Bevan in exasperation.

'What do you want me to do about it?' said Eric irritably.

'Well, he refuses to leave, he's inspiring the children to be naughty and there's just all hell let loose down here. You must come straight away.'

'Surely you can deal with it, Bevan?'

Mr Bevan started cursing in English this time and stamping his feet. The last thing Dunnet wanted right now was to bring attention to himself.

'All right, all right, I'll come straight away, but do let's hurry.' Dunnet donned a baseball cap and followed Mr Bevan to the basement. They avoided the lift, such was the hurry they were both in, and Dunnet kept a watchful eye out for any sign of Mr Big.

Mr Bevan was racing down the stairs, giving Eric a running commentary on the store's present situation. 'I don't know what things are coming to, Mr Dunnet, ever since those Americans took over things just aren't the same. Oh! Excuse me,' he said to the large-framed gentleman he was passing on the stairs, and promptly stood on the foot of the very small man hidden behind the giant.

'I beg your pardon,' said Mr Bevan. 'I didn't see you there. Anyway, as I was saying Mr Dunnet, you wouldn't get this sort of thing happening—' Mr Bevan would like to have said more on the subject, but lacked sufficient breath to do so having been shoved violently in the back by Dunnet as part of an exercise to save his life.

On hearing the name Dunnet, Mangle and Mr Big stopped in mid-upward flight and reversed direction when they realized the hairy hippie in the baseball cap was the very prey they were looking for.

Eric fled for his very existence, pursued by the two gangsters. He dashed down to the first floor and cut through the crowd in the music department. If he had had time to stop he would have seen Mr Caffey having an argument with a group of Hare Krishnas whose chanting was ruining his bagpipe concerto.

The four gentlemen were in the early stages of inserting the wailing instrument down Mr Caffey's throat and would have completed the manoeuvre if they had not caught sight of their prey racing by. Leaving Caffey to his own devices, they gave chase.

Dunnet managed to shake off his pursuers by ducking back along the first floor and up into Alfred's old office. Once inside he took the lift down to the basement and surfaced in the menswear section. Ignoring the puzzled looks from the staff, he headed for the toy department. Making sure his followers didn't see him, he slipped into the grotto and made his way to the front of the queue.

It was a bit difficult because a few extremely upset parents were now trying to give what-for to a Father Christmas severely the worse for wear. Children may be in awe of the magical figure from Lapland, but some of the wonder disappears when the bearded marvel throws up all over your Garfield T-shirt.

Eric fought his way to the front and grabbed Gerald. 'One moment, ladies and gentlemen, boys and girls, Santa Claus wants to have a word with his fairies to make sure you all get what you want for Christmas.' Dunnet forced Gerald into the changing room behind Santa's throne. Sitting the old actor in a chair he stripped him of his red robes and beard and exchanged them for the false hair he was wearing. Leaving Gerald mumbling Shakespeare verse, Eric re-emerged and sat down on the throne.

'Now then, boys and girls, what do you want me to bring you for Christmas?'

Inside and outside the grotto strange events were taking place. The queue now stretched anaconda-like right throughout the basement. The children had been waiting a long while to see Santa and the chewing gum had now taken full effect. Parents couldn't understand why their children were behaving like demons. A dozen or so were scaling the sides of the lift cage claiming they were Spiderman. Others were Superman and tried to prove it by running along the counter and flinging themselves into mid-air. Horrified parents were doing their best to catch them before they plummeted to the ground.

Children were hallucinating on a large scale. The models in the grotto were now monsters of immense proportion and had to be put to death. Kids were charging everywhere looking for guns and weapons of any sort to deal the ogres a fatal blow and save Father Christmas. Many of them came charging back from the china department with armfuls of crockery and started hurling them at the plaster figures.

Into this heaving mass of screaming spitting juveniles ran Mr Big and Mangle, who by now had teamed up with the Bishop and Rupert again. Following close behind were the Hare Krishna mob, determined to kidnap Mr Big and Dunnet at the earliest opportunity so they could dispose of them quickly and not work over Christmas.

The arrival of these eight weirdos was just oxygen to the flames. The children turned on them with venom. They swarmed over them like ants, biting and scratching, and it was all that the eightsome could do to remain upright.

With immaculate timing Jacko arrived in his lift at the basement. As he opened the door out tumbled Mr Caffey looking for the mob that jammed the bagpipes down his gullet.

The pipes were skirling and wailing under his arm infused with a new supply of gas. The pitch perfectly matched that of the screaming infants now busily tearing out the hair of the imagined monsters. Mr Caffey himself was immediately enveloped by the marauding midgets.

Watson and Miss Marchmont watched in silence from the back of the lift at the mayhem before them, not daring to leave the sanctuary of the lift cage. Inside the grotto the children had piled all the bits of scenery they could find into a funeral pyre for Snow White, whom they saw as the most wicked of beings. Setting light to the pile they ran round it in circles, whooping and yelling as Snow White began to smoulder away.

Dunnet, terrified as he was of being found by Mr Big, ventured from his throne room not only to escape the choking fumes but to see what the deafening cacophony of noise outside could possibly be.

At first he didn't recognize any of the people being attacked by the children but realized that the neanderthal Mangle could well be the foundation for the seven-foot pile of swarming humanity weaving through the department.

If this carnage wasn't enough, what happened next made what was going on look like a yoga class. The glassy-eyed euphoric children were dragging the remnants of the models from the grotto. As they hauled, thousands of fifty-pound notes were pouring from Sleepy, Dopey, Grumpy *et al* and fluttering down amongst the melée of bodies now in various states of raised and semi-consciousness.

Parents who were struggling to pull their limpet-like offspring off the unfortunate victims stopped momentarily at the sight of so much money. The older children, too, had sufficient greed instinct to rivet them to the cash swirling round their feet. The emphasis suddenly switched from inflicting pain to grabbing as much money as they could. With the respite, the eight attacked men took stock of the situation. The Krishnas saw Mr Big and grabbed him. Mangle, seeing his boss manhandled, grabbed them. Rupert and the Bishop looked round for an escape from this disaster but spied Dunnet, unmistakably Dunnet, although in red robes plus beard round his neck, stuffing money in the Santa Claus sack for all he was worth. They grabbed. Mr Caffey, now free from the swarm of children, saw the Krishnas and attacked them with his bagpipes.

Watson, waddling from the lift, couldn't resist the urge to attack and sallied forth into the fray, grabbing the first calf he came to. It was Rupert's. Rupert yelled out and tried to shake Watson free by hitting him with a pogo stick. Miss Marchmont went to Watson's rescue, wrenched the stick from Rupert's hand and started hitting him with it. Dunnet, now having only the Bishop to deal with, swung his sack of money on to the Bishop's head thereby gaining his release. He headed inside the lift.

'Quick, Jacko, beam me up!'

Jacko, only too pleased to get out of Hades, slammed the gates shut and shoved the level into the 'up' mode. The lift was four feet out of the basement when it came to an abrupt halt. Mangle, releasing his boss from his grip of the saffron-robed kidnappers, had opened the outer gate, thereby rendering the lift immobile. The gap between the lift and the basement floor was sufficient for Mangle to shove all four Krishnas through and down to the bottom of the lift shaft six feet below. He slammed the gate shut.

'Mangle, open the gate!' screamed Mr Big. 'Dunnet's in the lift!'

Dunnet was indeed in the lift, cowering in the back corner. 'Get moving, Jacko, for heaven's sake,' he whimpered.

Jacko slammed the lever across to get the lift moving upwards but in his panic moved it into the 'down' mode. The lift came to an automatic stop, level with the basement floor.

'Get him, Mangle!' cried Mr Big.

Mangle opened both the gates, ignoring Jacko's protestations that only he was allowed to touch the gates. He hauled Jacko out and let his boss enter. Rupert and the Bishop lunged for the lift, Rupert having finally shaken Watson from his calf.

Mangle ushered them all in and was about to enter himself when Watson, not to be out-done with losing one quarry, launched himself on to Mangle's leg to bag another. Mangle entered the lift with Watson attached. The Bishop took over the controls of the lift and set it in motion to leave the screaming mayhem behind and let it carry on in their absence. Mangle was furiously shaking his leg trying to dislodge Watson. Dunnet was equally deter-mined to hang on to his bag of money, which Mr Big was trying to prise from his grasp.

The ensuing struggles made the lift wave crazily from side to side. The shaking and shud-dering had now rendered the controls completely useless and the lift, with a will of its own, careered up and down with its occupants still fighting their personal battles.

No one was taking too much notice of the runaway lift because the entire store was being evacuated, due to the fire alarms now ringing round the building. Smoke was pouring up through the lift shaft and out into the other floors. The store's sprinkler system was trick-ling at its fullest stretch.

The juddering in the lift reached such a crescendo that the violent movement was too much for the ancient steel cables that kept it suspended. First one cable pinged, then another; the third and fourth held on for a fraction longer before giving way, leaving the centre cable the only one keeping the lift from hurtling down the shaft. Inside Mangle gave one last mighty shake of his leg to release the tenacious grip of the now rabid bulldog. The movement was just enough to strain the remaining cable past breaking point. The cage fell silently down the shaft at an ever-increasing rate of knots.

The four Hare Krishnas watched helplessly as the lift bore down upon them. It was a pity that they could not be informed that their presence at the impact saved the occupants of the lift considerably more injury than if they had not been there. As it was their demise was perhaps poetic justice much suited to the Karmic beliefs of Krishna followers.

The inmates of the lift were knocked completely unconscious.

The fire and ambulance crews had their work cut out rescuing reluctant, stoned children from the basement and dousing the piles of money and most of Walt Disney's favourite cartoon characters. Miraculously, no one but the Krishnas and the lift's survivors was hurt. Even Watson escaped unscathed. A combination of falling on the bodies of the gangsters and his rolls of fat saved him from any permanent damage. The following Sunday the Beehive made front page news.

23

Glory B, Jake, Kelsey and Miss Marchmont sat
in the departure lounge at Gatwick Airport
waiting to be called for the People's Express
flight to New York. With a glass of champagne
in one hand and a chip butty in the other, Kelsey
leaned across to Glory B, who had caused considerable consternation at the security check,
dressed as she was in a khaki micro skirt, army
fatigue jacket, black tights and Doc Marten
boots. Normally it's the passengers who stand
in line to be frisked by a heavy-handed guard.
When Glory B showed up it was the reverse.

On the other side of the lounge a matronly
American lady of indeterminate years but deter-
minable wealth — her earrings alone would keep
two-thirds of the subcontinent in chapatis for
a fortnight — snapped at her husband. 'For
Gahd's sake, Wilbur, close your mouth and take
your eyes off of that woman — you look like
a carp in heat!'

Gloria said, 'Do you think we'll stay in
touch?'

Kelsey answered, 'After all we've been through
together? Of course we'll stay in touch!'

'Well, I'm not so sure. You'll be stuck out in California—'

Jake interrupted, 'In California everybody's stuck out.'

Judith said, 'Why don't we all go to California?'

'And what would we do there?' said Gloria.

'We'd do in California what we do now,' said Kelsey, 'and what we do now is sell junk. We sell junk better than anybody in the world. We have global junk cred.'

'And what junk would we sell?'

Judith said, 'Let me tell them. Kelsey and I have this idea of opening a Sherlock Holmes shop in Santa Monica.'

'Right,' said Kelsey, 'within a year we're going to have every Yuppie on the West Coast smoking a meerschaum, walking a dog called Watson and picking up a few clues with a Moriarty pooper scooper.'

'And where are you going to get all the stuff – Judith's apartment?'

'To start with,' said Kelsey, 'and then we'll get it made for us.'

'You kidding?'

'No! We could go world-wide. Become the Macdonalds of ethnic junk. Sell franchises. What do you say?'

Jake stopped computing. 'Maybe this will convince Glory B. According to my user-friendly lap job here, we made a profit of two million dollars on junk in the last nine months.'

'That's incredible,' said Judith. 'How much have we got left?'

Kelsey reached into his bag and counted out forty severely burnt fifty-pound notes. 'If we can get the Bank of America to accept this lot, two thousand pounds, but if Nat West are anything to go by, zilch!'

The tannoy called their flight and the group picked up their bags to board the plane.

'I wonder what the Church will do with the Beehive now they've got it,' said Kelsey.

'They're going to turn it into a bingo hall,' said Judith.

'I don't think I'll ever understand Limeys,' said Kelsey, shaking his head.

'You will,' said Judith, pecking his cheek, 'you will.'

'I've got one!' cried Mangle in triumph.

Mr Big and Rupert looked disconsolately at each other.

'I can't eat another of the bloody things. Have it yourself.'

Mangle looked miffed. He'd spent a good fifteen minutes stalking the juicy rat he now held in his hand, and now these ungrateful people didn't want it. Oh well, he'd have it himself. He popped the lifeless rodent into his mouth and chewed happily.

Mr Big watched the masticating Mangle with dejection. He was utterly, thoroughly and terminally fed up. The Chinaman was after him for the money. Dunnet had done a runner leaving him to carry the can. He had gone into hiding to escape the Chinaman's attentions. The only safe hideout Mr Big had was the huge warehouse. Here, he and his two henchmen were safe, for no one could ever hope to find them among the huge piles and stacks of American junk, which were the only things in the world that Mr Big now owned. They had no food, hence Mangle's revolting rat diet. When things had calmed down a little, Mr Big knew that somehow, he would have to sell the stuff if he ever wanted to return to London and carry on living a normal criminal life.

He'd tried to do a deal with the Chinaman by offering to repay the debt in kind, but the Chinaman said he had no use for in-car saunas, talking kettles, horn-rimmed contact lenses and the like. No matter how much discount he offered. But there again, the Chinaman never was a reasonable man.

In the meantime, he, Rupert and Mangle sat morosely among the towering shelves full of plastic winking Jesus dolls, musical golf clubs and digital toothbrushes which they had to find buyers for in order not to end up at the bottom of the Thames. As Mangle prowled off in search of more wildlife to nibble, Mr Big put his head in his hands and cursed the day he'd ever heard of the Bishop, Eric Dunnet and the Beehive department store.

The sun glinted on the coarse Cornish granite that was used to build the eighteenth-century mansion that overlooked St Michael Mount in the busy village of Miragion. Originally built as a home for a Cornish lord, little had changed on the outside for hundreds of years. Apart from a television aerial and some outside cables it was much as it was when it was built. An extension had been added to the back but had been done tastefully and with respect. The same could not be said for the inside. Over the latter part of the century its usage had changed several times.

During the war it had been bought by the Ministry of Defence and had been turned into a naval training school specializing in submarine detection. During the early fifties it was sold to a couple who turned it into a bed and breakfast guest house. With all the fire regulations and other safety measures little of the original interior could be recognized. With the decline in the holiday trade due to the popularity of overseas holidays, it had been sold once more and had finally become a retirement home for service widows.

On the back lawns of the mansion a jolly crowd of old ladies mingled with the younger staff, and the sound of champagne corks could be heard. Several of the staff soon appeared with trays holding glasses filled with the French bubbly.

As the glasses were passed round the Matron of the home called everyone to order.

'Ladies and gentlemen, when you've received a glass of champagne, I would like to propose a toast.'

The nurses quickly made sure everyone had received their celebratory tipple.

'I think I'm right in saying,' boomed the Matron, making sure her voice could be heard over the incoming tide that washed up on to the beach that backed on to the property, 'that this is the first time we've ever had a wedding here at the Marshal De Havilland retirement home. And we couldn't have a happier couple.'

The crowd clapped and cheered the newlyweds standing by the Matron's side.

'Since we arrived here twelve months ago, I don't think we've ever had a more popular and caring male nurse than Mr Dunnet,' stated the Matron.

The old ladies in particular could not agree more; many of them present had good reason to know intimately how caring he could be. They smiled to themselves and clapped again to endorse the Matron's statement.

'And as for Mary,' said the Matron, turning to the lady next to her, 'I'm sure the last thing she thought when she arrived here just six weeks ago was that she would be getting married on her seventieth birthday. I'm sure they're going to be very happy and when they get back from their honeymoon, I know we're going to see lots of them. Ladies and gentlemen, please raise your glasses, I give you . . . Mr and Mrs Eric Dunnet.'

The gathering raised their glasses and toasted the happy couple.

Eric the groom, twenty-eight years her junior, looked fondly into his new wife's eyes. She was his perfect woman, the woman he'd longed to marry. Not too young, mature features, tight wavy grey hair and legs without a support hose in sight.

He leant over and whispered, 'I love you, Mary.' Mary turned her hearing aid up.

'Pardon, Eric?'

'I love you.'

'I love you too, my sweet.'

They were joined by wellwishers patting them on the back, congratulating them both and spraying them with confetti. They spent the next hour chatting gently to different members of the wedding party before they collected their honeymoon clothes and walked to the car.

'Where are you going for your honeymoon, Acapulco?' shouted one wag.

Mary sheepishly declined to reply and Eric, anticipating a night of sheer bliss, didn't even hear.

They climbed into the Metro and drove quickly out of the drive to waving and clapping from the cheering crowd.

'Where are we going, Eric?' asked Mary sweetly.

'Well, now we're alone and you can't tell anybody, I've found a small private hotel in Dawlish. It won't take long to get there and then watch out!' Eric leered excessively and Mary giggled, 'You'll have to show me what to do, it's been so long.'

'You won't have to do anything!' Eric chortled.

Several hours later they pulled up in front of a typical holiday hotel set back several hundred yards from the Devonshire town's sea front.

As they registered as Mr and Mrs Dunnet, Mary squeezed Eric's arm. 'I can't believe it,' she said. Eric winked, grabbed the luggage and led her off to room 101.

Over the pre-nuptial meal that evening, Eric was careful not to let Mary have too much Wincarnis; he didn't want anything to spoil their night. After coffee and mints, Eric hurriedly led his bride to the bedroom.

'You get undressed first, Mary. I'll get the appliances ready.' Mary padded off to the bathroom to change while Eric busied himself with the batteries.

Mary emerged from the bathroom, radiant in a pink wincyette nightgown with a picture of Frank Bough on it.

Eric, almost panting with desire, rushed into the bathroom to clean his teeth and swill his mouth out with Listerine. He quickly undressed and returned to the bedroom, banging his shin because Mary had turned the light out due to her shyness. He pulled back the bedclothes and slipped into the empty space beside his bride.

They snuggled together, Mary caressing Eric's bruised shin.

'Eric, have you had many women in your life? I don't mind if you have, it's just that I haven't and I'm worried in case you think I'm going to be inexperienced.'

Eric patted her reassuringly on her bottom. 'Look, don't worry about a thing, I've had a few women but not as lovely as you. Besides, I like women who are faithful.' He undid her top button.

'I did have one indiscretion while I was married and I've lived to regret it ever since. It put me off affairs for the rest of my life,' said Mary.

'What happened?' said Eric, nuzzling his nose down the top of her nightgown.

'Well, it was during the war while my husband was away fighting, I worked in this terrible department store in Ken High Street, right dump it was.'

Eric's nose came out of her nightgown. 'What was it called?'

'The Beehive. Silly name, isn't it?'

Eric shuffled about uncomfortably; should he tell her? No, best left unsaid, stick to the story about being an orderly in Rampton.

'Yes, silly name,' said Eric, 'so what happened?'

'Well, I fell for one of the bosses, Ronald was his name, right rogue I found out later, couldn't leave women alone. Looked a bit like you actually, Eric. I think that's what attracted me to you. Anyway I went and got pregnant, didn't I? Of course Ronald didn't want to know, scarpered off to America. When my husband returned from the war, he got a nasty shock when I told him we'd got a son. He didn't want to know. Took the little mite straight down to the store to give it to the father but it was too late, he'd gone!'

Eric was intrigued with this history of the Beehive's owners. 'What did he do?'

'Well, he dumped the kiddie with Ronald's brother, said he could look after it and for some reason that's what the man did.'

'What did Alfred do . . . I mean, what did the man do with the child?' said Eric.

'Last I heard he had someone adopt him. Lovely little baby he was, had this real funny birthmark on his bottom, like a one-legged frog!'

Eric leapt from the bed like a scalded cat.

'What did you say?' yelled Eric. 'Did you say a one-legged frog?'

'Yes.'

Eric switched the light on and turned his bare buttocks to Mary.

Mary stared for a moment and then screamed. It was not as large as she remembered it, but there was no mistaking the one-legged frog on Eric's backside.

'Son?'

'Mother!'

A Selection of Arrow Bestsellers

☐ The Lilac Bus	Maeve Binchy	£2.50
☐ 500 Mile Walkies	Mark Wallington	£2.50
☐ Staying Off the Beaten Track	Elizabeth Gundrey	£5.95
☐ A Better World Than This	Marie Joseph	£2.95
☐ No Enemy But Time	Evelyn Anthony	£2.95
☐ Rates of Exchange	Malcolm Bradbury	£3.50
☐ Colours Aloft	Alexander Kent	£2.95
☐ Speaker for the Dead	Orson Scott Card	£2.95
☐ Eon	Greg Bear	£4.95
☐ Talking to Strange Men	Ruth Rendell	£5.95
☐ Heartstones	Ruth Rendell	£2.50
☐ Rosemary Conley's Hip and Thigh Diet	Rosemary Conley	£2.50
☐ Communion	Whitley Strieber	£3.50
☐ The Ladies of Missalonghi	Colleen McCullough	£2.50
☐ Erin's Child	Sheelagh Kelly	£3.99
☐ Sarum	Edward Rutherfurd	£4.50

Prices and other details are liable to change

ARROW BOOKS, BOOKSERVICE BY POST, PO BOX 29, DOUGLAS, ISLE OF MAN, BRITISH ISLES

NAME...

ADDRESS...

....

....

Please enclose a cheque or postal order made out to Arrow Books Ltd. for the amount due and allow the following for postage and packing.

U.K. CUSTOMERS: Please allow 22p per book to a maximum of £3.00.

B.F.P.O. & EIRE: Please allow 22p per book to a maximum of £3.00

OVERSEAS CUSTOMERS: Please allow 22p per book.

Whilst every effort is made to keep prices low it is sometimes necessary to increase cover prices at short notice. Arrow Books reserve the right to show new retail prices on covers which may differ from those previously advertised in the text or elsewhere.

Bestselling Fiction

☐ Hiroshmia Joe	Martin Booth	£2.95
☐ The Pianoplayers	Anthony Burgess	£2.50
☐ Queen's Play	Dorothy Dunnett	£3.95
☐ Colours Aloft	Alexander Kent	£2.95
☐ Contact	Carl Sagan	£3.50
☐ Talking to Strange Men	Ruth Rendell	£5.95
☐ Heartstones	Ruth Rendell	£2.50
☐ The Ladies of Missalonghi	Colleen McCullough	£2.50
☐ No Enemy But Time	Evelyn Anthony	£2.95
☐ The Heart of the Country	Fay Weldon	£2.50
☐ The Stationmaster's Daughter	Pamela Oldfield	£2.95
☐ Erin's Child	Sheelagh Kelly	£3.99
☐ The Lilac Bus	Maeve Binchy	£2.50

Prices and other details are liable to change

ARROW BOOKS, BOOKSERVICE BY POST, PO BOX 29, DOUGLAS, ISLE OF MAN, BRITISH ISLES

NAME...

ADDRESS...

....

....

Please enclose a cheque or postal order made out to Arrow Books Ltd. for the amount due and allow the following for postage and packing.

U.K. CUSTOMERS: Please allow 22p per book to a maximum of £3.00.

B.F.P.O. & EIRE: Please allow 22p per book to a maximum of £3.00

OVERSEAS CUSTOMERS: Please allow 22p per book.

Whilst every effort is made to keep prices low it is sometimes necessary to increase cover prices at short notice. Arrow Books reserve the right to show new retail prices on covers which may differ from those previously advertised in the text or elsewhere.

Bestselling Fiction

☐ Saudi	Laurie Devine	£2.95
☐ Lisa Logan	Marie Joseph	£2.50
☐ The Stationmaster's Daughter	Pamela Oldfield	£2.95
☐ Duncton Wood	William Horwood	£3.50
☐ Aztec	Gary Jennings	£3.95
☐ The Pride	Judith Saxton	£2.99
☐ Fire in Heaven	Malcolm Bosse	£3.50
☐ Communion	Whitley Strieber	£3.50
☐ The Ladies of Missalonghi	Colleen McCullough	£2.50
☐ Skydancer	Geoffrey Archer	£2.50
☐ The Sisters	Pat Booth	£3.50
☐ No Enemy But Time	Evelyn Anthony	£2.95

Prices and other details are liable to change

ARROW BOOKS, BOOKSERVICE BY POST, PO BOX 29, DOUGLAS, ISLE
OF MAN, BRITISH ISLES

NAME...

ADDRESS..

....

....

Please enclose a cheque or postal order made out to Arrow Books Ltd. for the amount
due and allow the following for postage and packing.

U.K. CUSTOMERS: Please allow 22p per book to a maximum of £3.00.

B.F.P.O. & EIRE: Please allow 22p per book to a maximum of £3.00

OVERSEAS CUSTOMERS: Please allow 22p per book.

Whilst every effort is made to keep prices low it is sometimes necessary to increase cover
prices at short notice. Arrow Books reserve the right to show new retail prices on covers
which may differ from those previously advertised in the text or elsewhere.

Bestselling Humour

☐ Carrott Roots	Jasper Carrott	£3.50
☐ The Art of Course Office Life	Michael Green	£1.95
☐ Rambling On	Mike Harding	£2.50
☐ Sex Tips for Girls	Cynthia Heimel	£2.95
☐ Sex Tips for Boys	William Davis	£2.95
☐ Tales from a Long Room	Peter Tinniswood	£2.75
☐ Tales from Whitney Scrotum	Peter Tinniswood	£2.50
☐ Why Come to Slaka?	Malcolm Bradbury	£2.95
☐ Football is a Funny Game	Ian St. John & Jimmy Greaves	£3.95
☐ The Bedside Book of Sex	Rolf White	£2.95
☐ Palace	Neil Mackwood & Bryan Rostron	£2.50
☐ Tim Brooke-Taylor's Cricket Box	Tim Brooke-Taylor	£4.50

Prices and other details are liable to change

ARROW BOOKS, BOOKSERVICE BY POST, PO BOX 29, DOUGLAS, ISLE OF MAN, BRITISH ISLES

NAME ....

ADDRESS ....

....

....

Please enclose a cheque or postal order made out to Arrow Books Ltd. for the amount due and allow the following for postage and packing.

U.K. CUSTOMERS: Please allow 22p per book to a maximum of £3.00.

B.F.P.O. & EIRE: Please allow 22p per book to a maximum of £3.00

OVERSEAS CUSTOMERS: Please allow 22p per book.

Whilst every effort is made to keep prices low it is sometimes necessary to increase cover prices at short notice. Arrow Books reserve the right to show new retail prices on covers which may differ from those previously advertised in the text or elsewhere.